The Spoilers

The Spoilers

Rex Beach

MINT EDITIONS

The Spoilers was first published in 1906.

This edition published by Mint Editions 2021.

ISBN 9781513280509 | E-ISBN 9781513285528

Published by Mint Editions®

 MINT
EDITIONS

minteditionbooks.com

Publishing Director: Jennifer Newens
Design & Production: Rachel Lopez Metzger
Project Manager: Micaela Clark
Typesetting: Westchester Publishing Services

Contents

I. The Encounter 7

II. The Stowaway 15

III. In Which Glenister Errs 21

IV. The Killing 29

V. Wherein a Man Appears 38

VI. And a Mine is Jumped 46

VII. The "Bronco Kid's" Eavesdropping 52

VIII. Dextry Makes a Call 60

IX. Sluice Robbers 69

X. The Wit of an Adventuress 77

XI. Wherein a Writ and a Riot Fail 86

XII. Counterplots 94

XIII. In Which a Man is Possessed of a Devil 106

XIV. A Midnight Messenger 119

XV. Vigilantes 129

XVI. In Which the Truth Begins to Bare Itself 141

XVII. The Drip of Water in the Dark 152

XVIII. Wherein a Trap is Baited 164

XIX. DYNAMITE 173

XX. IN WHICH THREE GO TO THE SIGN OF THE
SLED AND BUT TWO RETURN 186

XXI. THE HAMMER-LOCK 197

XXII. THE PROMISE OF DREAMS 207

I

THE ENCOUNTER

G lenister gazed out over the harbor, agleam with the lights of anchored ships, then up at the crenelated mountains, black against the sky. He drank the cool air burdened with its taints of the sea, while the blood of his boyhood leaped within him.

"Oh, it's fine—fine," he murmured, "and this is my country—my country, after all, Dex. It's in my veins, this hunger for the North. I grow. I expand."

"Careful you don't bust," warned Dextry. "I've seen men get plumb drunk on mountain air. Don't expand too strong in one spot." He went back abruptly to his pipe, its villanous fumes promptly averting any danger of the air's too tonic quality.

"Gad! What a smudge!" sniffed the younger man. "You ought to be in quarantine."

"I'd rather smell like a man than talk like a kid. You desecrate the hour of meditation with rhapsodies on nature when your aesthetics ain't honed up to the beauties of good tobacco."

The other laughed, inflating his deep chest. In the gloom he stretched his muscles restlessly, as though an excess of vigor filled him.

They were lounging upon the dock, while before them lay the Santa Maria ready for her midnight sailing. Behind slept Unalaska, quaint, antique, and Russian, rusting amid the fogs of Bering Sea. Where, a week before, mild-eyed natives had dried their cod among the old bronze cannon, now a frenzied horde of gold-seekers paused in their rush to the new El Dorado. They had come like a locust cloud, thousands strong, settling on the edge of the Smoky Sea, waiting the going of the ice that barred them from their Golden Fleece—from Nome the new, where men found fortune in a night.

The mossy hills back of the village were ridged with graves of those who had died on the out-trip the fall before, when a plague had gripped the land—but what of that? Gold glittered in the sands, so said the survivors; therefore men came in armies. Glenister and Dextry had left Nome the autumn previous, the young man raving with fever. Now they returned to their own land.

"This air whets every animal instinct in me," Glenister broke out again. "Away from the cities I turn savage. I feel the old primitive passions—the fret for fighting."

"Mebbe you'll have a chance."

"How so?"

"Well, it's this way. I met Mexico Mullins this mornin'. You mind old Mexico, don't you? The feller that relocated Discovery Claim on Anvil Creek last summer?"

"You don't mean that 'tin-horn' the boys were going to lynch for claim-jumping?"

"Identical! Remember me tellin' you about a good turn I done him once down Guadalupe way?"

"Greaser shooting-scrape, wasn't it?"

"Yep! Well, I noticed first off that he's gettin fat; high-livin' fat, too, all in one spot, like he was playin' both ends ag'in the centre. Also he wore di'mon's fit to handle with ice-tongs.

"Says I, lookin' at his side elevation, 'What's accented your middle syllable so strong, Mexico?'

"'Prosperity, politics, an' the Waldorf-Astorier,' says he. It seems Mex hadn't forgot old days. He claws me into a corner an' says, 'Bill, I'm goin' to pay you back for that Moralez deal.'

"'It ain't comin' to me,' says I. 'That's a bygone!'

"'Listen here,' says he, an', seein' he was in earnest, I let him run on.

"'How much do you value that claim o' yourn at?'

"'Hard tellin',' says I. 'If she holds out like she run last fall, there'd ought to be a million clear in her."

"'How much'll you clean up this summer?'

"''Bout four hundred thousand, with luck.'

"'Bill,' says he, 'there's hell a-poppin' an' you've got to watch that ground like you'd watch a rattle-snake. Don't never leave 'em get a grip on it or you're down an' out.'

"He was so plumb in earnest it scared me up, 'cause Mexico ain't a gabby man.

"'What do you mean?' says I.

"'I can't tell you nothin' more. I'm puttin' a string on my own neck, sayin' THIS much. You're a square man, Bill, an' I'm a gambler, but you saved my life oncet, an' I wouldn't steer you wrong. For God's sake, don't let 'em jump your ground, that's all.'

"'Let who jump it? Congress has give us judges an' courts an' marshals—' I begins.

"'That's just it. How you goin' to buck that hand? Them's the best cards in the deck. There's a man comin' by the name of McNamara. Watch him clost. I can't tell you no more. But don't never let 'em get a grip on your ground.' That's all he'd say."

"Bah! He's crazy! I wish somebody would try to jump the Midas; we'd enjoy the exercise."

The siren of the Santa Maria interrupted, its hoarse warning throbbing up the mountain.

"We'll have to get aboard," said Dextry.

"Sh-h! What's that?" the other whispered.

At first the only sound they heard was a stir from the deck of the steamer. Then from the water below them came the rattle of rowlocks and a voice cautiously muffled.

"Stop! Stop there!"

A skiff burst from the darkness, grounding on the beach beneath. A figure scrambled out and up the ladder leading to the wharf. Immediately a second boat, plainly in pursuit of the first one, struck on the beach behind it.

As the escaping figure mounted to their level the watchers perceived with amazement that it was a young woman. Breath sobbed from her lungs, and, stumbling, she would have fallen but for Glenister, who ran forward and helped her to her feet.

"Don't let them get me," she panted.

He turned to his partner in puzzled inquiry, but found that the old man had crossed to the head of the landing ladder up which the pursuers were climbing.

"Just a minute—you there! Back up or I'll kick your face in." Dextry's voice was sharp and unexpected, and in the darkness he loomed tall and menacing to those below.

"Get out of the way. That woman's a runaway," came from the one highest on the ladder.

"So I jedge."

"She broke qu—"

"Shut up!" broke in another. "Do you want to advertise it? Get out of the way, there, ye damn fool! Climb up, Thorsen." He spoke like a bucko mate, and his words stirred the bile of Dextry.

Thorsen grasped the dock floor, trying to climb up, but the old miner stamped on his fingers and the sailor loosened his hold with a yell, carrying the under men with him to the beach in his fall.

"This way! Follow me!" shouted the mate, making up the bank for the shore end of the wharf.

"You'd better pull your freight, miss," Dextry remarked; "they'll be here in a minute."

"Yes, yes! Let us go! I must get aboard the Santa Maria. She's leaving now. Come, come!"

Glenister laughed, as though there were a humorous touch in her remark, but did not stir.

"I'm gettin' awful old an' stiff to run," said Dextry, removing his mackinaw, "but I allow I ain't too old for a little diversion in the way of a rough-house when it comes nosin' around." He moved lightly, though the girl could see in the half-darkness that his hair was silvery.

"What do you mean?" she questioned, sharply.

"You hurry along, miss; we'll toy with 'em till you're aboard." They stepped across to the dockhouse, backing against it. The girl followed.

Again came the warning blast from the steamer, and the voice of an officer:

"Clear away that stern line!"

"Oh, we'll be left!" she breathed, and somehow it struck Glenister that she feared this more than the men whose approaching feet he heard.

"You can make it all right," he urged her, roughly. "You'll get hurt if you stay here. Run along and don't mind us. We've been thirty days on shipboard, and were praying for something to happen." His voice was boyishly glad, as if he exulted in the fray that was to come; and no sooner had he spoken than the sailors came out of the darkness upon them.

During the space of a few heart-beats there was only a tangle of whirling forms with the sound of fist on flesh, then the blot split up and forms plunged outward, falling heavily. Again the sailors rushed, attempting to clinch. They massed upon Dextry only to grasp empty air, for he shifted with remarkable agility, striking bitterly, as an old wolf snaps. It was baffling work, however, for in the darkness his blows fell short or overreached.

Glenister, on the other hand, stood carelessly, beating the men off as they came to him. He laughed gloatingly, deep in his throat, as though the encounter were merely some rough sport. The girl shuddered, for the desperate silence of the attacking men terrified her more than a din, and yet she stayed, crouched against the wall.

Dextry swung at a dim target, and, missing it, was whirled off his balance. Instantly his antagonist grappled with him, and they fell to the floor, while a third man shuffled about them. The girl throttled a scream.

"I'm goin' to kick 'im, Bill," the man panted hoarsely. "Le' me fix 'im." He swung his heavy shoe, and Bill cursed with stirring eloquence.

"Ow! You're kickin' me! I've got 'im, safe enough. Tackle the big un."

Bill's ally then started towards the others, his body bent, his arms flexed yet hanging loosely. He crouched beside the girl, ignoring her, while she heard the breath wheezing from his lungs; then silently he leaped. Glenister had hurled a man from him, then stepped back to avoid the others, when he was seized from behind and felt the man's arms wrapped about his neck, the sailor's legs locked about his thighs. Now came the girl's first knowledge of real fighting. The two spun back and forth so closely entwined as to be indistinguishable, the others holding off. For what seemed many minutes they struggled, the young man striving to reach his adversary, till they crashed against the wall near her and she heard her champion's breath coughing in his throat at the tightening grip of the sailor. Fright held her paralyzed, for she had never seen men thus. A moment and Glenister would be down beneath their stamping feet—they would kick his life out with their heavy shoes. At thought of it, the necessity of action smote her like a blow in the face. Her terror fell away, her shaking muscles stiffened, and before realizing what she did she had acted.

The seaman's back was to her. She reached out and gripped him by the hair, while her fingers, tense as talons, sought his eyes. Then the first loud sound of the battle arose. The man yelled in sudden terror; and the others as suddenly fell back. The next instant she felt a hand upon her shoulder and heard Dextry's voice.

"Are ye hurt? No? Come on, then, or we'll get left." He spoke quietly, though his breath was loud, and, glancing down, she saw the huddled form of the sailor whom he had fought.

"That's all right—he ain't hurt. It's a Jap trick I learned. Hurry up!"

They ran swiftly down the wharf, followed by Glenister and by the groans of the sailors in whom the lust for combat had been quenched. As they scrambled up the Santa Maria's gang-plank, a strip of water widened between the boat and the pier.

"Close shave, that," panted Glenister, feeling his throat gingerly, "but I wouldn't have missed it for a spotted pup."

"I've been through b'iler explosions and snowslides, not to mention a triflin' jail-delivery, but fer real sprightly diversions I don't recall nothin' more pleasin' than this." Dextry's enthusiasm was boylike.

"What kind of men are you?" the girl laughed nervously, but got no answer.

They led her to their deck cabin, where they switched on the electric light, blinking at each other and at their unknown guest.

They saw a graceful and altogether attractive figure in a trim, short skirt and long, tan boots. But what Glenister first saw was her eyes; large and gray, almost brown under the electric light. They were active eyes, he thought, and they flashed swift, comprehensive glances at the two men. Her hair had fallen loose and crinkled to her waist, all agleam. Otherwise she showed no sign of her recent ordeal.

Glenister had been prepared for the type of beauty that follows the frontier; beauty that may stun, but that has the polish and chill of a new-ground bowie. Instead, this girl with the calm, reposeful face struck a note almost painfully different from her surroundings, suggesting countless pleasant things that had been strange to him for the past few years.

Pure admiration alone was patent in the older man's gaze.

"I make oration," said he, "that you're the gamest little chap I ever fought over, Mexikin, Injun, or white. What's the trouble?"

"I suppose you think I've done something dreadful, don't you?" she said. "But I haven't. I had to get away from the Ohio to-night for—certain reasons. I'll tell you all about it to-morrow. I haven't stolen anything, nor poisoned the crew—really I haven't." She smiled at them, and Glenister found it impossible not to smile with her, though dismayed by her feeble explanation.

"Well, I'll wake up the steward and find a place for you to go," he said at length. "You'll have to double up with some of the women, though; it's awfully crowded aboard."

She laid a detaining hand on his arm. He thought he felt her tremble.

"No, no! I don't want you to do that. They mustn't see me to-night. I know I'm acting strangely and all that, but it's happened so quickly I haven't found myself yet. I'll tell you to-morrow, though, really. Don't let any one see me or it will spoil everything. Wait till to-morrow, please."

She was very white, and spoke with eager intensity.

"Help you? Why, sure Mike!" assured the impulsive Dextry, "an', see here, Miss—you take your time on explanations. We don't care a cuss what you done. Morals ain't our long suit, 'cause 'there's never a law of God or man runs north of Fifty-three,' as the poetry man remarked, an' he couldn't have spoke truer if he'd knowed what he was sayin'. Everybody is privileged to 'look out' his own game up here. A square deal an' no questions asked."

She looked somewhat doubtful at this till she caught the heat of Glenister's gaze. Some boldness of his look brought home to her the actual situation, and a stain rose in her cheek. She noted him more carefully; noted his heavy shoulders and ease of bearing, an ease and looseness begotten of perfect muscular control. Strength was equally suggested in his face, she thought, for he carried a marked young countenance, with thrusting chin, aggressive thatching brows, and mobile mouth that whispered all the changes from strength to abandon. Prominent was a look of reckless energy. She considered him handsome in a heavy, virile, perhaps too purely physical fashion.

"You want to stowaway?" he asked.

"I've had a right smart experience in that line," said Dextry, "but I never done it by proxy. What's your plan?"

"She will stay here to-night," said Glenister quickly. "You and I will go below. Nobody will see her."

"I can't let you do that," she objected. "Isn't there some place where I can hide?" But they reassured her and left.

When they had gone, she crouched trembling upon her seat for a long time, gazing fixedly before her. "I'm afraid!" she whispered; "I'm afraid. What am I getting into? Why do men look so at me? I'm frightened. Oh, I'm sorry I undertook it." At last she rose wearily. The close cabin oppressed her; she felt the need of fresh air. So, turning out the lights, she stepped forth into the night. Figures loomed near the rail and she slipped astern, screening herself behind a life-boat, where the cool breeze fanned her face.

The forms she had seen approached, speaking earnestly. Instead of passing, they stopped abreast of her hiding-place; then, as they began to talk, she saw that her retreat was cut off and that she must not stir.

"What brings her here?" Glenister was echoing a question of Dextry's. "Bah! What brings them all? What brought 'the Duchess,' and Cherry Malotte, and all the rest?"

"No, no," said the old man. "She ain't that kind—she's too fine, too delicate—too pretty."

"That's just it—too pretty! Too pretty to be alone—or anything except what she is."

Dextry growled sourly. "This country has plumb ruined you, boy. You think they're all alike—an' I don't know but they are—all but this girl. Seems like she's different, somehow—but I can't tell."

Glenister spoke musingly:

"I had an ancestor who buccaneered among the Indies, a long time ago—so I'm told. Sometimes I think I have his disposition. He comes and whispers things to me in the night. Oh, he was a devil, and I've got his blood in me—untamed and hot—I can hear him saying something now—something about the spoils of war. Ha, ha! Maybe he's right. I fought for her to-night—Dex—the way he used to fight for his sweethearts along the Mexicos. She's too beautiful to be good—and 'there's never a law of God or man runs north of Fifty-three.'"

They moved on, his vibrant, cynical laughter stabbing the girl till she leaned against the yawl for support.

She held herself together while the blood beat thickly in her ears, then fled to the cabin, hurling herself into her berth, where she writhed silently, beating the pillow with hands into which her nails had bitten, staring the while into the darkness with dry and aching eyes.

II

The Stowaway

S he awoke to the throb of the engines, and, gazing cautiously through her stateroom window, saw a glassy, level sea, with the sun brightly agleam on it.

So this was Bering? She had clothed it always with the mystery of her school-days, thinking of it as a weeping, fog-bound stretch of gray waters. Instead, she saw a flat, sunlit main, with occasional sea-parrots flapping their fat bodies out of the ship's course. A glistening head popped up from the waters abreast, and she heard the cry of "seal!"

Dressing, the girl noted minutely the personal articles scattered about the cabin, striving to derive therefrom some fresh hint of the characteristics of the owners. First, there was an elaborate, copper-backed toilet-set, all richly ornamented and leather-bound. The metal was magnificently hand-worked and bore Glenister's initial. It spoke of elegant extravagance, and seemed oddly out of place in an Arctic miner's equipment, as did also a small set of De Maupassant.

Next, she picked up Kipling's Seven Seas, marked liberally, and felt that she had struck a scent. The roughness and brutality of the poems had always chilled her, though she had felt vaguely their splendid pulse and swing. This was the girl's first venture from a sheltered life. She had not rubbed elbows with the world enough to find that Truth may be rough, unshaven, and garbed in homespun. The book confirmed her analysis of the junior partner.

Pendent from a hook was a worn and blackened holster from which peeped the butt of a large Colt's revolver, showing evidence of many years' service. It spoke mutely of the white-haired Dextry, who, before her inspection was over, knocked at the door, and, when she admitted him, addressed her cautiously:

"The boy's down forrad, teasin' grub out of a flunky. He'll be up in a minute. How'd ye sleep?"

"Very well, thank you," she lied, "but I've been thinking that I ought to explain myself to you."

"Now, see here," the old man interjected, "there ain't no explanations needed till you feel like givin' them up. You was in trouble—that's unfortunate; we help you—that's natural; no questions asked—that's Alaska."

"Yes—but I know you must think—"

"What bothers me," the other continued irrelevantly, "is how in blazes we're goin' to keep you hid. The steward's got to make up this room, and somebody's bound to see us packin' grub in."

"I don't care who knows if they won't send me back. They wouldn't do that, would they?" She hung anxiously on his words.

"Send you back? Why, don't you savvy that this boat is bound for Nome? There ain't no turnin' back on gold stampedes, and this is the wildest rush the world ever saw. The captain wouldn't turn back—he couldn't—his cargo's too precious and the company pays five thousand a day for this ship. No, we ain't puttin' back to unload no stowaways at five thousand per. Besides, we passengers wouldn't let him—time's too precious." They were interrupted by the rattle of dishes outside, and Dextry was about to open the door when his hand wavered uncertainly above the knob, for he heard the hearty greeting of the ship's captain.

"Well, well, Glenister, where's all the breakfast going?"

"Oo!" whispered the old man—"that's Cap' Stephens."

"Dextry isn't feeling quite up to form this morning," replied Glenister easily.

"Don't wonder! Why weren't you aboard sooner last night? I saw you—'most got left, eh? Served you right if you had." Then his voice dropped to the confidential: "I'd advise you to cut out those women. Don't misunderstand me, boy, but they're a bad lot on this boat. I saw you come aboard. Take my word for it—they're a bad lot. Cut 'em out. Guess I'll step inside and see what's up with Dextry."

The girl shrank into her corner, gazing apprehensively at the other listener.

"Well—er—he isn't up yet," they heard Glenister stammer; "better come around later."

"Nonsense; it's time he was dressed." The master's voice was gruffly good-natured. "Hello, Dextry! Hey! Open up for inspection." He rattled the door.

There was nothing to be done. The old miner darted an inquiring glance at his companion, then, at her nod, slipped the bolt, and the captain's blue bulk filled the room.

His grizzled, close-bearded face was genially wrinkled till he spied the erect, gray figure in the corner, when his cap came off involuntarily.

There his courtesy ended, however, and the smile died coldly from his face. His eyes narrowed, and the good-fellowship fell away, leaving him the stiff and formal officer.

"Ah," he said, "not feeling well, eh? I thought I had met all of our lady passengers. Introduce me, Dextry."

Dextry squirmed under his cynicism.

"Well—I—ah—didn't catch the name myself."

"What?"

"Oh, there ain't much to say. This is the lady—we brought aboard last night—that's all."

"Who gave you permission?"

"Nobody. There wasn't time."

"There wasn't TIME, eh? Which one of you conceived the novel scheme of stowing away ladies in your cabin? Whose is she? Quick! Answer me." Indignation was vibrant in his voice.

"Oh!" the girl cried—her eyes widening darkly. She stood slim and pale and slightly trembling.

His words had cut her bitterly, though through it all he had scrupulously avoided addressing her.

The captain turned to Glenister, who had entered and closed the door.

"Is this your work? Is she yours?"

"No," he answered quietly, while Dextry chimed in:

"Better hear details, captain, before you make breaks like that. We helped the lady side-step some sailors last night and we most got left doing it. It was up to her to make a quick get-away, so we helped her aboard."

"A poor story! What was she running away from?" He still addressed the men, ignoring her completely, till, with hoarse voice, she broke in:

"You mustn't talk about me that way—I can answer your questions. It's true—I ran away. I had to. The sailors came after me and fought with these men. I had to get away quickly, and your friends helped me on here from gentlemanly kindness, because they saw me unprotected. They are still protecting me. I can't explain how important it is for me to reach Nome on the first boat, because it isn't my secret. It was important enough to make me leave my uncle at Seattle at an hour's notice when we found there was no one else who could go. That's all I can say. I took my maid with me, but the sailors caught her just as she was following me down the ship's ladder. She had my bag of clothes when they seized her. I cast off the rope and rowed ashore as fast as I could, but they lowered another boat and followed me."

The captain eyed her sharply, and his grim lines softened a bit, for she was clean-cut and womanly, and utterly out of place, He took her in, shrewdly, detail by detail, then spoke directly to her:

"My dear young lady—the other ships will get there just as quickly as ours, maybe more quickly. To-morrow we strike the ice-pack and then it is all a matter of luck."

"Yes, but the ship I left won't get there."

At this the commander started, and, darting a great, thick-fingered hand at her, spoke savagely:

"What's that? What ship? Which one did you come from? Answer me."

"The Ohio," she replied, with the effect of a hand-grenade. The master glared at her.

"The Ohio! Good God! You DARE to stand there and tell me that?" He turned and poured his rage upon the others.

"She says the Ohio, d'ye hear? You've ruined me! I'll put you in irons—all of you. The Ohio!"

"What d'ye mean? What's up?"

"What's up? There's small-pox aboard the Ohio! This girl has broken quarantine. The health inspectors bottled up the boat at six o'clock last night! That's why I pulled out of Unalaska ahead of time, to avoid any possible delay. Now we'll all be held up when we get to Nome. Great Heavens! do you realize what this means—bringing this hussy aboard?"

His eyes burned and his voice shook, while the two partners stared at each other in dismay. Too well they knew the result of a small-pox panic aboard this crowded troop-ship. Not only was every available cabin bulging with passengers, but the lower decks were jammed with both humanity and live stock all in the most unsanitary conditions. The craft, built for three hundred passengers, was carrying triple her capacity; men and women were stowed away like cattle. Order and a half-tolerable condition were maintained only by the efforts of the passengers themselves, who held to the thought that imprisonment and inconvenience would last but a few days longer. They had been aboard three weeks and every heart was aflame with the desire to reach Nome— to reach it ahead of the pressing horde behind.

What would be the temper of this gold-frenzied army if thrown into quarantine within sight of their goal? The impatient hundreds would have to lie packed in their floating prison, submitting to the foul disease. Long they must lie thus, till a month should have passed after the disappearance of the last symptom. If the disease recurred sporadically, that might mean endless weeks of maddening idleness. It might even be impossible to impose the necessary restraint; there would be violence, perhaps mutiny.

The fear of the sickness was nothing to Dextry and Glenister, but of their mine they thought with terror. What would happen in their absence, where conditions were as unsettled as in this new land; where titles were held only by physical possession of the premises? During the long winter of their absence, ice had held their treasure inviolate, but with the warming summer the jewel they had fought for so wearily would lie naked and exposed to the first comer. The Midas lay in the valley of the richest creek, where men had schemed and fought and slain for the right to inches. It was the fruit of cheerless, barren years of toil, and if they could not guard it—they knew the result.

The girl interrupted their distressing reflections.

"Don't blame these men, sir," she begged the captain. "I am the only one at fault. Oh! I HAD to get away. I have papers here that must be delivered quickly." She laid a hand upon her bosom. "They couldn't be trusted to the unsettled mail service. It's almost life and death. And I assure you there is no need of putting me in quarantine. I haven't the smallpox. I wasn't even exposed to it."

"There's nothing else to do," said Stephens. "I'll isolate you in the deck smoking-cabin. God knows what these madmen on board will do when they hear about it, though. They're apt to tear you to shreds. They're crazy!"

Glenister had been thinking rapidly.

"If you do that, you'll have mutiny in an hour. This isn't the crowd to stand that sort of thing."

"Bah! Let 'em try it. I'll put 'em down." The officer's square jaws clicked.

"Maybe so; but what then? We reach Nome and the Health Inspector hears of small-pox suspects, then we're all quarantined for thirty days; eight hundred of us. We'll lie at Egg Island all summer while your company pays five thousand a day for this ship. That's not all. The firm is liable in damages for your carelessness in letting disease aboard."

"MY CARELESSNESS!" The old man ground his teeth.

"Yes; that's what it amounts to. You'll ruin your owners, all right. You'll tie up your ship and lose your job, that's a cinch!"

Captain Stephens wiped the moisture from his brow angrily.

"My carelessness! Curse you—you say it well. Don't you realize that I am criminally liable if I don't take every precaution?" He paused for a moment, considering. "I'll hand her over to the ship's doctor."

"See here, now," Glenister urged. "We'll be in Nome in a week—before the young lady would have time to show symptoms of the disease, even if she were going to have it—and a thousand to one she hasn't been exposed, and will never show a trace of it. Nobody knows she's aboard but we three. Nobody will see her get off. She'll stay in this cabin, which will be just as effectual as though you isolated her in any other part of the boat. It will avoid a panic—you'll save your ship and your company—no one will be the wiser—then if the girl comes down with small-pox after she gets ashore, she can go to the pest-house and not jeopardize the health of all the people aboard this ship. You go up forrad to your bridge, sir, and forget that you stepped in to see old Bill Dextry this morning. We'll take care of this matter all right. It means as much to us as it does to you. We've GOT to be on Anvil Creek before the ground thaws or we'll lose the Midas. If you make a fuss, you'll ruin us all."

For some moments they watched him breathlessly as he frowned in indecision, then—

"You'll have to look out for the steward," he said, and the girl sank to a stool while two great tears rolled down her cheeks. The captain's eyes softened and his voice was gentle as he laid his hand on her head.

"Don't feel hurt over what I said, miss. You see, appearances don't tell much, hereabouts—most of the pretty ones are no good. They've fooled me many a time, and I made a mistake. These men will help you through; I can't. Then when you get to Nome, make your sweetheart marry you the day you land. You are too far north to be alone."

He stepped out into the passage and closed the door carefully.

III

In Which Glenister Errs

Well, bein' as me an' Glenister is gougin' into the bowels of Anvil Creek all last summer, we don't really get the fresh-grub habit fastened on us none. You see, the gamblers down-town cop out the few aigs an' green vegetables that stray off the ships, so they never get out as far as the Creek none; except, maybe, in the shape of anecdotes.

"We don't get intimate with no nutriments except hog-boosum an' brown beans, of which luxuries we have unstinted measure, an' bein' as this is our third year in the country we hanker for bony fido grub, somethin' scan'lous. Yes, ma'am—three years without a taste of fresh fruit nor meat nor nuthin'—except pork an' beans. Why, I've et bacon till my immortal soul has growed a rind.

"When it comes time to close down the claim, the boy is sick with the fever an' the only ship in port is a Point Barrow whaler, bound for Seattle. After I book our passage, I find they have nothin' aboard to eat except canned salmon, it bein' the end of a two years' cruise, so when I land in the States after seventeen days of a fish diet, I am what you might call sated with canned grub, and have added salmon to the list of things concernin' which I am goin' to economize.

"Soon's ever I get the boy into a hospital, I gallop up to the best restarawnt in town an' prepare for the huge pot-latch. This here, I determine, is to be a gormandizin' jag which shall live in hist'ry, an' wharof in later years the natives of Puget Sound shall speak with bated breath.

"First, I call for five dollars' worth of pork an' beans an' then a full-grown platter of canned salmon. When the waiter lays 'em out in front of me, I look them vittles coldly in their disgustin' visages, an' say in sarcastic accents:

"'Set there, damn you! an' watch me eat REAL grub,' which I proceed to do, cleanin' the menu from soda to hock. When I have done my worst, I pile bones an' olive seeds an' peelin's all over them articles of nourishment, stick toothpicks into 'em, an' havin' offered 'em what other indignities occur to me, I leave the place."

Dextry and the girl were leaning over the stern-rail, chatting idly in the darkness. It was the second night out and the ship lay dead in the ice-pack. All about them was a flat, floe-clogged sea, leprous and mottled in the deep twilight that midnight brought in this latitude. They had threaded into the ice-field as long as the light lasted, following the lanes of blue water till they closed, then drifting idly till others appeared; worming out into leagues of open sea, again creeping into the shifting labyrinth till darkness rendered progress perilous.

Occasionally they had passed herds of walrus huddled sociably upon ice-pans, their wet hides glistening in the sunlight. The air had been clear and pleasant, while away on all quarters they had seen the smoke of other ships toiling through the barrier. The spring fleet was knocking at the door of the Golden North.

Chafing at her imprisonment, the girl had asked the old man to take her out on deck under the shelter of darkness; then she had led him to speak of his own past experiences, and of Glenister's; which he had done freely. She was frankly curious about them, and she wondered at their apparent lack of interest in her own identity and her secret mission. She even construed their silence as indifference, not realizing that these Northmen were offering her the truest evidence of camaraderie.

The frontier is capable of no finer compliment than this utter disregard of one's folded pages. It betokens that highest faith in one's fellow-man, the belief that he should be measured by his present deeds, not by his past. It says, translated: "This is God's free country where a man is a man, nothing more. Our land is new and pure, our faces are to the front. If you have been square, so much the better; if not, leave behind the taints of artificial things and start again on the level—that's all."

It had happened, therefore, that since the men had asked her no questions, she had allowed the hours to pass and still hesitated to explain further than she had explained to Captain Stephens. It was much easier to let things continue as they were; and there was, after all, so little that she was at liberty to tell them.

In the short time since meeting them, the girl had grown to like Dextry, with his blunt chivalry and boyish, whimsical philosophy, but she avoided Glenister, feeling a shrinking, hidden terror of him, ever since her eavesdropping of the previous night. At the memory of that scene she grew hot, then cold—hot with anger, icy at the sinister power and sureness which had vibrated in his voice. What kind of life was she entering where men spoke of strange women with this assurance and hinted thus of ownership? That he was handsome and unconscious of it, she acknowledged, and had she met him in her accustomed circle of friends, garbed in the conventionalities, she would perhaps have thought of him as a striking man, vigorous and intelligent; but here he seemed naturally to take on the attributes of his surroundings, acquiring a picturesque negligee of dress and morals, and suggesting rugged, elemental, chilling potentialities. While with him—and he had sought her repeatedly that day—she was uneasily aware of his strong personality tugging at her; aware of the unbridled passionate flood of a nature unbrooking of delay and heedless of denial. This it was that antagonized her and set her every mental sinew in rigid resistance.

During Dextry's garrulous ramblings, Glenister emerged from the darkness and silently took his place beside her, against the rail.

"What portent do you see that makes you stare into the night so anxiously?" he inquired.

"I am wishing for a sight of the midnight sun or the aurora borealis," she replied.

"Too late for one an' too fur south for the other," Dextry interposed. "We'll see the sun further north, though."

"Have you ever heard the real origin of the Northern Lights?" the young man inquired.

"Naturally, I never have," she answered.

"Well, here it is. I have it from the lips of a great hunter of the Tananas. He told it to me when I was sick, once, in his cabin, and inasmuch as he is a wise Indian and has a reputation for truth, I have no doubt that it is scrupulously correct.

"In the very old days, before the white man or corned beef had invaded this land, the greatest tribe in all the North was the Tananas. The bravest hunter of these was Itika, the second chief. He could follow a moose till it fell exhausted in the snow and he had many belts made from the claws of the brown bear which is deadly wicked and, as every one knows, inhabited by the spirits of 'Yabla-men,' or devils.

"One winter a terrible famine settled over the Tanana Valley. The moose departed from the gulches and the caribou melted from the hills like mist. The dogs grew gaunt and howled all night, the babies cried, the women became hollow-eyed and peevish.

"Then it was that Itika decided to go hunting over the saw-tooth range which formed the edge of the world. They tried to dissuade him, saying it was certain death because a pack of monstrous white wolves, taller than the moose and swifter than the eagle, was known to range these mountains, running madly in chase. Always, on clear, cold nights, could be seen the flashing of the moonbeams from their gleaming hungry sides, and although many hunters had crossed the passes in other years, they never returned, for the pack slew them.

"Nothing could deter Itika, however, so he threaded his way up through the range and, night coming, burrowed into a drift to sleep in his caribou-skin. Peering out into the darkness, he saw the flashing lights a thousand times brighter than ever before. The whole heavens were ablaze with shifting streamers that raced and writhed back and forth in wild revel. Listening, he heard the hiss and whine of dry snow under the feet of the pack, and a distant noise as of rushing winds, although the air was deathly still.

"With daylight, he proceeded through the range, till he came out above a magnificent valley. Descending the slope, he entered a forest of towering spruce, while on all sides the snow was trampled with tracks as wide as a snow-shoe. There came to him a noise which, as he proceeded, increased till it filled the woods. It was a frightful din, as though a thousand wolves were howling with the madness of the kill. Cautiously creeping nearer, he found a monstrous white animal struggling beneath a spruce which had fallen upon it in such fashion as to pinion it securely.

"All brave men are tender-hearted, so Itika set to work with his axe and cleared away the burden, regardless of the peril to himself. When he had released it, the beast arose and instead of running away addressed him in the most polite and polished Indian, without a trace of accent.

"'You have saved my life. Now, what can I do for you?'

"'I want to hunt in this valley. My people are starving,' said Itika, at which the wolf was greatly pleased and rounded up the rest of the pack to help in the kill.

"Always thereafter when Itika came to the valley of the Yukon the giant drove hunted with him. To this day they run through the mountains on cold, clear nights, in a multitude, while the light of the moon flickers from their white sides, flashing up into the sky in weird, fantastic figures. Some people call it Northern Lights, but old Isaac assured me earnestly, toothlessly, and with the light of ancient truth, as I lay snow-blind in his lodge, that it is nothing more remarkable than the spirit of Itika and the great white wolves."

"What a queer legend!" she said. "There must be many of them in this country. I feel that I am going to like the North."

"Perhaps you will," Glenister replied, "although it is not a woman's land."

"Tell me what led you out here in the first place. You are an Eastern man. You have had advantages, education—and yet you choose this. You must love the North."

"Indeed I do! It calls to a fellow in some strange way that a gentler country never could. When once you've lived the long, lazy June days that never end, and heard geese honking under a warm, sunlit midnight; or when once you've hit the trail on a winter morning so sharp and clear that the air stings your lungs, and the whole white, silent world glistens like a jewel; yes—and when you've seen the dogs romping in harness till the sled runners ring; and the distant mountain-ranges come out like beautiful carvings, so close you can reach them—well, there's something in it that brings you back—that's all, no matter where you've lost yourself. It means health and equality and unrestraint. That's what I like best, I dare say—the utter unrestraint.

"When I was a school-boy, I used to gaze at the map of Alaska for hours. I'd lose myself in it. It wasn't anything but a big, blank corner in the North then, with a name, and mountains, and mystery. The word 'Yukon' suggested to me everything unknown and weird—hairy mastodons, golden river bars, savage Indians with bone arrow-heads and seal-skin trousers. When I left college I came as fast as ever I could—the adventure, I suppose. . .

"The law was considered my destiny. How the shades of old Choate and Webster and Patrick Henry must have wailed when I forswore it. I'll bet Blackstone tore his whiskers."

"I think you would have made a success," said the girl, but he laughed.

"Well, anyhow, I stepped out, leaving the way to the United States Supreme bench unobstructed, and came North. I found it was where I belonged. I fitted in. I'm not contented—don't think that. I'm ambitious, but I prefer these surroundings to the others—that's all. I'm realizing my desires. I've made a fortune—now I'll see what else the world has."

He suddenly turned to her. "See here," he abruptly questioned, "what's your name?"

She started, and glanced towards where Dextry had stood, only to find that the old frontiersman had slipped away during the tale.

"Helen Chester," she replied.

"Helen Chester," he repeated, musingly. "What a pretty name! It seems almost a pity to change it—to marry, as you will."

"I am not going to Nome to get married."

He glanced at her quickly.

"Then you won't like this country. You are two years too early; you ought to wait till there are railroads and telephones, and tables d'hote, and chaperons. It's a man's country yet."

"I don't see why it isn't a woman's country, too. Surely we can take a part in taming it. Yonder on the Oregon is a complete railroad, which will be running from the coast to the mines in a few weeks. Another ship back there has the wire and poles and fixings for a telephone system, which will go up in a night. As to tables d'hote, I saw a real French count in Seattle with a monocle. He's bringing in a restaurant outfit, imported snails, and pate de joies gras. All that's wanting is the chaperon. In my flight from the Ohio I left mine. The sailors caught her. You see I am not far ahead of schedule."

"What part are you going to take in this taming process?" he asked.

She paused long before replying, and when she did her answer sounded like a jest.

"I herald the coming of the law," she said.

"The law! Bah! Red tape, a dead language, and a horde of shysters! I'm afraid of law in this land; we're too new and too far away from things. It puts too much power in too few hands. Heretofore we men up here have had recourse to our courage and our Colts, but we'll have to unbuckle them both when the law comes. I like the court that hasn't any appeal." He laid hand upon his hip.

"The Colts may go, but the courage never will," she broke in.

"Perhaps. But I've heard rumors already of a plot to prostitute the law. In Unalaska a man warned Dextry, with terror in his eye, to beware of it; that beneath the cloak of Justice was a drawn dagger whetted for us fellows who own the rich diggings. I don't think there's any truth in it, but you can't tell."

"The law is the foundation—there can't be any progress without it. There is nothing here now but disorder."

"There isn't half the disorder you think there is. There weren't any crimes in this country till the tenderfeet arrived. We didn't know what a thief was. If you came to a cabin you walked in without knocking. The owner filled up the coffee-pot and sliced into the bacon; then when he'd started your meal, he shook hands and asked your name. It was just the same whether his cache was full or whether he'd packed his few pounds of food two hundred miles on his back. That was hospitality to make your Southern article look pretty small. If there was no one at home, you ate what you needed. There was but one unpardonable breach of etiquette—to fail to leave dry kindlings. I'm afraid of the transitory stage we're coming to—that epoch of chaos between the death of the old and the birth of the new. Frankly, I like the old way best. I love the license of it. I love to wrestle with nature; to snatch, and guard, and fight for what I have. I've been beyond the law for years and I want to stay there, where life is just what it was intended to be—a survival of the fittest."

His large hands, as he gripped the bulwark, were tense and corded, while his rich voice issued softly from his chest with the hint of power unlimited behind it. He stood over her, tall, virile, and magnetic. She saw now why he had so joyously hailed the fight of the previous night; to one of his kind it was as salt air to the nostrils. Unconsciously she approached him, drawn by the spell of his strength.

"My pleasures are violent and my hate is mighty bitter in my mouth. What I want, I take. That's been my way in the old life, and I'm too selfish to give it up."

He was gazing out upon the dimly lucent miles of ice; but now he turned towards her, and, doing so, touched her warm hand next his on the rail.

She was staring up at him unaffectedly, so close that the faint odor from her hair reached him. Her expression was simply one of wonder and curiosity at this type, so different from any she had known. But the man's eyes were hot and blinded with the sight of her, and he felt only her beauty heightened in the dim light, the brush of her garments, and the small, soft hand beneath his. The thrill from the touch of it surged over him—mastered him.

"What I want—I take," he repeated, and then suddenly he reached forth and, taking her in his arms, crushed her to him, kissing her softly, fiercely, full upon the lips. For an instant she lay gasping and stunned against his breast, then she tore her fist free and, with all her force, struck him full in the face.

It was as though she beat upon a stone. With one movement he forced her arm to her side, smiling into her terrified eyes; then, holding her like iron, he kissed her again and again upon the mouth, the eyes, the hair—and released her.

"I am going to love you—Helen," said he.

"And may God strike me dead if I ever stop HATING you!" she cried, her voice coming thick and hoarse with passion.

Turning, she walked proudly forward towards her cabin, a trim, straight, haughty figure; and he did not know that her knees were shaking and weak.

IV

The Killing

For four days the Santa Maria felt blindly through the white fields, drifting north with the spring tide that sets through Behring Strait, till, on the morning of the fifth, open water showed to the east. Creeping through, she broke out into the last stage of the long race, amid the cheers of her weary passengers; and the dull jar of her engines made welcome music to the girl in the deck state-room.

Soon they picked up a mountainous coast which rose steadily into majestic, barren ranges, still white with the melting snows; and at ten in the evening under a golden sunset, amid screaming whistles, they anchored in the roadstead of Nome. Before the rumble of her chains had ceased or the echo from the fleet's salute had died from the shoreward hills, the ship was surrounded by a swarm of tiny craft clamoring about her iron sides, while an officer in cap and gilt climbed the bridge and greeted Captain Stephens. Tugs with trailing lighters circled discreetly about, awaiting the completion of certain formalities. These over, the uniformed gentleman dropped back into his skiff and rowed away.

"A clean bill of health, captain," he shouted, saluting the commander.

"Thank ye, sir," roared the sailor, and with that the row-boats swarmed inward pirate-like, boarding the steamer from all quarters.

As the master turned, he looked down from his bridge to the deck below, full into the face of Dextry, who had been an intent witness of the meeting. With unbending dignity, Captain Stephens let his left eyelid droop slowly, while a boyish grin spread widely over his face. Simultaneously, orders rang sharp and fast from the bridge, the crew broke into feverish life, the creak of booms and the clank of donkey-hoists arose.

"We're here, Miss Stowaway," said Glenister, entering the girl's cabin. "The inspector passed us and it's time for you to see the magic city. Come, it's a wonderful sight."

This was the first time they had been alone since the scene on the after-deck, for, besides ignoring Glenister, she had managed that he should not even see her except in Dextry's presence. Although he had ever since been courteous and considerate, she felt the leaping emotions that were hidden within him and longed to leave the ship, to fly from the spell of his personality. Thoughts of him made her writhe, and yet when he was near she could not hate him as she willed—he overpowered her, he would not be hated, he paid no heed to her slights. This very quality reminded her how willingly and unquestioningly he had fought off the sailors from the Ohio at a word from her. She knew he would do so again, and more, and it is hard to be bitter to one who would lay down his life for you, even though he has offended—particularly when he has the magnetism that sweeps you away from your moorings.

"There's no danger of being seen," he continued, "The crowd's crazy, and, besides, we'll go ashore right away. You must be mad with the confinement—it's on my nerves, too."

As they stepped outside, the door of an adjacent cabin opened, framing an angular, sharp-featured woman, who, catching sight of the girl emerging from Glenister's state-room, paused with shrewdly narrowed eyes, flashing quick, malicious glances from one to the other. They came later to remember with regret this chance encounter, for it was fraught with grave results for them both.

"Good evening, Mr. Glenister," the lady said with acid cordiality.

"Howdy, Mrs. Champian?" He moved away.

She followed a step, staring at Helen.

"Are you going ashore to-night or wait for morning?"

"Don't know yet, I'm sure." Then aside to the girl he muttered, "Shake her, she's spying on us."

"Who is she?" asked Miss Chester, a moment later.

"Her husband manages one of the big companies. She's an old cat."

Gaining her first view of the land, the girl cried out, sharply. They rode on an oily sea, tinted like burnished copper, while on all sides, amid the faint rattle and rumble of machinery, scores of ships were belching cargoes out upon living swarms of scows, tugs, stern-wheelers, and dories. Here and there Eskimo oomiaks, fat, walrus-hide boats, slid about like huge, many-legged water-bugs. An endless, ant-like stream of tenders, piled high with freight, plied to and from the shore. A mile distant lay the city, stretched like a white ribbon between the gold of the ocean sand and the dun of the moss-covered tundra. It was like no other in the world. At first glance it seemed all made of new white canvas. In a week its population had swelled from three to thirty thousand. It now wandered in a slender, sinuous line along the coast for miles, because only the beach afforded dry camping ground. Mounting to the bank behind, one sank knee-deep in moss and water, and, treading twice in the same tracks, found a bog of oozing, icy mud. Therefore, as the town doubled daily in size, it grew endwise like a string of dominoes, till the shore from Cape Nome to Penny River was a long reach of white, glinting in the low rays of the arctic sunset like foamy breakers on a tropic island.

"That's Anvil Creek up yonder," said Glenister. "There's where the Midas lies. See!" He indicated a gap in the buttress of mountains rolling back from the coast. "It's the greatest creek in the world. You'll see gold by the mule-load, and hillocks of nuggets. Oh, I'm glad to get back. This is life. That stretch of beach is full of gold. These hills are seamed with quartz. The bed-rock of that creek is yellow. There's gold, gold, gold, everywhere—more than ever was in old Solomon's mines—and there's mystery and peril and things unknown."

"Let us make haste," said the girl. "I have something I must do to-night. After that, I can learn to know these things."

Securing a small boat, they were rowed ashores the partners plying their ferryman with eager questions. Having arrived five days before, he was exploding with information and volunteered the fruits of his ripe experience till Dextry stated that they were "sourdoughs" themselves, and owned the Midas, whereupon Miss Chester marvelled at the awe which sat upon the man and the wondering stare with which he devoured the partners, to her own utter exclusion.

"Sufferin' cats! Look at the freight!" exclaimed Dextry. "If a storm come up it would bust the community!"

The beach they neared was walled and crowded to the high-tide mark with ramparts of merchandise, while every incoming craft deposited its quota upon whatever vacant foot was close at hand, till bales, boxes, boilers, and baggage of all kinds were confusedly intermixed in the narrow space. Singing longshoremen trundled burdens from the lighters and piled them on the heap, while yelling, cursing crowds fought over it all, selecting, sorting, loading.

There was no room for more, yet hourly they added to the mass. Teams splashed through the lapping surf or stuck in the deep sand between hillocks of goods. All was noise, profanity, congestion, and feverish hurry. This burning haste rang in the voice of the multitude, showed in its violence of gesture and redness of face, permeated the atmosphere with a magnetic, electrifying energy.

"It's somethin' fierce ashore," said the oarsman. "I been up fer three days an' nights steady—there ain't no room, nor time, nor darkness to sleep in. Ham an' eggs is a dollar an' a half, an' whiskey's four bits a throw." He wailed the last, sadly, as a complaint unspeakable.

"Any trouble doin'?" inquired the old man.

"You Know it!" the other cried, colloquially. "There was a massacree in the Northern last night."

"Gamblin' row?"

"Yep. Tin-horn called 'Missou' done it."

"Sho!" said Dextry. "I know him. He's a bad actor." All three men nodded sagely, and the girl wished for further light, but they volunteered no explanation.

Leaving the skiff, they plunged into turmoil. Dodging through the tangle, they came out into fenced lots where tents stood wall to wall and every inch was occupied. Here and there was a vacant spot guarded jealously by its owner, who gazed sourly upon all men with the forbidding eye of suspicion. Finding an eddy in the confusion, the men stopped.

"Where do you want to go?" they asked Miss Chester.

There was no longer in Glenister's glance that freedom with which he had come to regard the women of the North. He had come to realize dully that here was a girl driven by some strong purpose into a position repellent to her. In a man of his type, her independence awoke only admiration and her coldness served but to inflame him the more. Delicacy, in Glenister, was lost in a remarkable singleness of purpose. He could laugh at her loathing, smile under her abuse, and remain utterly ignorant that anything more than his action in seizing her that night lay at the bottom of her dislike. He did not dream that he possessed characteristics abhorrent to her; and he felt a keen reluctance at parting.

She extended both hands.

"I can never thank you enough for what you have done—you two; but I shall try. Good-bye!"

Dextry gazed doubtfully at his own hand, rough and gnarly, then taking hers as he would have handled a robin's egg, waggled it limply.

"We ain't goin' to turn you adrift this-a-way. Whatever your destination is, we'll see you to it."

"I can find my friends," she assured him.

"This is the wrong latitude in which to dispute a lady, but knowin' this camp from soup to nuts, as I do, I su'gests a male escort."

"Very well! I wish to find Mr. Struve, of Dunham & Struve, lawyers."

"I'll take you to their offices," said Glenister. "You see to the baggage, Dex. Meet me at the Second Class in half an hour and we'll run out to the Midas." They pushed through the tangle of tents, past piles of lumber, and emerged upon the main thoroughfare, which ran parallel to the shore.

Nome consisted of one narrow street, twisted between solid rows of canvas and half-erected frame buildings, its every other door that of a saloon. There were fair-looking blocks which aspired to the dizzy height of three stories, some sheathed in corrugated iron, others gleaming and galvanized. Lawyers' signs, doctors', surveyors', were in the upper windows. The street was thronged with men from every land—Helen Chester heard more dialects than she could count. Laplanders in quaint, three-cornered, padded caps idled past. Men with the tan of the tropics rubbed elbows with yellow-haired Norsemen, and near her a carefully groomed Frenchman with riding-breeches and monocle was in pantomime with a skin-clad Eskimo. To her left was the sparkling sea, alive with ships of every class. To her right towered timberless mountains, unpeopled, unexplored, forbidding, and desolate—their hollows inlaid with snow. On one hand were the life and the world she knew; on the other, silence, mystery, possible adventure.

The roadway where she stood was a crush of sundry vehicles from bicycles to dog-hauled water-carts, and on all sides men were laboring busily, the echo of hammers mingling with the cries of teamsters and the tinkle of music within the saloons.

"And this is midnight!" exclaimed Helen, breathlessly. "Do they ever rest?"

"There isn't time—this is a gold stampede. You haven't caught the spirit of it yet." They climbed the stairs in a huge, iron-sheeted building to the office of Dunham.

"Anybody else here besides you?" asked her escort of the lawyer.

"No. I'm runnin' the law business unassisted. Don't need any help. Dunham's in Wash'n'ton, D. C., the lan' of the home, the free of the brave. What can I do for you?"

He made to cross the threshold hospitably, but tripped, plunged forward, and would have rolled down the stairs had not Glenister gathered him up and borne him back into the office, where he tossed him upon a bed in a rear room.

"Now what, Miss Chester?" asked the young man, returning.

"Isn't that dreadful?" she shuddered. "Oh, and I must see him to-night!" She stamped impatiently. "I must see him alone."

"No, you mustn't," said Glenister, with equal decision. "In the first place, he wouldn't know what you were talking about, and in the second place—I know Struve. He's too drunk to talk business and too sober to—well, to see you alone."

"But I Must see him," she insisted. "It's what brought me here. You don't understand."

"I understand more than he could. He's in no condition to act on any important matter. You come around to-morrow when he's sober."

"It means so much," breathed the girl. "The beast!"

Glenister noted that she had not wrung her hands nor even hinted at tears, though plainly her disappointment and anxiety were consuming her.

"Well, I suppose I'll have to wait, but I don't know where to go—some hotel, I suppose."

"There aren't any. They're building two, but to-night you couldn't hire a room in Nome for money. I was about to say 'love or money.' Have you no other friends here—no women? Then you must let me find a place for you. I have a friend whose wife will take you in."

She rebelled at this. Was she never to have done with this man's favors? She thought of returning to the ship, but dismissed that. She undertook to decline his aid, but he was half-way down the stairs and paid no attention to her beginning—so she followed him.

It was then that Helen Chester witnessed her first tragedy of the frontier, and through it came to know better the man whom she disliked and with whom she had been thrown so fatefully. Already she had thrilled at the spell of this country, but she had not learned that strength and license carry blood and violence as corollaries.

Emerging from the doorway at the foot of the stairs, they drifted slowly along the walk, watching the crowd. Besides the universal tension, there were laughter and hope and exhilaration in the faces. The enthusiasm of this boyish multitude warmed one. The girl wished to get into this spirit—to be one of them. Then suddenly from the babble at their elbows came a discordant note, not long nor loud, only a few words, penetrating and harsh with the metallic quality lent by passion.

Helen glanced over her shoulder to find that the smiles of the throng were gone and that its eyes were bent on some scene in the street, with an eager interest she had never seen mirrored before. Simultaneously Glenister spoke:

"Come away from here."

With the quickened eye of experience he foresaw trouble and tried to drag her on, but she shook off his grasp impatiently, and, turning, gazed absorbed at the spectacle which unfolded itself before her. Although not comprehending the play of events, she felt vaguely the quick approach of some crisis, yet was unprepared for the swiftness with which it came.

Her eyes had leaped to the figures of two men in the street from whom the rest had separated like oil from water. One was slim and well dressed; the other bulky, mackinawed, and lowering of feature. It was the smaller who spoke, and for a moment she misjudged his bloodshot eyes and swaying carriage to be the result of alcohol, until she saw that he was racked with fury.

"Make good, I tell you, quick! Give me that bill of sale, you—."

The unkempt man swung on his heel with a growl and walked away, his course leading him towards Glenister and the girl. With two strides he was abreast of them; then, detecting the flashing movement of the other, he whirled like a wild animal. His voice had the snarl of a beast in it.

"Ye had to have it, didn't ye? Well, there!"

The actions of both men were quick as light, yet to the girl's taut senses they seemed theatrical and deliberate. Into her mind was seared forever the memory of that second, as though the shutter of a camera had snapped, impressing upon her brain the scene, sharp, clear-cut, and vivid. The shaggy back of the large man almost brushing her, the rage-drunken, white shirted man in the derby hat, the crowd sweeping backward like rushes before a blast, men with arms flexed and feet raised in flight, the glaring yellow sign of the "Gold Belt Dance Hall" across the way—these were stamped upon her retina, and then she was jerked violently backward, two strong arms crushed her down upon her knees against the wall, and she was smothered in the arms of Roy Glenister.

"My God! Don't move! We're in line!"

He crouched over her, his cheek against her hair, his weight forcing her down into the smallest compass, his arms about her, his body forming a living shield against the flying bullets. Over them the big man stood, and the sustained roar of his gun was deafening. In an instant they heard the thud and felt the jar of lead in the thin boards against which they huddled. Again the report echoed above their heads, and they saw the slender man in the street drop his weapon and spin half round as though hit with some heavy hand. He uttered a cry and, stooping for his gun, plunged forward, burying his face in the sand.

The man by Glenister's side shouted curses thickly, and walked towards his prostrate enemy, firing at every step. The wounded man rolled to his side, and, raising himself on his elbow, shot twice, so rapidly that the reports blended—but without checking his antagonist's approach. Four more times the relentless assailant fired deliberately, his last missile sent as he stood over the body which twitched and shuddered at his feet, its garments muddy and smeared. Then he turned and retraced his steps. Back within arm's-length of the two who pressed against the building he came, and as he went by they saw his coarse and sullen features drawn and working pallidly, while the breath whistled through his teeth. He held his course to the door they had just quitted, then as he turned he coughed bestially, spitting out a mouthful of blood. His knees wavered. He vanished within the portals and, in the sickly silence that fell, they heard his hob-nailed boots clumping slowly up the stairs.

Noise awoke and rioted down the thoroughfare. Men rushed forth from every quarter, and the ghastly object in the dirt was hidden by a seething mass of miners.

Glenister raised the girl, but her head rolled limply, and she would have slipped to her knees again had he not placed his arm about her waist. Her eyes were staring and horror-filled.

"Don't be frightened," said he, smiling at her reassuringly; but his own lips shook and the sweat stood out like dew on him; for they had both been close to death. There came a surge and swirl through the crowd, and Dextry swooped upon them like a hawk.

"Be ye hurt? Holy Mackinaw! When I see 'em blaze away I yells at ye fit to bust my throat. I shore thought you was gone. Although I can't say but this killin' was a sight for sore eyes—so neat an' genteel—still, as a rule, in these street brawls it's the innocuous bystander that has flowers sent around to his house afterwards."

"Look at this," said Glenister. Breast-high in the wall against which they had crouched, not three feet apart, were bullet holes.

"Them's the first two he unhitched," Dextry remarked, jerking his head towards the object in the street. "Must have been a new gun an' pulled hard—throwed him to the right. See!"

Even to the girl it was patent that, had she not been snatched as she was, the bullet would have found her.

"Come away quick," she panted, and they led her into a near-by store, where she sank upon a seat and trembled until Dextry brought her a glass of whiskey.

"Here, Miss," he said. "Pretty tough go for a 'cheechako.' I'm afraid you ain't gettin' enamoured of this here country a whole lot."

For half an hour he talked to her, in his whimsical way, of foreign things, till she was quieted. Then the partners arose to go. Although Glenister had arranged for her to stop with the wife of the merchant for the rest of the night, she would not.

"I can't go to bed. Please don't leave me! I'm too nervous. I'll go MAD if you do. The strain of the last week has been too much for me. If I sleep I'll see the faces of those men again."

Dextry talked with his companion, then made a purchase which he laid at the lady's feet.

"Here's a pair of half-grown gum boots. You put 'em on an' come with us. We'll take your mind off of things complete. An' as fer sweet dreams, when you get back you'll make the slumbers of the just seem as restless as a riot, or the antics of a mountain-goat which nimbly leaps from crag to crag, and—well, that's restless enough. Come on!"

As the sun slanted up out of Behring Sea, they marched back towards the hills, their feet ankle-deep in the soft fresh moss, while the air tasted like a cool draught and a myriad of earthy odors rose up and encircled them. Snipe and reed birds were noisy in the hollows and from the misty tundra lakes came the honking of brant. After their weary weeks on shipboard, the dewy freshness livened them magically, cleansing from their memories the recent tragedy, so that the girl became herself again.

"Where are we going?" she asked, at the end of an hour, pausing for breath.

"Why, to the Midas, of course," they said; and one of them vowed recklessly, as he drank in the beauty of her clear eyes and the grace of her slender, panting form, that he would gladly give his share of all its riches to undo what he had done one night on the Santa Maria.

V

Wherein a Man Appears

In the lives of countries there are crises where, for a breath, destinies lie in the laps of the gods and are jumbled, heads or tails. Thus are marked distinctive cycles like the seven ages of a man, and though, perhaps, they are too subtle to be perceived at the time, yet, having swung past the shadowy milestones, the epochs disclose themselves.

Such a period in the progress of the Far Northwest was the nineteenth day of July, although to those concerned in the building of this new empire the day appealed only as the date of the coming of the law. All Nome gathered on the sands as lighters brought ashore Judge Stillman and his following. It was held fitting that the Senator should be the ship to safeguard the dignity of the first court and to introduce Justice into this land of the wild.

The interest awakened by His Honor was augmented by the fact that he was met on the beach by a charming girl, who flung herself upon him with evident delight.

"That's his niece," said some one. "She came up on the first boat—name's Chester—swell looker, eh?"

Another new-comer attracted even more notice than the limb of the law; a gigantic, well-groomed man, with keen, close-set eyes, and that indefinable easy movement and polished bearing that come from confidence, health, and travel. Unlike the others, he did not dally on the beach nor display much interest in his surroundings; but, with purposeful frown strode through the press, up into the heart of the city. His companion was Struve's partner, Dunham, a middle-aged, pompous man. They went directly to the offices of Dunham & Struve, where they found the white-haired junior partner.

"Mighty glad to meet you, Mr. McNamara," said Struve. "Your name is a household word in my part of the country. My people were mixed up in Dakota politics somewhat, so I've always had a great admiration for you and I'm glad you've come to Alaska. This is a big country and we need big men."

"Did you have any trouble?" Dunham inquired when the three had adjourned to a private room.

"Trouble," said Struve, ruefully; "well, I wonder if I did. Miss Chester brought me your instructions O.K. and I got busy right off. But, tell me this—how did you get the girl to act as messenger?"

"There was no one else to send," answered McNamara. "Dunham intended sailing on the first boat, but he was detained in Washington with, me, and the Judge had to wait for us at Seattle. We were afraid to trust a stranger for fear he might get curious and examine the papers. That would have meant—" He moved his hand eloquently.

Struve nodded. "I see. Does she know what was in the documents?"

"Decidedly not. Women and business don't mix. I hope you didn't tell her anything."

"No; I haven't had a chance. She seemed to take a dislike to me for some reason, I haven't seen her since the day after she got here."

"The Judge told her it had something to do with preparing the way for his court," said Dunham, "and that if the papers were not delivered before he arrived it might cause a lot of trouble—litigation, riots, bloodshed, and all that. He filled her up on generalities till the girl was frightened to death and thought the safety of her uncle and the whole country depended on her."

"Well," continued Struve, "it's dead easy to hire men to jump claims and it's dead easy to buy their rights afterwards, particularly when they know they haven't got any—but what course do you follow when owners go gunning for you?"

McNamara laughed.

"Who did that?"

"A benevolent, silver-haired old Texan pirate by the name of Dextry. He's one half owner in the Midas and the other half mountain-lion; as peaceable, you'd imagine, as a benediction, but with the temperament of a Geronimo. I sent Galloway out to relocate the claim, and he got his notices up in the night when they were asleep, but at 6 A.M. he came flying back to my room and nearly hammered the door down. I've seen fright in varied forms and phases, but he had them all, with some added starters.

"'Hide me out, quick!' he panted.

"'What's up?' I asked.

"'I've stirred up a breakfast of grizzly bear, smallpox, and sudden death and it don't set well on my stummick. Let me in.'

"I had to keep him hidden three days, for this gentle-mannered old cannibal roamed the streets with a cannon in his hand, breathing fire and pestilence."

"Anybody else act up?" queried Dunham.

"No; all the rest are Swedes and they haven't got the nerve to fight. They couldn't lick a spoon if they tried. These other men are different, though. There are two of them, the old one and a young fellow. I'm a little afraid to mix it up with them, and if their claim wasn't the best in the district, I'd say let it alone."

"I'll attend to that," said McNamara.

Struve resumed:

"Yes, gentlemen, I've been working pretty hard and also pretty much in the dark so far. I'm groping for light. When Miss Chester brought in the papers I got busy instanter. I clouded the title to the richest placers in the region, but I'm blamed if I quite see the use of it. We'd be thrown out of any court in the land if we took them to law. What's the game—blackmail?"

"Humph!" exclaimed McNamara. "What do you take me for?"

"Well, it does seem small for Alec McNamara, but I can't see what else you're up to."

"Within a week I'll be running every good mine in the Nome district."

McNamara's voice was calm but decisive, his glance keen and alert, while about him clung such a breath of power and confidence that it compelled belief even in the face of this astounding speech.

In spite of himself, Wilton Struve, lawyer, rake, and gentlemanly adventurer, felt his heart leap at what the other's daring implied. The proposition was utterly past belief, and yet, looking into the man's purposeful eyes, he believed.

"That's big—awful big—Too big," the younger man murmured. "Why, man, it means you'll handle fifty thousand dollars a day!"

Dunham shifted his feet in the silence and licked his dry lips.

"Of course it's big, but Mr. McNamara's the biggest man that ever came to Alaska," he said.

"And I've got the biggest scheme that ever came north, backed by the biggest men in Washington," continued the politician. "Look here!" He displayed a type-written sheet bearing parallel lists of names and figures. Struve gasped incredulously.

"Those are my stockholders and that is their share in the venture. Oh, yes; we're incorporated—under the laws of Arizona—secret, of course; it would never do for the names to get out. I'm showing you this only because I want you to be satisfied who's behind me."

"Lord! I'm satisfied," said Struve, laughing nervously. "Dunham was with you when you figured the scheme out and he met some of your friends in Washington and New York. If he says it's all right, that settles it. But say, suppose anything went wrong with the company and it leaked out who those stockholders are?"

"There's no danger. I have the books where they will be burned at the first sign. We'd have had our own land laws passed but for Sturtevant of Nevada, damn him. He blocked us in the Senate. However, my plan is this." He rapidly outlined his proposition to the listeners, while a light of admiration grew and shone in the reckless face of Struve.

"By heavens! you're a wonder!" he cried, at the close, "and I'm with you body and soul. It's dangerous—that's why I like it."

"Dangerous?" McNamara shrugged his shoulders. "Bah! Where is the danger? We've got the law—or rather, we ARE the law. Now, let's get to work."

It seemed that the Boss of North Dakota was no sluggard. He discarded coat and waistcoat and tackled the documents which Struve laid before him, going through them like a whirlwind. Gradually he infected the others with his energy, and soon behind the locked doors of Dunham & Struve there were only haste and fever and plot and intrigue.

As Helen Chester led the Judge towards the flamboyant, three-storied hotel she prattled to him light-heartedly. The fascination of a new land already held her fast, and now she felt, in addition, security and relief. Glenister saw them from a distance and strode forward to greet them.

He beheld a man of perhaps threescore years, benign of aspect save for the eyes, which were neither clear nor steady, but had the trick of looking past one. Glenister thought the mouth, too, rather weak and vacillating; but the clean-shaven face was dignified by learning a acumen and was wrinkled in pleasant fashion.

"My niece has just told me of your service to her," the old gentleman began. "I am happy to know you, sir."

"Besides being a brave knight and assisting ladies in distress, Mr. Glenister is a very great and wonderful man," Helen explained, lightly. "He owns the Midas."

"Indeed!" said the old man, his shifting eyes now resting full on the other with a flash of unmistakable interest. "I hear that is a wonderful mine. Have you begun work yet?"

"No. We'll commence sluicing day after to-morrow. It has been a late spring. The snow in the gulch was deep and the ground thaws slowly. We've been building houses and doing dead work, but we've got our men on the ground, waiting."

"I am greatly interested. Won't you walk with us to the hotel? I want to hear more about these wonderful placers."

"Well, they ARE great placers," said the miner, as the three walked on together; "nobody knows How great because we've only scratched at them yet. In the first place the ground is so shallow and the gold is so easy to get, that if nature didn't safeguard us in the winter we'd never dare leave our claims for fear of 'snipers.' They'd run in and rob us."

"How much will the Anvil Creek mines produce this summer?" asked the Judge.

"It's hard to tell, sir; but we expect to average five thousand a day from the Midas alone, and there are other claims just as good."

"Your title is all clear, I dare say, eh?"

"Absolutely, except for one jumper, and we don't take him seriously. A fellow named Galloway relocated us one night last month, but he didn't allege any grounds for doing so, and we could never find trace of him. If we had, our title would be as clean as snow again." He said the last with a peculiar inflection.

"You wouldn't use violence, I trust?"

"Sure! Why not? It has worked all right heretofore."

"But, my dear sir, those days are gone. The law is here and it is the duty of every one to abide by it."

"Well, perhaps it is; but in this country we consider a man's mine as sacred as his family. We didn't know what a lock and key were in the early times and we didn't have any troubles except famine and hardship. It's different now, though. Why, there have been more claims jumped around here this spring than in the whole length and history of the Yukon."

They had reached the hotel, and Glenister paused, turning to the girl as the Judge entered. When she started to follow, he detained her.

"I came down from the hills on purpose to see you. It has been a long week—"

"Don't talk that way," she interrupted, coldly. "I don't care to hear it."

"See here—what makes you shut me out and wrap yourself up in your haughtiness? I'm sorry for what I did that night—I've told you so repeatedly. I've wrung my soul for that act till there's nothing left but repentance."

"It is not that," she said, slowly. "I have been thinking it over during the past month, and now that I have gained an insight into this life I see that it wasn't an unnatural thing for you to do. It's terrible to think of, but it's true. I don't mean that it was pardonable," she continued, quickly, "for it wasn't, and I hate you when I think about it, but I suppose I put myself into a position to invite such actions. No; I'm sufficiently broad-minded not to blame you unreasonably, and I think I could like you in spite of it, just for what you have done for me; but that isn't all. There is something deeper. You saved my life and I'm grateful, but you frighten me, always. It is the cruelty in your strength, it is something away back in you—lustful, and ferocious, and wild, and crouching."

He smiled wryly.

"It is my local color, maybe—absorbed from this country. I'll try to change, though, if you want me to. I'll let them rope and throw and brand me. I'll take on the graces of civilization and put away revenge and ambition and all the rest of it, if it will make you like me any better. Why, I'll even promise not to violate the person of our claim-jumper if I catch him; and Heaven knows THAT means that Samson has parted with his locks."

"I think I could like you if you did," she said, "but you can't do it. You are a savage."

There are no clubs nor marts where men foregather for business in the North—nothing but the saloon, and this is all and more than a club. Here men congregate to drink, to gamble, and to traffic.

It was late in the evening when Glenister entered the Northern and passed idly down the row of games, pausing at the crap-table, where he rolled the dice when his turn came. Moving to the roulette-wheel, he lost a stack of whites, but at the faro "lay-out" his luck was better, and he won a gold coin on the "high-card." Whereupon he promptly ordered a round of drinks for the men grouped about him, a formality always precedent to overtures of general friendship.

As he paused, glass in hand, his eyes were drawn to a man who stood close by, talking earnestly. The aspect of the stranger challenged notice, for he stood high above his companions with a peculiar grace of attitude in place of the awkwardness common in men of great stature. Among those who were listening intently to the man's carefully modulated tones, Glenister recognized Mexico Mullins, the ex-gambler who had given Dextry the warning at Unalaska. As he further studied the listening group, a drunken man staggered uncertainly through the wide doors of the saloon and, gaining sight of the tall stranger, blinked, then approached him, speaking with a loud voice:

"Well, if 'tain't ole Alec McNamara! How do, ye ole pirate!"

McNamara nodded and turned his back coolly upon the new-comer.

"Don't turn your dorsal fin to me; I wan' to talk to ye."

McNamara continued his calm discourse till he received a vicious whack on the shoulder; then he turned for a moment to interrupt his assailant's garrulous profanity:

"Don't bother me. I am engaged."

"Ye won' talk to me, eh? Well, I'm goin' to talk to You, see? I guess you'd listen if I told these people all I know about you. Turn around here."

His voice was menacing and attracted general notice. Observing this, McNamara addressed him, his words dropping clear, concise, and cold:

"Don't talk to me. You are a drunken nuisance. Go away before something happens to you."

Again he turned away, but the drunken man seized and whirled him about, repeating his abuse, encouraged by this apparent patience.

"Your pardon for an instant, gentlemen." McNamara laid a large white and manicured hand upon the flannel sleeve of the miner and gently escorted him through the entrance to the sidewalk, while the crowd smiled.

As they cleared the threshold, however, he clenched his fist without a word and, raising it, struck the sot fully and cruelly upon the jaw. His victim fell silently, the back of his head striking the boards with a hollow thump; then, without even observing how he lay, McNamara re-entered the saloon and took up his conversation where he had been interrupted. His voice was as evenly regulated as his movements, betraying not a sign of anger, excitement, or bravado. He lit a cigarette, extracted a note-book, and jotted down certain memoranda supplied him by Mexico Mullins.

All this time the body lay across the threshold without a sign of life. The buzz of the roulette-wheel was resumed and the crap-dealer began his monotonous routine. Every eye was fixed on the nonchalant man at the bar, but the unconscious creature outside the threshold lay unheeded, for in these men's code it behooves the most humane to practise a certain aloofness in the matter of private brawls.

Having completed his notes, McNamara shook hands gravely with his companions and strode out through the door, past the bulk that sprawled across his path, and, without pause or glance, disappeared.

A dozen willing, though unsympathetic, hands laid the drunkard on the roulette-table, where the bartender poured pitcher upon pitcher of water over him.

"He ain't hurt none to speak of," said a bystander; then added, with enthusiasm:

"But say! There's a MAN in this here camp!"

VI

AND A MINE IS JUMPED

W ho's your new shift boss?" Glenister inquired of his partner, a few days later, indicating a man in the cut below, busied in setting a line of sluices.

"That's old 'Slapjack' Simms, friend of mine from up Dawson way."

Glenister laughed immoderately, for the object was unusually tall and loose-jointed, and wore a soiled suit of yellow mackinaw. He had laid off his coat, and now the baggy, bilious trousers hung precariously from his angular shoulders by suspenders of alarming frailty. His legs were lost in gum boots, also loose and cavernous, and his entire costume looked relaxed and flapping, so that he gave the impression of being able to shake himself out of his raiment, and to rise like a burlesque Aphrodite. His face was overgrown with a grizzled tangle that looked as though it had been trimmed with button-hole scissors, while above the brush heap grandly soared a shiny, dome-like head.

"Has he always been bald?"

"Naw! He ain't bald at all. He shaves his nob. In the early days he wore a long flowin' mane which was inhabited by crickets, tree-toads, and such fauna. It got to be a hobby with him finally, so that he growed superstitious about goin' uncurried, and would back into a corner with both guns drawed if a barber came near him. But once Hank—that's his real name—undertook to fry some slapjacks, and in givin' the skillet a heave, the dough lit among his forest primeval, jest back of his ears, soft side down. Hank polluted the gulch with langwidge which no man had ought to keep in himself without it was fumigated. Disreppitableness oozed out through him like sweat through an ice-pitcher, an' since then he's been known as Slapjack Simms, an' has kept his head shingled smooth as a gun bar'l. He's a good miner, though; ain't none better—an' square as a die."

Sluicing had begun on the Midas. Long sinuous lengths of canvas hose wound down the creek bottom from the dam, like gigantic serpents, while the roll of gravel through the flumes mingled musically with the rush of waters, the tinkle of tools, and the song of steel on rock. There were four "strings" of boxes abreast, and the heaving line of shovellers ate rapidly into the creek bed, while teams with scrapers splashed through the tail races in an atmosphere of softened profanity. In the big white tents which sat back from the bluffs, fifty men of the night shift were asleep; for there is no respite here—no night, no Sunday, no halt, during the hundred days in which the Northland lends herself to pillage.

The mine lay cradled between wonderful, mossy, willow-mottled mountains, while above and below the gulch was dotted with tents and huts, and everywhere, from basin to hill crest, men dug and blasted, punily, patiently, while their tracks grew daily plainer over the face of this inscrutable wilderness.

A great contentment filled the two partners as they looked on this scene. To wrest from reluctant earth her richest treasures, to add to the wealth of the world, to create—here was satisfaction.

"We ain't robbin' no widders an' orphans doin' it, neither," Dextry suddenly remarked, expressing his partner's feelings closely. They looked at each other and smiled with that rare understanding that exceeds words.

Descending into the cut, the old man filled a gold-pan with dirt taken from under the feet of the workers, and washed it in a puddle, while the other watched his dexterous whirling motions. When he had finished, they poked the stream of yellow grains into a pile, then, with heads together, guessed its weight, laughing again delightedly, in perfect harmony and contentment.

"I've been waitin' a turrible time fer this day," said the elder. "I've suffered the plagues of prospectin' from the Mexicos to the Circle, an' yet I don't begretch it none, now that I've struck pay."

While they spoke, two miners struggled with a bowlder they had unearthed, and having scraped and washed it carefully, staggered back to place it on the cleaned bed-rock behind. One of them slipped, and it crashed against a brace which held the sluices in place. These boxes stand more than a man's height above the bed-rock, resting on supporting posts and running full of water. Should a sluice fall, the rushing stream carries out the gold which has lodged in the riffles and floods the bed-rock, raising havoc. Too late the partners saw the string of boxes sway and bend at the joint. Then, before they could reach the threatened spot to support it, Slapjack Simms, with a shriek, plunged flapping down into the cut and seized the flume. His great height stood him in good stead now, for where the joint had opened, water poured forth in a cataract, He dived under the breach unhesitatingly and, stooping, lifted the line as near to its former level as possible, holding the entire burden upon his naked pate. He gesticulated wildly for help, while over him poured the deluge of icy, muddy water. It entered his gaping waistband, bulging out his yellow trousers till they were fat and full and the seams were bursting, while his yawning boot-tops became as boiling springs. Meanwhile he chattered forth profanity in such volume that the ear ached under it as must have ached the heroic Slapjack under the chill of the melting snow. He was relieved quickly, however, and emerged triumphant, though blue and puckered, his wilderness of whiskers streaming like limber stalactites, his boots loosely "squishing," while oaths still poured from him in such profusion that Dextry whispered:

"Ain't he a ring-tailed wonder? It's plumb solemn an' reverent the way he makes them untamed cuss-words sit up an' beg. It's a privilege to be present. That's a GIFT, that is."

"You'd better get some dry clothes," they suggested, and Slapjack proceeded a few paces towards the tents, hobbling as though treading on pounded glass.

"Ow—w!" he yelled. "These blasted boots is full of gravel."

He seated himself and tugged at his foot till the boot came away with a sucking sound, then, instead of emptying the accumulation at random, he poured the contents into Dextry's empty gold-pan, rinsing it out carefully. The other boot he emptied likewise. They held a surprising amount of sediment, because the stream that had emerged from the crack in the sluices had carried with it pebbles, sand, and all the concentration of the riffles at this point. Standing directly beneath the cataract, most of it had dived fairly into his inviting waistband, following down the lines of least resistance into his boot-legs and boiling out at the knees.

"Wash that," he said. "You're apt to get a prospect."

With artful passes Dextry settled it in the pan bottom and washed away the gravel, leaving a yellow, glittering pile which raised a yell from the men who had lingered curiously.

"He pans forty dollars to the boot-leg," one shouted.

"How much do you run to the foot, Slapjack?"

"He's a reg'lar free-milling ledge."

"No, he ain't—he's too thin. He's nothing but a stringer, but he'll pay to work."

The old miner grinned toothlessly.

"Gentlemen, there ain't no better way to save fine gold than with undercurrents an' blanket riffles. I'll have to wash these garments of mine an' clean up the soapsuds 'cause there's a hundred dollars in gold-dust clingin' to my person this minute." He went dripping up the bank, while the men returned to their work singing.

After lunch Dextry saddled his bronco.

"I'm goin' to town for a pair of gold-scales, but I'll be back by supper, then we'll clean up between shifts. She'd ought to give us a thousand ounces, the way that ground prospects." He loped down the gulch, while his partner returned to the pit, the flashing shovel blades, and the rumbling undertone of the big workings that so fascinated him. It was perhaps four o'clock when he was aroused from his labors by a shout from the bunk-tent, where a group of horsemen had clustered. As Glenister drew near, he saw among them Wilton Struve, the lawyer, and the big, well-dressed tenderfoot of the Northern—McNamara—the man of the heavy hand. Struve straightway engaged him.

"Say, Glenister, we've come out to see about the title to this claim."

"What about it?"

"Well, it was relocated about a month ago." He paused.

"Yes. What of that?"

"Galloway has commenced suit."

"The ground belongs to Dextry and me. We discovered it, we opened it up, we've complied with the law, and we're going to hold it." Glenister spoke with such conviction and heat as to nonplus Struve, but McNamara, who had sat his horse silently until now, answered:

"Certainly, sir; if your title is good you will be protected, but the law has arrived in Alaska and we've got to let it take its course. There's no need of violence—none whatever—but, briefly, the situation is this: Mr. Galloway has commenced action against you; the court has enjoined you from working and has appointed me as receiver to operate the mine until the suit is settled. It's an extraordinary procedure, of course, but the conditions are extraordinary in this country. The season is so short that it would be unjust to the rightful owner if the claim lay idle all summer—so, to avoid that, I've been put in charge, with instructions to operate it and preserve the proceeds subject to the court's order. Mr. Voorhees here is the United States Marshal. He will serve the papers."

Glenister threw up his hand in a gesture of restraint.

"Hold on! Do you mean to tell me that any court would recognize such a claim as Galloway's?"

"The law recognizes everything. If his grounds are no good, so much the better for you."

"You can't put in a receiver without notice to us. Why, good Lord! we never heard of a suit being commenced. We've never even been served with a summons and we haven't had a chance to argue in our own defence."

"I have just said that this is a remarkable state of affairs and unusual action had to be taken," McNamara replied, but the young miner grew excited.

"Look here—this gold won't get away. It's safe in the ground. We'll knock off work and let the claim lie idle till the thing is settled. You can't really expect us to surrender possession of our mine on the mere allegation of some unknown man. That's ridiculous. We won't do it. Why, you'll have to let us argue our case, at least, before you try to put us off."

Voorhees shook his head. "We'll have to follow instructions. The thing for you to do is to appear before the court to-morrow and have the receiver dismissed. If your title is as good as you say it is, you won't have any trouble."

"You're not the only ones to suffer," added McNamara. "We've taken possession of all the mines below here." He nodded down the gulch. "I'm an officer of the court and under bond—"

"How much?"

"Five thousand dollars for each claim."

"What! Why, heavens, man, the poorest of these mines is producing that much every day!"

While he spoke, Glenister was rapidly debating what course to follow.

"The place to argue this thing is before Judge Stillman," said Struve—but with little notion of the conflict going on within Glenister. The youth yearned to fight—not with words nor quibbles nor legal phrases, but with steel and blows. And he felt that the impulse was as righteous as it was natural, for he knew this process was unjust, an outrage. Mexico Mullins's warning recurred to him. And yet—. He shifted slowly as he talked till his back was to the door of the big tent. They were watching him carefully, for all their apparent languor and looseness in saddle; then as he started to leap within and rally his henchmen, his mind went back to the words of Judge Stillman and his niece. Surely that old man was on the square. He couldn't be otherwise with her beside him, believing in him; and a suspicion of deeper plots behind these actions was groundless. So far, all was legal, he supposed, with his scant knowledge of law; though the methods seemed unreasonable. The men might be doing what they thought to be right. Why be the first to resist? The men on the mines below had not done so. The title to this ground was capable of such easy proof that he and Dex need have no uneasiness. Courts do not rob honest people nowadays, he argued, and moreover, perhaps the girl's words were true, perhaps she WOULD think more of him if he gave up the old fighting ways for her sake. Certainly armed resistance to her uncle's first edict would not please her. She had said he was too violent, so he would show her he could lay his savagery aside. She might smile on him approvingly, and that was worth taking a chance for—anyway it would mean but a few days' delay in the mine's run. As he reasoned he heard a low voice speaking within the open door. It was Slapjack Simms.

"Step aside, lad. I've got the big un covered."

Glenister saw the men on horseback snatch at their holsters, and, just in time, leaped at his foreman, for the old man had moved out into the open, a Winchester at shoulder, his cheek cuddling the stock, his eyes cold and narrow. The young man flung the barrel up and wrenched the weapon from his hands.

"None of that, Hank!" he cried, sharply. "I'll say when to shoot." He turned to look into the muzzles of guns held in the hands of every horseman—every horseman save one, for Alec McNamara sat unmoved, his handsome features, nonchalant and amused, nodding approval. It was at him that Hank's weapon had been levelled.

"This is bad enough at the best. Don't let's make it any worse," said he.

Slapjack inhaled deeply, spat with disgust, and looked over his boss incredulously.

"Well, of all the different kinds of damn fools," he snorted, "you are the kindest." He marched past the marshal and his deputies down to the cut, put on his coat, and vanished down the trail towards town, not deigning a backward glance either at the mine or at the man unfit to fight for.

VII

The "Bronco Kid's" Eavesdropping

L ate in July it grows dark as midnight approaches, so that the many lights from doorway and window seem less garish and strange than they do a month earlier. In the Northern there was good business doing. The new bar fixtures, which had cost a king's ransom, or represented the one night's losings of a Klondike millionaire, shone rich, dark, and enticing, while the cut glass sparkled with iridescent hues, reflecting, in a measure, the prismatic moods, the dancing spirits of the crowd that crushed past, halting at the gambling games, or patronizing the theatre in the rear. The old bar furniture, brought down by dog team from "Up River," was established at the rear extremity of the long building, just inside the entrance to the dancehall, where patrons of the drama might, with a modicum of delay and inconvenience, quaff as deeply of the beaker as of the ballet.

Now, however, the show had closed, the hall had been cleared of chairs and canvas, exposing a glassy, tempting surface, and the orchestra had moved to the stage. They played a rollicking, blood-stirring two-step, while the floor swam with dancers.

At certain intervals the musicians worked feverishly up to a crashing crescendo, supported by the voices of the dancers, until all joined at the top note in a yell, while the drummer fired a .44 Colt into a box of wet sawdust beside his chair—all in time, all in the swinging spirit of the tune.

The men, who were mostly young, danced like college boys, while the women, who were all young and good dancers, floated through the measures with the ease of rose-leaves on a summer stream. Faces were flushed, eyes were bright, and but rarely a voice sounded that was not glad. Most of the noise came from the men, and although one caught, here and there, a hint of haggard lines about the girlish faces, and glimpsed occasional eyes that did not smile, yet as a whole the scene was one of genuine enjoyment.

Suddenly the music ceased and the couples crowded to the bar. The women took harmless drinks, the men, mostly whiskey. Rarely was the choice of potations criticised, though occasionally some ruddy eschewer of sobriety insisted that his lady "take the same," avowing that "hootch," having been demonstrated beneficial in his case, was good for her also. Invariably the lady accepted without dispute, and invariably the man failed to note her glance at the bartender, or the silent substitution by that capable person of ginger-ale for whiskey or of plain water for gin. In turn, the mixers collected one dollar from each man, flipping to the girl a metal percentage-check which she added to her store. In the curtained boxes overhead, men bought bottles with foil about the corks, and then subterfuge on the lady's part was idle, but, on the other hand, she was able to pocket for each bottle a check redeemable at five dollars.

A stranger, straight from the East, would have remarked first upon the good music, next upon the good looks of the women, and then upon the shabby clothes of the men—for some of them were in "mukluk," others in sweaters with huge initials and winged emblems, and all were collarless.

Outside in the main gambling-room there were but few women. Men crowded in dense masses about the faro lay-out, the wheel, craps, the Klondike game, pangingi, and the card-tables. They talked of business, of home, of women, bought and sold mines, and bartered all things from hams to honor. The groomed and clean, the unkempt and filthy jostled shoulder to shoulder, equally affected by the license of the goldfields and the exhilaration of the New. The mystery of the North had touched them all. The glad, bright wine of adventure filled their veins, and they spoke mightily of things they had resolved to do, or recounted with simple diffidence the strange stories of their accomplishment.

The "Bronco Kid," familiar from Atlin to Nome as the best "bank" dealer on the Yukon, worked the shift from eight till two. He was a slender man of thirty, dexterous in movement, slow to smile, soft of voice, and known as a living flame among women. He had dealt the biggest games of the early days, and had no enemies. Yet, though many called him friend, they wondered inwardly.

It was a strong play the Kid had to-night, for Swede Sam, of Dawson, ventured many stacks of yellow chips, and he was a quick, aggressive gambler. A Jew sat at the king end with ten neatly creased one-thousand-dollar bills before him, together with piles of smaller currency. He adventured viciously and without system, while outsiders to the number of four or five cut in sporadically with small bets. The game was difficult to follow; consequently the lookout, from his raised dais, was leaning forward, chin in hand, while the group was hedged about by eager on-lookers.

Faro is a closed book to most people, for its intricacies are confusing. Lucky is he who has never persevered in solving its mysteries nor speculated upon the "systems" of beating it. From those who have learned it, the game demands practice, dexterity, and coolness. The dealer must run the cards, watch the many shifting bets, handle the neatly piled checks, figure, lightning-like, the profits and losses. It was his unerring, clock like regularity in this that had won the Kid his reputation. This night his powers were taxed. He dealt silently, scowlingly, his long white fingers nervously caressing the cards.

This preoccupation prevented his noticing the rustle and stir of a new-comer who had crowded up behind him, until he caught the wondering glances of those in front and saw that the Israelite was staring past him, his money forgotten, his eyes beady and sharp, his rat-like teeth showing in a grin of admiration. Swede Sam glared from under his unkempt shock and felt uncertainly towards the open collar of his flannel shirt where a kerchief should have been. The men who were standing gazed at the new-comer, some with surprise, others with a half smile of recognition.

Bronco glanced quickly over his shoulder, and as he did so the breath caught in his throat—but for only an instant. A girl stood so close beside him that the lace of her gown brushed his sleeve. He was shuffling at the moment and dropped a card, then nodded to her. speaking quietly, as he stooped to regain the pasteboard:

"Howdy, Cherry?"

She did not answer—only continued to look at the "lay-out." "What a woman!" he thought. She was not too tall, with smoothly rounded bust and hips, and long waist, all well displayed by her perfectly fitting garments. Her face was oval, the mouth rather large, the eyes of dark, dark-blue, prominently outlined under thin, silken lids. Her dull-gold hair was combed low over the ears, and her smile showed rows of sparkling teeth before it dived into twin dimples. Strangest of all, it was an innocent face, the face and smile of a school-girl.

The Kid finished his shuffling awkwardly and slid the cards into the box. Then the woman spoke:

"Let me have your place, Bronco."

The men gasped, the Jew snickered, the lookout straightened in his chair.

"Better not. It's a hard game," said the Kid, but her voice was imperious as she commanded him:

"Hurry up. Give me your place."

Bronco arose, whereupon she settled in his chair, tucked in her skirts, removed her gloves, and twisted into place the diamonds on her hands.

"What the devil's this?" said the lookout, roughly. "Are you drunk, Bronco? Get out of that chair, miss."

She turned to him slowly. The innocence had fled from her features and the big eyes flashed warningly. A change had coarsened her like a puff of air on a still pool. Then, while she stared at him, her lids drooped dangerously and her lip curled.

"Throw him out, Bronco," she said, and her tones held the hardness of a mistress to her slave.

"That's all right," the Kid reassured the lookout. "She's a better dealer than I am. This is Cherry Malotte."

Without noticing the stares this evoked, the girl commenced. Her hands, beautifully soft and white, flashed over the board. She dealt rapidly, unfalteringly, with the finish of one bred to the cards, handling chips and coppers with the peculiar mannerisms that spring from long practice. It was seen that she never looked at her check-rack, but, when a bet required paying, picked up a stack without turning her head; and they saw further that she never reached twice, nor took a large pile and sized it up against its mate, removing the extra disks, as is the custom. When she stretched forth her hand she grasped the right number unerringly. This is considered the acme of professional finish, and the Bronco Kid smiled delightedly as he saw the wonder spread from the lookout to the spectators and heard the speech of the men who stood on chairs and tables for sight of the woman dealer.

For twenty minutes she continued, until the place became congested, and never once did the lookout detect an error.

While she was busy, Glenister entered the front-door and pushed his way back towards the theatre. He was worried and distrait, his manner perturbed and unnatural. Silently and without apparent notice he passed friends who greeted him.

"What ails Glenister to-night?" asked a by-stander. "He acts funny,"

"Ain't you heard? Why, the Midas has been jumped. He's in a bad way—all broke up."

The girl suddenly ceased without finishing the deck, and arose.

"Don't stop," said the Kid, while a murmur of dismay came from the spectators. She only shook her head and drew on her gloves with a show of ennui.

Gliding through the crowd, she threaded about aimlessly, the recipient of many stares though but few greetings, speaking with no one, a certain dignity serving her as a barrier even here. She stopped a waiter and questioned him.

"He's up-stairs in a gallery box."

"Alone?"

"Yes'm. Anyhow, he was a minute ago, unless some of the rustlers has broke in on him."

A moment later Glenister, watching the scene below, was aroused from his gloomy absorption by the click of the box door and the rustle of silken skirts.

"Go out, please," he said, without turning. "I don't want company." Hearing no answer, he began again, "I came here to be alone"—but there he ceased, for the girl had come forward and laid her two hot hands upon his cheeks.

"Boy," she breathed—and he arose swiftly.

"Cherry! When did you come?"

"Oh, Days ago," she said, impatiently, "from Dawson. They told me you had struck it. I stood it as long as I could—then I came to you. Now, tell me about yourself. Let me see you first, quick!"

She pulled him towards the light and gazed upward, devouring him hungrily with her great, languorous eyes. She held to his coat lapels, standing close beside him, her warm breath beating up into his face.

"Well," she said, "kiss me!"

He took her wrists in his and loosed her hold, then looked down on her gravely and said:

"No—that's all over. I told you so when I left Dawson."

"All over! Oh no, it isn't, boy. You think so, but it isn't—it can't be. I love you too much to let you go."

"Hush!" said he. "There are people in the next box."

"I don't care! Let them hear," she cried, with feminine recklessness. "I'm proud of my love for you. I'll tell it to them—to the whole world."

"Now, see here, little girl," he said, quietly, "we had a long talk in Dawson and agreed that it was best to divide our ways. I was mad over you once, as a good many other men have been, but I came to my senses. Nothing could ever result from it, and I told you so."

"Yes, yes—I know. I thought I could give you up, but I didn't realize till you had gone how I wanted you. Oh, it's been a TORTURE to me every day for the past two years." There was no semblance now to the cold creature she had appeared upon entering the gambling-hall. She spoke rapidly, her whole body tense with emotion, her voice shaken with passion. "I've seen men and men and men, and they've loved me, but I never cared for anybody in the world till I saw you. They ran after me, but you were cold. You made me come to you. Perhaps that was it. Anyhow, I can't stand it. I'll give up everything—I'll do anything just to be where you are. What do you think of a woman who will beg? Oh, I've lost my pride—I'm a fool—a fool—but I can't help it."

"I'm sorry you feel this way," said Glenister. "It isn't my fault, and it isn't of any use."

For an instant she stood quivering, while the light died out of her face; then, with a characteristic change, she smiled till the dimples laughed in her cheeks. She sank upon a seat beside him and pulled together the curtains, shutting out the sight below.

"Very well"—then she put his hand to her cheek and cuddled it. "I'm glad to see you just the same, and you can't keep me from loving you."

With his other hand he smoothed her hair, while, unknown to him and beneath her lightness, she shrank and quivered at his touch like a Barbary steed under the whip.

"Things are very bad with me," he said. "We've had our mine jumped."

"Bah! You know what to do. You aren't a cripple—you've got five fingers on your gun hand."

"That's it! They all tell me that—all the old-timers; but I don't know what to do. I thought I did—but I don't. The law has come into this country and I've tried to meet it half-way. They jumped us and put in a receiver—a big man—by the name of McNamara. Dex wasn't there and I let them do it. When the old man learned of it he nearly went crazy. We had our first quarrel. He thought I was afraid—"

"Not he," said the girl. "I know him and he knows you."

"That was a week ago. We've hired the best lawyer in Nome—Bill Wheaton—and we've tried to have the injunction removed. We've offered bond in any sum, but the Judge refuses to accept it. We've argued for leave to appeal, but he won't give us the right. The more I look into it the worse it seems, for the court wasn't convened in accordance with law, we weren't notified to appear in our own behalf, we weren't allowed a chance to argue our own case—nothing. They simply slapped on a receiver, and now they refuse to allow us redress. From a legal standpoint, it's appalling, I'm told—but what's to be done? What's the game? That's the thing. What are they up to? I'm nearly out of my mind, for it's all my fault. I didn't think it meant anything like this or I'd have made a fight for possession and stood them off at least. As it is, my partner's sore and he's gone to drinking—first time in twelve years. He says I gave the claim away, and now it's up to me and the Almighty to get it back. If he gets full he'll drive a four-horse wagon into some church, or go up and pick the Judge to pieces with his fingers to see what makes him go round."

"What've they got against you and Dextry—some grudge?" she questioned.

"No, no! We're not the only ones in trouble; they've jumped the rest of the good mines and put this McNamara in as receiver on all of them, but that's small comfort. The Swedes are crazy; they've hired all the lawyers in town, and are murdering more good American language than would fill Bering Strait. Dex is in favor of getting our friends together and throwing the receiver off. He wants to kill somebody, but we can't do that. They've got the soldiers to fall back on. We've been warned that the troops are instructed to enforce the court's action. I don't know what the plot is, for I can't believe the old Judge is crooked—the girl wouldn't let him."

"Girl?"

Cherry Malotte leaned forward where the light shone on the young man's worried face.

"The girl? What girl? Who is she?"

Her voice had lost its lazy caress, her lips had thinned. Never was a woman's face more eloquent, mused Glenister as he noted her. Every thought fled to this window to peer forth, fearful, lustful, hateful, as the case might be. He had loved to play with her in the former days, to work upon her passions and watch the changes, to note her features mirror every varying emotion from tenderness to flippancy, from anger to delight, and, at his bidding, to see the pale cheeks glow with love's fire, the eyes grow heavy, the dainty lips invite kisses. Cherry was a perfect little spoiled animal, he reflected, and a very dangerous one.

"What girl?" she questioned again, and he knew beforehand the look that went with it.

"The girl I intend to marry," he said, slowly, looking her between the eyes.

He knew he was cruel—he wanted to be—it satisfied the clamor and turmoil within him, while he also felt that the sooner she knew and the colder it left her the better. He could not note the effect of the remark on her, however, for, as he spoke, the door of the box opened and the head of the Bronco Kid appeared, then retired instantly with apologies.

"Wrong stall," he said, in his slow voice. "Looking for another party." Nevertheless, his eyes had covered every inch of them—noted the drawn curtains and the breathless poise of the woman—while his ears had caught part of Glenister's speech.

"You won't marry her," said Cherry, quietly. "I don't know who she is, but I won't let you marry her."

She rose and smoothed her skirts.

"It's time nice people were going now." She said it with a sneer at herself. "Take me out through this crowd. I'm living quietly and I don't want these beasts to follow me."

As they emerged from the theatre the morning air was cool and quiet, while the sun was just rising. The Bronco Kid lighted a cigar as they passed, nodding silently at their greeting. His eyes followed them, while his hands were so still that the match burned through to his fingers—then when they had gone his teeth met and ground savagely through the tobacco so that the cigar fell, while he muttered:

"So that's the girl you intend to marry? We'll see, by God!"

VIII

DEXTRY MAKES A CALL

The water front had a strong attraction for Helen Chester, and rarely did a fair day pass without finding her in some quiet spot from which she could watch the shifting life along its edge, the ships at anchor, and the varied incidents of the surf.

This morning she sat in a dory pulled high up on the beach, bathed in the bright sunshine, and staring at the rollers, while lines of concentration wrinkled her brow. The wind had blown for some days till the ocean beat heavily across the shallow bar, and now, as it became quieter, longshoremen were launching their craft, preparing to resume their traffic.

Not until the previous day had the news of her friends' misfortune come to her, and although she had heard no hint of fraud, she began to realize that they were involved in a serious tangle. To the questions which she anxiously put to her uncle he had replied that their difficulty arose from a technicality in the mining laws which another man had been shrewd enough to profit by. It was a complicated question, he said, and one requiring time to thrash out to an equitable settlement. She had undertaken to remind him of the service these men had done her, but, with a smile, he interrupted; he could not allow such things to influence his judicial attitude, and she must not endeavor to prejudice him in the discharge of his duty. Recognizing the justice of this, she had desisted.

For many days the girl had caught scattered talk between the Judge and McNamara, and between Struve and his associates, but it all seemed foreign and dry, and beyond the fact that it bore on the litigation over the Anvil Creek mines, she understood nothing and cared less, particularly as a new interest had but recently come into her life, an interest in the form of a man—McNamara.

He had begun with quiet, half-concealed admiration of her, which had rapidly increased until his attentions had become of a singularly positive and resistless character.

Judge Stillman was openly delighted, while the court of one like Alec McNamara could but flatter any girl. In his presence, Helen felt herself rebelling at his suit, yet as distance separated them she thought ever more kindly of it. This state of mind contrasted oddly with her feelings towards the other man she had met, for in this country there were but two. When Glenister was with her she saw his love lying nakedly in his eyes and it exercised some spell which drew her to him in spite of herself, but when he had gone, back came the distrust, the terror of the brute she felt was there behind it all. The one appealed to her while present, the other pled strongest while away. Now she was attempting to analyze her feelings and face the future squarely, for she realized that her affairs neared a crisis, and this, too, not a month after meeting the men. She wondered if she would come to love her uncle's friend. She did not know. Of the other she was sure—she never could.

Busied with these reflections, she noticed the familiar figure of Dextry wandering aimlessly. He was not unkempt, and yet his air gave her the impression of prolonged sleeplessness. Spying her, he approached and seated himself in the sand against the boat, while at her greeting he broke into talk as if he was needful only of her friendly presence to stir his confidential chords into active vibration.

"We're in turrible shape, miss," he said. "Our claim's jumped. Somebody run in and talked the boy out of it while I was gone, and now we can't get 'em off. He's been tryin' this here new law game that you-all brought in this summer. I've been drunk—that's what makes me look so ornery."

He said the last, not in the spirit of apology, for rarely does your frontiersman consider that his self-indulgences require palliation, but rather after the manner of one purveying news of mild interest, as he would inform you that his surcingle had broken or that he had witnessed a lynching.

"What made them jump your claim?"

"I don't know. I don't know nothin' about it, because, as I remarked previous, I 'ain't follered the totterin' footsteps of the law none too close. Nor do I intend to. I simply draws out of the game fer a spell, and lets the youngster have his fling; then if he can't make good, I'll take the cards and finish it for him.

"It's like the time I was ranchin' with an Englishman up in Montana. This here party claimed the misfortune of bein' a younger son, whatever that is, and is grubstaked to a ranch by his people back home. Havin' acquired an intimate knowledge of the West by readin' Bret Harte, and havin' assim'lated the secrets of ranchin' by correspondence school, he is fitted, ample, to teach us natives a thing or two—and he does it. I am workin' his outfit as foreman, and it don't take long to show me that he's a good-hearted feller, in spite of his ridin'-bloomers an' pinochle eye-glass. He ain't never had no actual experience, but he's got a Henry Thompson Seton book that tells him all about everything from field-mice to gorrillys.

"We're troubled a heap with coyotes them days, and finally this party sends home for some Rooshian wolf-hounds. I'm fer pizenin' a sheep carcass, but he says:

"'No, no, me deah man; that's not sportsman-like; we'll hunt 'em. Ay, hunt 'em! Only fawncy the sport we'll have, ridin' to hounds!'

"'We will not,' says I. 'I ain't goin' to do no Simon Legree stunts. It ain't man's size. Bein' English, you don't count, but I'm growed up.'

"Nothin' would do him but those Uncle Tom's Cabin dogs, however, and he had 'em imported clean from Berkshire or Sibeery or thereabouts, four of 'em, great, big, blue ones. They was as handsome and imposin' as a set of solid-gold teeth, but somehow they didn't seem to savvy our play none. One day the cook rolled a rain bar'l down-hill from the kitchen, and when them blooded critters saw it comin' they throwed down their tails and tore out like rabbits. After that I couldn't see no good in 'em with a spy-glass.

"'They 'ain't got no grit. What makes you think they can fight?' I asked one day.

"'Fight?' says H'Anglish. 'My deah man, they're full-blooded. Cost seventy pun each. They're dreadful creatures when they're roused—they'll tear a wolf to pieces like a rag—kill bears—anything. Oh! Rully, perfectly dreadful!'

"Well, it wasn't a week later that he went over to the east line with me to mend a barb wire. I had my pliers and a hatchet and some staples. About a mile from the house we jumped up a little brown bear that scampered off when he seen us, but bein' agin' a bluff where he couldn't get away, he climbed a cotton-wood. H'Anglish was simply frothin' with excitement.

"'What a misfortune! Neyther gun nor hounds.'

"'I'll scratch his back and talk pretty to him,' says I, 'while you run back and get a Winchester and them ferocious bull-dogs.'

"'Wolf-hounds,' says he, with dignity, 'full-blooded, seventy pun each. They'll rend the poor beast limb from limb. I hate to do it, but it'll be good practice for them.'

"'They may be good renders,' says I, 'but don't forget the gun.'

"Well, I throwed sticks at the critter when he tried to unclimb the tree, till finally the boss got back with his dogs. They set up an awful holler when they see the bear—first one they'd ever smelled, I reckon—and the little feller crawled up in some forks and watched things, cautious, while they leaped about, bayin' most fierce and blood-curdlin'.

"'How you goin' to get him down?' says I.

"'I'll shoot him in the lower jaw,' says the Britisher, 'so he cawn't bite the dogs. It'll give 'em cawnfidence.'

"He takes aim at Mr. Bear's chin and misses it three times runnin', he's that excited.

"'Settle down, H'Anglish,' says I. 'He 'ain't got no double chins. How many shells left in your gun?'" When he looks he finds there's only one more, for he hadn't stopped to fill the magazine, so I cautions him.

"'You're shootin' too low. Raise her.'

"He raised her all right, and caught Mr. Bruin in the snout. What followed thereafter was most too quick to notice, for the poor bear let out a bawl, dropped off his limb into the midst of them ragin', tur'ble, seventy-pun hounds, an' hugged 'em to death, one after another, like he was doin' a system of health exercises. He took 'em to his boosum as if he'd just got back off a long trip, then, droppin' the last one, he made at that younger son an' put a gold fillin' in his leg. Yes, sir; most chewed it off. H'Anglish let out a Siberian-wolf holler hisself, an' I had to step in with the hatchet and kill the brute though I was most dead from laughin'.

"That's how it is with me an' Glenister," the old man concluded. "When he gets tired experimentin' with this new law game of hisn, I'll step in an' do business on a common-sense basis."

"You talk as if you wouldn't get fair play," said Helen.

"We won't," said he, with conviction. "I look on all lawyers with suspicion, even to old bald-face—your uncle, askin' your pardon an' gettin' it, bein' as I'm a friend an' he ain't no real relation of yours, anyhow. No, sir; they're all crooked."

Dextry held the Western distrust of the legal profession—comprehensive, unreasoning, deep.

"Is the old man all the kin you've got?" he questioned, when she refused to discuss the matter.

"He is—in a way. I have a brother, or I hope I have, somewhere. He ran away when we were both little tads and I haven't seen him since. I heard about him, indirectly, at Skagway—three years ago—during the big rush to the Klondike, but he has never been home. When father died, I went to live with Uncle Arthur—some day, perhaps, I'll find my brother. He's cruel to hide from me this way, for there are only we two left and I've loved him always."

She spoke sadly and her mood blended well with the gloom of her companion, so they stared silently out over the heaving green waters.

"It's a good thing me an' the kid had a little piece of money ahead," Dextry resumed later, reverting to the thought that lay uppermost in his mind, "'cause we'd be up against it right if we hadn't. The boy couldn't have amused himself none with these court proceedings, because they come high. I call 'em luxuries, like brandied peaches an' silk undershirts.

"I don't trust these Jim Crow banks no more than I do lawyers, neither. No, sirree! I bought a iron safe an' hauled it out to the mine. She weighs eighteen hundred, and we keep our money locked up there. We've got a feller named Johnson watchin' it now. Steal it? Well, hardly. They can't bust her open without a stick of 'giant' which would rouse everybody in five miles, an' they can't lug her off bodily—she's too heavy. No; it's safer there than any place I know of. There ain't no abscondin' cashiers an' all that. Tomorrer I'm goin' back to live on the claim an' watch this receiver man till the thing's settled."

When the girl arose to go, he accompanied her up through the deep sand of the lane-like street to the main, muddy thoroughfare of the camp. As yet, the planked and gravelled pavements, which later threaded the town, were unknown, and the incessant traffic had worn the road into a quagmire of chocolate-colored slush, almost axle-deep, with which the store fronts, show-windows, and awnings were plentifully shot and spattered from passing teams. Whenever a wagon approached, pedestrians fled to the shelter of neighboring doorways, watching a chance to dodge out again. When vehicles passed from the comparative solidity of the main street out into the morasses that constituted the rest of the town, they adventured perilously, their horses plunging, snorting, terrified, amid an atmosphere of profanity. Discouraged animals were down constantly, and no foot-passenger, even with rubber boots, ventured off the planks that led from house to house.

To avoid a splashing team, Dextry pulled his companion close in against the entrance to the Northern saloon, standing before her protectingly.

Although it was late in the afternoon the Bronco Kid had just arisen and was now loafing preparatory to the active duties of his profession. He was speaking with the proprietor when Dextry and the girl sought shelter just without the open door, so he caught a fair though fleeting glimpse of her as she flashed a curious look inside. She had never been so close to a gambling-hall before, and would have liked to peer in more carefully had she dared, but her companion moved forward. At the first look the Bronco Kid had broken off in his speech and stared at her as though at an apparition. When she had vanished, he spoke to Reilly:

"Who's that?"

Reilly shrugged his shoulders, then without further question the Kid turned back towards the empty theatre and out of the back door.

He moved nonchalantly till he was outside, then with the speed of a colt ran down the narrow planking between the buildings, turned parallel to the front street, leaped from board to board, splashed through puddles of water till he reached the next alley. Stamping the mud from his shoes and pulling down his sombrero, he sauntered out into the main thoroughfare.

Dextry and his companion had crossed to the other side and were approaching, so the gambler gained a fair view of them. He searched every inch of the girl's face and figure, then, as she made to turn her eyes in his direction, he slouched away. He followed, however, at a distance, till he saw the man leave her, then on up to the big hotel he shadowed her. A half-hour later he was drinking in the Golden Gate bar-room with an acquaintance who ministered to the mechanical details behind the hotel counter.

"Who's the girl I saw come in just now?" he inquired.

"I guess you mean the Judge's niece."

Both men spoke in the dead, restrained tones that go with their callings.

"What's her name?"

"Chester, I think. Why? Look good to you, Kid?"

Although the other neither spoke nor made sign, the bartender construed his silence as acquiescence and continued, with a conscious glance at his own reflection while he adjusted his diamond scarf-pin: "Well, she can have ME! I've got it fixed to meet her."

"Bah! I guess not," said the Kid, suddenly, with an inflection that startled the other from his preening. Then, as he went out, the man mused:

"Gee! Bronco's got the worst eye in the camp! Makes me creep when he throws it on me with that muddy look. He acted like he was jealous."

At noon the next day, as he prepared to go to the claim, Dextry's partner burst in upon him. Glenister was dishevelled, and his eyes shone with intense excitement.

"What d'you think they've done now?" he cried, as greeting.

"I dunno. What is it?"

"They've broken open the safe and taken our money."

"What!"

The old man in turn was on his feet, the grudge which he had felt against Glenister in the past few days forgotten in this common misfortune.

"Yes, by Heaven, they've swiped our money—our tents, tools, teams, books, hose, and all of our personal property—everything! They threw Johnson off and took the whole works. I never heard of such a thing. I went out to the claim and they wouldn't let me go near the workings. They've got every mine on Anvil Creek guarded the same way, and they aren't going to let us come around even when they clean up. They told me so this morning."

"But, look here," demanded Dextry, sharply, "the money in that safe belongs to us. That's money we brought in from the States. The court 'ain't got no right to it. What kind of a damn law is that?"

"Oh, as to law, they don't pay any attention to it any more," said Glenister, bitterly. "I made a mistake in not killing the first man that set foot on the claim. I was a sucker, and now we're up against a stiff game. The Swedes are in the same fix, too. This last order has left them groggy."

"I don't understand it yet," said Dextry.

"Why, it's this way. The Judge has issued what he calls an order enlarging the powers of the receiver, and it authorizes McNamara to take possession of everything on the claims—tents, tools, stores, and personal property of all kinds. It was issued last night without notice to our side, so Wheaton says, and they served it this morning early. I went out to see McNamara, and when I got there I found him in our private tent with the safe broken open."

"'What does this mean?' I said. And then he showed me the new order.

"'I'm responsible to the court for every penny of this money,' said he, 'and for every tool on the claim. In view of that I can't allow you to go near the workings.'

"'Not go near the workings?' said I. 'Do you mean you won't let us see the clean-ups from our own mine? How do we know we're getting a square deal if we don't see the gold weighed?'

"'I'm an officer of the court and under bond,' said he, and the smiling triumph in his eyes made me crazy.

"'You're a lying thief,' I said, looking at him square. 'And you're going too far. You played me for a fool once and made it stick, but it won't work twice.'

"He looked injured and aggrieved and called in Voorhees, the marshal. I can't grasp the thing at all; everybody seems to be against us, the Judge, the marshal, the prosecuting attorney—everybody. Yet they've done it all according to law, they claim, and have the soldiers to back them up."

"It's just as Mexico Mullins said," Dextry stormed; "there's a deal on of some kind. I'm goin' up to the hotel an' call on the Judge myself. I 'ain't never seen him nor this McNamara, either. I allus want to look a man straight in the eyes once, then I know what course to foller in my dealings."

"You'll find them both," said Glenister, "for McNamara rode into town behind me."

The old prospector proceeded to the Golden Gate Hotel and inquired for Judge Stillman's room. A boy attempted to take his name, but he seized him by the scruff of the neck and sat him in his seat, proceeding unannounced to the suite to which he had been directed. Hearing voices, he knocked, and then, without awaiting a summons, walked in.

The room was fitted like an office, with desk, table, type-writer, and law-books. Other rooms opened from it on both sides. Two men were talking earnestly—one gray-haired, smooth-shaven, and clerical, the other tall, picturesque, and masterful. With his first glance the miner knew that before him were the two he had come to see, and that in reality he had to deal with but one, the big man who shot at him the level glances.

"We are engaged," said the Judge, "very busily engaged, sir. Will you call again in half an hour?"

Dextry looked him over carefully from head to foot, then turned his back on him and regarded the other. Neither he nor McNamara spoke, but their eyes were busy and each instinctively knew that here was a foe.

"What do you want?" McNamara inquired, finally.

"I just dropped in to get acquainted. My name is Dextry—Joe Dextry—from everywhere west of the Missouri—an' your name is McNamara, ain't it? This here, I reckon, is your little French poodle—eh?" indicating Stillman.

"What do you mean?" said McNamara, while the Judge murmured indignantly.

"Just what I say. However, that ain't what I want to talk about. I don't take no stock in such truck as judges an' lawyers an' orders of court. They ain't intended to be took serious. They're all right for children an' Easterners an' non compos mentis people, I s'pose, but I've always been my own judge, jury, an' hangman, an' I aim to continue workin' my legislatif, executif, an' judicial duties to the end of the string. You look out! My pardner is young an' seems to like the idee of lettin' somebody else run his business, so I'm goin' to give him rein and let him amuse himself for a while with your dinky little writs an' receiverships. But don't go too far—you can rob the Swedes, 'cause Swedes ain't entitled to have no money, an' some other crook would get it if you didn't, but don't play me an' Glenister fer Scandinavians. It's a mistake. We're white men, an' I'm apt to come romancin' up here with one of these an' bust you so you won't hold together durin' the ceremonies."

With his last words he made the slightest shifting movement, only a lifting shrug of the shoulder, yet in his palm lay a six-shooter. He had slipped it from his trousers band with the ease of long practice and absolute surety. Judge Stillman gasped and backed against the desk, but McNamara idly swung his leg as he sat sidewise on the table. His only sign of interest was a quickening of the eyes, a fact of which Dextry made mental note.

"Yes," said the miner, disregarding the alarm of the lawyer, "you can wear this court in your vest-pocket like a Waterbury, if you want to, but if you don't let me alone, I'll uncoil its main-spring. That's all."

He replaced his weapon and, turning, walked out the door.

IX

SLUICE ROBBERS

"We must have money," said Glenister a few days later. "When McNamara jumped our safe he put us down and out. There's no use fighting in this court any longer, for the Judge won't let us work the ground ourselves, even if we give bond, and he won't grant an appeal. He says his orders aren't appealable. We ought to send Wheaton out to 'Frisco and have him take the case to the higher courts. Maybe he can get a writ of supersedeas."

"I don't rec'nize the name, but if it's as bad as it sounds it's sure horrible. Ain't there no cure for it?"

"It simply means that the upper court would take the case away from this one."

"Well, let's send him out quick. Every day means ten thousand dollars to us. It'll take him a month to make the round trip, so I s'pose he ought to leave tomorrow on the Roanoke."

"Yes, but where's the money to do it with? McNamara has ours. My God! What a mess we're in! What fools we've been, Dex! There's a conspiracy here. I'm beginning to see it now that it's too late. This man is looting our country under color of law, and figures on gutting all the mines before we can throw him off. That's his game. He'll work them as hard and as long as he can, and Heaven only knows what will become of the money. He must have big men behind him in order to fix a United States judge this way. Maybe he has the 'Frisco courts corrupted, too."

"If he has, I'm goin' to kill him," said Dextry. "I've worked like a dog all my life, and now that I've struck pay I don't aim to lose it. If Bill Wheaton can't win out accordin' to law, I'm goin' to proceed accordin' to justice."

During the past two days the partners had haunted the court-room where their lawyer, together with the counsel for the Scandinavians, had argued and pleaded, trying every possible professional and unprofessional artifice in search of relief from the arbitrary rulings of the court, while hourly they had become more strongly suspicious of some sinister plot—some hidden, powerful understanding back of the Judge and the entire mechanism of justice. They had fought with the fury of men who battle for life, and had grown to hate the lines of Stillman's vacillating face, the bluster of the district-attorney, and the smirking confidence of the clerks, for it seemed that they all worked mechanically, like toys, at the dictates of Alec McNamara. At last, when they had ceased, beaten and exhausted, they were too confused with technical phrases to grasp anything except the fact that relief was denied them; that their claims were to be worked by the receiver; and, as a crowning defeat, they learned that the Judge would move his court to St. Michael's and hear no cases until he returned, a month later.

Meanwhile, McNamara hired every idle man he could lay hand upon, and ripped the placers open with double shifts. Every day a stream of yellow dust poured into the bank and was locked in his vaults, while those mine-owners who attempted to witness the clean-ups were ejected from their claims. The politician had worked with incredible swiftness and system, and a fortnight after landing he had made good his boast to Struve, and was in charge of every good claim in the district, the owners were ousted, their appeals argued and denied, and the court gone for thirty days, leaving him a clear field for his operations. He felt a contempt for most of his victims, who were slow-witted Swedes, grasping neither the purport nor the magnitude of his operation, and as to those litigants who were discerning enough to see its enormity, he trusted to his organization to thwart them.

The two partners had come to feel that they were beating against a wall, and had also come squarely to face the proposition that they were without funds wherewith to continue their battle. It was maddening for them to think of the daily robbery that they suffered, for the Midas turned out many ounces of gold at every shift; and more maddening to realize the receiver's shrewdness in crippling them by his theft of the gold in their safe. That had been his crowning stroke.

"We Must get money quick," said Glenister. "Do you think we can borrow?"

"Borrow?" sniffed Dextry. "Folks don't lend money in Alaska."

They relapsed into a moody silence.

"I met a feller this mornin' that's workin' on the Midas," the old man resumed. "He came in town fer a pair of gum boots, an' he says they've run into awful rich ground—so rich that they have to clean up every morning when the night shift goes off 'cause the riffles clog with gold."

"Think of it!" Glenister growled. "If we had even a part of one of those clean-ups we could send Wheaton outside."

In the midst of his bitterness a thought struck him. He made as though to speak, then closed his mouth; but his partner's eyes were on him, filled with a suppressed but growing fire. Dextry lowered his voice cautiously:

"There'll be twenty thousand dollars in them sluices to-night at midnight."

Glenister stared back while his pulse pounded at something that lay in the other's words.

"It belongs to us," the young man said. "There wouldn't be anything wrong about it, would there?"

Dextry sneered. "Wrong! Right! Them is fine an' soundin' titles in a mess like this. What do they mean? I tell you, at midnight to-night Alec McNamara will have twenty thousand dollars of our money—"

"God! What would happen if they caught us?" whispered the younger, following out his thought. "They'd never let us get off the claim alive. He couldn't find a better excuse to shoot us down and get rid of us. If we came up before this Judge for trial, we'd go to Sitka for twenty years."

"Sure! But it's our only chance. I'd rather die on the Midas in a fair fight than set here bitin' my hangnails. I'm growin' old and I won't never make another strike. As to bein' caught—them's our chances. I won't be took alive—I promise you that—and before I go I'll get my satisfy. Castin' things up, that's about all a man gets in this vale of tears, jest satisfaction of one kind or another. It'll be a fight in the open, under the stars, with the clean, wet moss to lie down on, and not a scrappin'-match of freak phrases and law-books inside of a stinkin' court-room. The cards is shuffled and in the box, pardner, and the game is started. If we're due to win, we'll win. If we're due to lose, we'll lose. These things is all figgered out a thousand years back. Come on, boy. Are you game?"

"Am I game?" Glenister's nostrils dilated and his voice rose a tone. "Am I game? I'm with you till the big cash-in, and Lord have mercy on any man that blocks our game to-night."

"We'll need another hand to help us," said Dextry. "Who can we get?"

At that moment, as though in answer, the door opened with the scant ceremony that friends of the frontier are wont to observe, admitting the attenuated, flapping, dome-crowned figure of Slapjack Simms, and Dextry fell upon him with the hunger of a wolf.

It was midnight and over the dark walls of the valley peered a multitude of stars, while away on the southern horizon there glowed a subdued effulgence as though from hidden fires beneath the Gold

God's caldron, or as though the phosphorescence of Bering had spread upward into the skies. Although each night grew longer, it was not yet necessary to light the men at work in the cuts. There were perhaps two hours in which it was difficult to see at a distance, but the dawn came early, hence no provision had been made for torches.

Five minutes before the hour the night-shift boss lowered the gates in the dam, and, as the rush from the sluices subsided, his men quit work and climbed the bluff to the mess tent. The dwellings of the Midas, as has already been explained, sat back from the creek at a distance of a city block, the workings being thus partially hidden under the brow of the steep bank.

It is customary to leave a watchman in the pit during the noon and midnight hours, not only to see that strangers preserve a neutral attitude, but also to watch the waste-gates and water supply. The night man of the Midas had been warned of his responsibility, and, knowing that much gold lay in his keeping, was disposed to gaze on the curious-minded with the sourness of suspicion. Therefore, as a man leading a pack-horse approached out of the gloom of the creek-trail, his eyes were on him from the moment he appeared. The road wound along the gravel of the bars and passed in proximity to the flumes. However, the wayfarer paid no attention to them, and the watchman detected an explanatory weariness in his slow gait.

"Some prospector getting in from a trip," he thought.

The stranger stopped, scratched a match, and, as he undertook to light his pipe, the observer caught the mahogany shine of a negro's face. The match sputtered out and then came impatient blasphemy as he searched for another.

"Evenin', sah! You-all oblige me with a match?"

He addressed the watcher on the bank above, and, without waiting a reply, began to climb upward.

No smoker on the trail will deny the luxury of a light to the most humble, so as the negro gained his level the man reached forth to accommodate him. Without warning, the black man leaped forward with the ferocity of an animal and struck the other a fearful blow. The watchman sank with a faint, startled cry, and the African dragged him out of sight over the brow of the bank, where he rapidly tied him hand and foot, stuffing a gag into his mouth. At the same moment two other figures rounded the bend below and approached. They were mounted and leading a third saddle-horse, as well as other pack-animals. Reaching the workings, they dismounted. Then began a strange procedure, for one man clambered upon the sluices and, with a pick, ripped out the riffles. This was a matter of only a few seconds; then, seizing a shovel, he transferred the concentrates which lay in the bottom of the boxes into canvas sacks which his companion held. As each bag was filled, it was tied and dumped into the cut. They treated but four boxes in this way, leaving the lower two-thirds of the flume untouched, for Anvil Creek gold is coarse and the heart of the clean-up lies where it is thrown in. Gathering the sacks together, they lashed them upon the pack-animals, then mounted the second string of sluices and began as before. Throughout it all they worked with feverish haste and in unbroken silence, every moment flashing quick glances at the figure of the lookout who stood on the crest above, half dimmed in the shadow of a willow clump. Judging by their rapidity and sureness, they were expert miners.

From the tent came the voices of the night shift at table, and the faint rattle of dishes, while the canvas walls glowed from the lights within like great fire-flies hidden in the grass. The foreman, finishing his meal, appeared at the door of the mess tent, and, pausing to accustom his eyes to the gloom, peered perfunctorily towards the creek. The watchman detached himself from the shadow, moving out into plain sight, and the boss turned back. The two men below were now working on the sluices which lay close under the bank and were thus hidden from the tent.

McNamara's description of Anvil Creek's riches had fired Helen Chester with the desire to witness a clean-up, so they had ridden out from town in time for supper at the claim. She had not known whither he led her, only understanding that provision for her entertainment would be made with the superintendent's wife. Upon recognizing the Midas, she had endeavored to question him as to why her friends had been dispossessed, and he had answered, as it seemed, straight and true.

The ground was in dispute, he said—another man claimed it—and while the litigation pended he was in charge for the court, to see that neither party received injury. He spoke adroitly, and it satisfied her to have the proposition resolved into such simplicity.

She had come prepared to spend the night and witness the early morning operation, so the receiver made the most of his opportunity. He showed her over the workings, explaining the many things that were strange to her. Not only was he in himself a fascinating figure to any woman, but wherever he went men regarded him deferentially, and nothing affects a woman's judgment more promptly than this obvious sign of power. He spent the evening with her, talking of his early days and the things he had done in the West, his story matching the picturesqueness of her canvas-walled quarters with their rough furnishings of skins and blankets. Being a keen observer as well as a finished raconteur, he had woven a spell of words about the girl, leaving her in a state of tumult and indecision when at last, towards midnight, he retired to his own tent. She knew to what end all this was working, and yet knew not what her answer would be when the question came which lay behind it all. At moments she felt the wonderful attraction of the man, and still there was some distrust of him which she could not fathom. Again her thoughts reverted to Glenister, the impetuous, and she compared the two, so similar in some ways, so utterly opposed in others.

It was when she heard the night shift at their meal that she threw a silken shawl about her head, stepped into the cool night, and picked her way down towards the roar of the creek. "A breath of air and then to bed," she thought. She saw the tall figure of the watchman and made for him. He seemed oddly interested in her approach, watching her very closely, almost as though alarmed. It was doubtless because there were so few women out here, or possibly on account of the lateness of the hour. Away with conventions! This was the land of instinct and impulse. She would talk to him. The man drew his hat more closely about his face and moved off as she came up. Glenister had been in her thoughts a moment since, and she now noted that here was another with the same great, square shoulders and erect head. Then she saw with a start that this one was a negro. He carried a Winchester and seemed to watch her carefully, yet with indecision.

To express her interest and to break the silence, she questioned him, but at the sound of her voice he stepped towards her and spoke roughly.

"What!"

Then he paused, and stammered in a strangely altered and unnatural voice:

"Yass'm. I'm the watchman."

She noted two other darkies at work below and was vaguely surprised, not so much at their presence, as at the manner in which they moved, for they seemed under stress of some great haste, running hither and yon. She saw horses standing in the trail and sensed something indefinably odd and alarming in the air. Turning to the man, she opened her mouth to speak, when from the rank grass under her feet came a noise which set her a-tingle, and at which her suspicions leaped full to the solution. It was the groan of a man. Again he gave voice to his pain, and she knew that she stood face to face with something sinister. Tales of sluice robbers had come to her, and rumors of the daring raids into which men were lured by the yellow sheen—and yet this was incredible. A hundred men lay within sound of her voice; she could hear their laughter; one was whistling a popular refrain. A quarter-mile away on every hand were other camps; a scream from her would bring them all. Nonsense, this was no sluice robbery—and then the man in the bushes below moaned for the third time.

"What is that?" she said.

Without reply the negro lowered the muzzle of his rifle till it covered her breast and at the same time she heard the double click of the hammer.

"Keep still and don't move," he warned. "We're desperate and we can't take any chances, Miss."

"Oh, you are stealing the gold—"

She was wildly frightened, yet stood still while the lookout anxiously divided his attention between her and the tents above until his companions signalled him that they were through and the horses were loaded. Then he spoke:

"I don't know what to do with you, but I guess I'll tie you up."

"What!" she said.

"I'm going to tie and gag you so you can't holler."

"Oh, don't you DARE!" she cried, fiercely. "I'll stand right here till you've gone and I won't scream. I promise." She looked up at him appealingly, at which he dipped his head, so that she caught only a glimpse of his face, and then backed away.

"All right! Don't try it, because I'll be hidden in those bushes yonder at the bend and I'll keep you covered till the others are gone." He leaped down the bank, ran to the cavalcade, mounted quickly, and the three lashed their horses into a run, disappearing up the trail around the sharp curve. She heard the blows of their quirts as they whipped the pack-horses.

They were long out of sight before the girl moved or made sound, although she knew that none of the three had paused at the bend. She only stood and gazed, for as they galloped off she had heard the scrap of a broken sentence. It was but one excited word, sounding through the rattle of hoofs—her own name—"Helen"; and yet because of it she did not voice the alarm, but rather began to piece together, bit by bit, the strange points of this adventure. She recalled the outlines of her captor with a wrinkle of perplexity. Her fright disappeared entirely, giving place to intense excitement. "No, no—it can't be—and yet I wonder if it Is!" she cried. "Oh, I wonder if it could be!" She opened her lips to cry aloud, then hesitated. She started towards the tents, then paused, and for many moments after the hoof-beats had died out she stayed undecided. Surely she wished to give the signal, to force the fierce pursuit. What meant this robbery, this defiance of the law, of her uncle's edicts and of McNamara? They were common thieves, criminals, outlaws, these men, deserving punishment, and yet she recalled a darker night, when she herself had sobbed and quivered with the terrors of pursuit and two men had shielded her with their bodies.

She turned and sped towards the tents, bursting in through the canvas door; instantly every man rose to his feet at sight of her pallid face, her flashing eyes, and rumpled hair.

"Sluice robbers!" she cried, breathlessly. "Quick! A hold-up! The watchman is hurt!"

A roar shook the night air, and the men poured out past her, while the day shift came tumbling forth from every quarter in various stages of undress.

"Where? Who did it? Where did they go?"

McNamara appeared among them, fierce and commanding, seeming to grasp the situation intuitively, without explanation from her.

"Come on, men. We'll run 'em down. Get out the horses. Quick!"

He was mounted even as he spoke, and others joined him. Then turning, he waved his long arm up the valley towards the mountains. "Divide into squads of five and cover the hills! Run down to Discovery, one of you, and telephone to town for Voorhees and a posse."

As they made ready to ride away, the girl cried:

"Stop! Not that way. They went Down the gulch—three negroes."

She pointed out of the valley, towards the dim glow on the southern horizon, and the cavalcade rode away into the gloom.

X

THE WIT OF AN ADVENTURESS

U p creek the three negroes fled, past other camps, to where the stream branched. Here they took to the right and urged their horses along a forsaken trail to the head-waters of the little tributary and over the low saddle. They had endeavored to reach unfrequented paths as soon as possible in order that they might pass unnoticed. Before quitting the valley they halted their heaving horses, and, selecting a stagnant pool, scoured the grease paint from their features as best they could. Their ears were strained for sounds of pursuit, but, as the moments passed and none came, the tension eased somewhat and they conversed guardedly. As the morning light spread they crossed the moss-capped summit of the range, but paused again, and, removing two saddles, hid them among the rocks. Slapjack left the others here and rode southward down the Dry Creek Trail towards town, while the partners shifted part of the weight from the overloaded pack-mules to the remaining saddle-animals and continued eastward along the barren comb of hills on foot, leading the five horses.

"It don't seem like we'll get away this easy," said Dextry, scanning the back trail. "If we do, I'll be tempted to foller the business reg'lar. This grease paint on my face makes me smell like a minstrel man. I bet we'll get some bully press notices to-morrow."

"I wonder what Helen was doing there," Glenister answered, irrelevantly, for he had been more shaken by his encounter with her than at his part in the rest or the enterprise, and his mind, which should have been busied with the flight, held nothing but pictures of her as she stood in the half darkness under the fear of his Winchester. "What if she ever learned who that black ruffian was!" He quailed at the thought.

"Say, Dex, I am going to marry that girl."

"I dunno if you be or not," said Dextry. "Better watch McNamara."

"What!" The younger man stopped and stared. "What do you mean?"

"Go on. Don't stop the horses. I ain't blind. I kin put two an' two together."

"You'll never put those two together. Nonsense! Why, the man's a rascal. I wouldn't let him have her. Besides, it couldn't be. She'll find him out. I love her so much that—oh, my feelings are too big to talk about." He moved his hands eloquently. "You can't understand."

"Um-m! I s'pose not," grunted Dextry, but his eyes were level and held the light of the past.

"He may be a rascal," the old man continued, after a little; "I'll put in with you on that; but he's a handsome devil, and, as for manners, he makes you look like a logger. He's a brave man, too. Them three qualities are trump-cards and warranted to take most any queen in the human deck—red, white, or yellow."

"If he dares," growled Glenister, while his thick brows came forward and ugly lines hardened in his face.

In the gray of the early morning they descended the foot-hills into the wide valley of the Nome River and filed out across the rolling country to the river bluffs where, cleverly concealed among the willows, was a rocker. This they set up, then proceeded to wash the dirt from the sacks carefully, yet with the utmost speed, for there was serious danger of discovery. It was wonderful, this treasure of the richest ground since the days of '49, and the men worked with shining eyes and hands a-tremble. The gold was coarse, and many ragged, yellow lumps, too large to pass through the screen, rolled in the hopper, while the aprons bellied with its weight. In the pans which they had provided there grew a gleaming heap of wet, raw gold.

Shortly, by divergent routes, the partners rode unnoticed into town, and into the excitement of the hold-up news, while the tardy still lingered over their breakfasts. Far out in the roadstead lay the Roanoke, black smoke pouring from her stack. A tug was returning from its last trip to her.

Glenister forced his lathered horse down to the beach and questioned the longshoremen who hung about.

"No; it's too late to get aboard—the last tender is on its way back," they informed him. "If you want to go to the 'outside' you'll have to wait for the fleet. That only means another week, and—there she blows now."

A ribbon of white mingled with the velvet from the steamer's funnel and there came a slow, throbbing, farewell blast.

Glenister's jaw clicked and squared.

"Quick! You men!" he cried to the sailors. "I want the lightest dory on the beach and the strongest oarsmen in the crowd. I'll be back in five minutes. There's a hundred dollars in it for you if we catch that ship."

He whirled and spurred up through the mud of the streets. Bill Wheaton was snoring luxuriously when wrenched from his bed by a dishevelled man who shook him into wakefulness and into a portion of his clothes, with a storm of excited instructions. The lawyer had neither time nor opportunity for expostulation, for Glenister snatched a valise and swept into it a litter of documents from the table.

"Hurry up, man," he yelled, as the lawyer dived frantically about his office in a rabbit-like hunt for items. "My Heavens! Are you dead? Wake up! The ship's leaving." With sleep still in his eyes Wheaton was dragged down the street to the beach, where a knot had assembled to witness the race. As they tumbled into the skiff, willing hands ran it out into the surf on the crest of a roller. A few lifting heaves and they were over the bar with the men at the oars bending the white ash at every swing.

"I guess I didn't forget anything," gasped Wheaton as he put on his coat. "I got ready yesterday, but I couldn't find you last night, so I thought the deal was off."

Glenister stripped off his coat and, facing the bow, pushed upon the oars at every stroke, thus adding his strength to that of the oarsmen. They crept rapidly out from the beach, eating up the two miles that lay towards the ship. He urged the men with all his power till the sweat soaked through their clothes and, under their clinging shirts, the muscles stood out like iron. They had covered half the distance when Wheaton uttered a cry and Glenister desisted from his work with a curse. The Roanoke was moving slowly.

The rowers rested, but the young man shouted at them to begin again, and, seizing a boat-hook, stuck it into the arms of his coat. He waved this on high while the men redoubled their efforts. For many moments they hung in suspense, watching the black hull as it gathered speed, and then, as they were about to cease their effort, a puff of steam burst from its whistle and the next moment a short toot of recognition reached them. Glenister wiped the moisture from his brow and grinned at Wheaton.

A quarter of an hour later, as they lay heaving below the ship's steel sides, he thrust a heavy buckskin sack into the lawyer's hand.

"There's money to win the fight, Bill. I don't know how much, but it's enough. God bless you. Hurry back!"

A sailor cast them a whirling rope, up which Wheaton clambered; then, tying the gripsack to its end, they sent it after.

"Important!" the young man yelled at the officer on the bridge. "Government business." He heard a muffled clang in the engine-room, the thrash of the propellers followed, and the big ship glided past.

As Glenister dragged himself up the beach, upon landing, Helen Chester called to him, and made room for him beside her. It had never been necessary to call him to her side before; and equally unfamiliar was the abashment, or perhaps physical weariness, that led the young man to sink back in the warm sand with a sigh of relief. She noted that, for the first time, the audacity was gone from his eyes.

"I watched your race," she began. "It was very exciting and I cheered for you."

He smiled quietly.

"What made you keep on after the ship started? I should have given up—and cried."

"I never give up anything that I want," he said.

"Have you never been forced to? Then it is because you are a man. Women have to sacrifice a great deal."

Helen expected him to continue to the effect that he would never give her up—it was in accordance with his earlier presumption—but he was silent; and she was not sure that she liked him as well thus as when he overwhelmed her with the boldness of his suit. For Glenister it was delightful, after the perils of the night, to rest in the calm of her presence and to feel dumbly that she was near. She saw him secretly caress a fold of her dress.

If only she had not the memory of that one night on the ship. "Still, he is trying to make amends in the best way he can," she thought. "Though, of course, no woman could care for a man who would do such a thing." Yet she thrilled at the thought of how he had thrust his body between her and danger; how, but for his quick, insistent action, she would have failed in escaping from the pest ship, failed in her mission, and met death on the night of her landing. She owed him much.

"Did you hear what happened to the good ship Ohio?" she asked.

"No; I've been too busy to inquire. I was told the health officers quarantined her when she arrived, that's all."

"She was sent to Egg Island with every one aboard. She has been there more than a month now and may not get away this summer."

"What a disappointment for the poor devils on her!"

"Yes, and only for what you did, I should be one of them," Helen remarked.

"I didn't do much," he said. "The fighting part is easy. It's not half so hard as to give up your property and lie still while—"

"Did you do that because I asked you to—because I asked you to put aside the old ways?" A wave of compassion swept over her.

"Certainly," he answered. "It didn't come easy, but—"

"Oh, I thank you," said she. "I know it is all for the best. Uncle Arthur wouldn't do anything wrong, and Mr. McNamara is an honorable man."

He turned towards her to speak, but refrained. He could not tell her what he felt certain of. She believed in her own blood and in her uncle's friends—and it was not for him to speak of McNamara. The rules of the game sealed his lips.

She was thinking again, "If only you had not acted as you did." She longed to help him now in his trouble as he had helped her, but what could she do? The law was such a confusing, intricate, perplexing thing.

"I spent last night at the Midas," she told him, "and rode back early this morning. That was a daring hold-up, wasn't it?"

"What hold-up?"

"Why, haven't you heard the news?"

"No" he answered, steadily. "I just got up."

"Your claim was robbed. Three men overcame the watchman at midnight and cleaned the boxes."

His simulation of excited astonishment was perfect and he rained a shower of questions upon her. She noted with approval that he did not look her in the eye, however. He was not an accomplished liar. Now McNamara had a countenance of iron. Unconsciously she made comparison, and the young man at her side did not lose thereby.

"Yes, I saw it all," she concluded, after recounting the details. "The negro wanted to bind me so that I couldn't give the alarm, but his chivalry prevented. He was a most gallant darky."

"What did you do when they left?"

"Why, I kept my word and waited until they were out of sight, then I roused the camp, and set Mr. McNamara and his men right after them down the gulch."

"Down the gulch!" spoke Glenister, off his guard.

"Yes, of course. Did you think they went Up-stream?" She was looking squarely at him now, and he dropped his eyes. "No, the posse started in that direction, but I put them right." There was an odd light in her glance, and he felt the blood drumming in his ears.

She sent them down-stream! So that was why there had been no pursuit! Then she must suspect—she must know everything! Glenister was stunned. Again his love for the girl surged tumultuously within him and demanded expression. But Miss Chester, no longer feeling sure that she had the situation in hand, had already started to return to the hotel. "I saw the men distinctly," she told him, before they separated, "and I could identify them all."

At his own house Glenister found Dextry removing the stains of the night's adventure.

"Miss Chester recognized us last night," he announced.

"How do you know?"

"She told me so just now, and, what's more, she sent McNamara and his crowd down the creek instead of up. That's why we got away so easily."

"Well, well—ain't she a brick? She's even with us now. By-the-way, I wonder how much we cleaned up, anyhow—let's weigh it." Going to the bed, Dextry turned back the blankets, exposing four moose-skin sacks, wet and heavy, where he had thrown them.

"There must have been twenty thousand dollars with what I gave Wheaton," said Glenister.

At that moment, without warning, the door was flung open, and as the young man jerked the blankets into place he whirled, snatched the six-shooter that Dextry had discarded, and covered the entrance.

"Don't shoot, boy!" cried the new-comer, breathlessly. "My, but you're nervous!"

Glenister dropped his gun. It was Cherry Malotte; and, from her heaving breast and the flying colors in her cheeks, the men saw she had been running. She did not give them time to question, but closed and locked the door while the words came tumbling from her:

"They're on to you, boys—you'd better duck out quick. They're on their way up here now."

"What!"

"Who?"

"Quick! I heard McNamara and Voorhees, the marshal, talking. Somebody has spotted you for the hold-ups. They're on their way now, I tell you. I sneaked out by the back way and came here through the mud. Say, but I'm a sight!" She stamped her trimly booted feet and flirted her skirt.

"I don't savvy what you mean," said Dextry, glancing at his partner warningly. "We ain't done nothin'."

"Well, it's all right then. I took a long chance so you could make a get-away if you wanted to, because they've got warrants for you for that sluice robbery last night. Here they are now." She darted to the window, the men peering over her shoulder. Coming up the narrow walk they saw Voorhees, McNamara, and three others.

The house stood somewhat isolated and well back on the tundra, so that any one approaching it by the planking had an unobstructed view of the premises. Escape was impossible, for the back door led out into the ankle-deep puddles of the open prairie; and it was now apparent that a sixth man had made a circuit and was approaching from the rear.

"My God! They'll search the place," said Dextry, and the men looked grimly in each other's faces.

Then in a flash Glenister stripped back the blankets and seized the "pokes," leaping into the back room. In another instant he returned with them and faced desperately the candid bareness of the little room that they lived and slept in. Nothing could be hidden; it was folly to think of it. There was a loft overhead, he remembered, hopefully, then realized that the pursuers would search there first of all.

"I told you he was a hard fighter," said Dextry, as the quick footsteps grew louder. "He ain't no fool neither. 'Stead of our bein' caught in the mountains, I reckon we'll shoot it out here. We should have cached that gold somewhere."

He spun the cylinder of his blackened Colt, while his face grew hard and vulture-like.

Meanwhile, Cherry Malotte watched the hunted look in Glenister's face grow wilder and then stiffen into the stubbornness of a man at bay. The posse was at the door now, knocking. The three inside stood rigid and strained. Then Glenister tossed his burden on the bed.

"Go into the back room, Cherry; there's going to be trouble."

"Who's there?" inquired Dextry through the door, to gain time. Suddenly, without a word, the girl glided to the hot-blast heater, now cold and empty, which stood in a corner of the room. These stoves, used widely in the North, are vertical iron cylinders into which coal is poured from above. She lifted the lid and peered in to find it a quarter full of dead ashes, then turned with shining eyes and parted lips to Glenister. He caught the hint, and in an instant the four sacks were dropped softly into the feathery bottom and the ashes raked over. The daring manoeuvre was almost as quick as the flash of woman's wit that prompted it, and was carried through while the answer to Dextry's question was still unspoken.

Then Glenister opened the door carelessly and admitted the group of men.

"We've got a search-warrant to look through your house," said Voorhees.

"What are you looking for?"

"Gold-dust from Anvil Creek."

"All right—search away."

They rapidly scoured the premises, covering every inch, paying no heed to the girl, who watched them with indifferent eyes, nor to the old man, who glared at their every movement. Glenister was carelessly sarcastic, although he kept his right arm free, while beneath his sang-froid was a thoroughly trained alertness.

McNamara directed the search with a manner wholly lacking in his former mock courtesy. It was as though he had been soured by the gall of defeat. The mask had fallen off now, and his character showed— insistent, overbearing, cruel. Towards the partners he preserved a contemptuous silence.

The invaders ransacked thoroughly, while a dozen times the hearts of Cherry Malotte and her two companions stopped, then lunged onward, as McNamara or Voorhees approached, then passed the stove. At last Voorhees lifted the lid and peered into its dark interior. At the same instant the girl cried out, sharply, flinging herself from her position, while the marshal jerked his head back in time to see her dash upon Dextry.

"Don't! Don't!" She cried her appeal to the old man. "Keep cool. You'll be sorry, Dex—they're almost through."

The officer had not seen any movement on Dextry's part, but doubtless her quick eye had detected signs of violence. McNamara emerged, glowering, from the back room at that moment.

"Let them hunt," the girl was saying, while Dextry stared dazedly over her head. "They won't find anything. Keep cool and don't act rash."

Voorhees's duties sat uncomfortably upon him at the best, and, looking at the smouldering eyes of the two men, he became averse to further search in a powdery household whose members itched to shoot him in the back.

"It isn't here," he reported; but the politician only scowled, then spoke for the first time directly to the partners:

"I've got warrants for both of you and I'm tempted to take you in, but I won't. I'm not through yet—not by any means. I'll get you—get you both." He turned out of the door, followed by the marshal, who called off his guards, and the group filed back along the walk.

"Say, you're a jewel, Cherry. You've saved us twice. You caught Voorhees just in time. My heart hit my palate when he looked into that stove, but the next instant I wanted to laugh at Dextry's expression."

Impulsively Glenister laid his hands upon her shoulders. At his look and touch her throat swelled, her bosom heaved, and the silken lids fluttered until she seemed choked by a very flood of sweet womanliness. She blushed like a little maid and laughed a timid, broken laugh; then pulling herself together, the merry, careless tone came into her voice and her cheeks grew cool and clear.

"You wouldn't trust me at first, eh? Some day you'll find that your old friends are the best, after all."

And as she left them she added, mockingly:

"Say, you're a pair of 'shine' desperadoes. You need a governess."

XI

Wherein a Writ and a Riot Fail

A Raw, gray day with a driving drizzle from seaward and a leaden rack of clouds drifting low matched the sullen, fitful mood of Glenister.

During the last month he had chafed and fretted like an animal in leash for word of Wheaton. This uncertainty, this impotent waiting with folded hands, was maddening to one of his spirit. He could apply himself to no fixed duty, for the sense of his wrong preyed on him fiercely, and he found himself haunting the vicinity of the Midas, gazing at it from afar, grasping hungrily for such scraps of news as chanced to reach him. McNamara allowed access to none but his minions, so the partners knew but vaguely of what happened on their property, even though, under fiction of law, it was being worked for their protection.

No steps regarding a speedy hearing of the case were allowed, and the collusion between Judge Stillman and the receiver had become so generally recognized that there were uneasy mutterings and threats in many quarters. Yet, although the politician had by now virtually absorbed all the richest properties in the district and worked them through his hirelings, the people of Nome as a whole did not grasp the full turpitude of the scheme nor the system's perfect working.

Strange to say, Dextry, the fire-eater, had assumed an Oriental patience quite foreign to his peppery disposition, and spent much of his time in the hills prospecting.

On this day, as the clouds broke, about noon, close down on the angry horizon a drift of smoke appeared, shortly resolving itself into a steamer. She lay to in the offing, and through his glasses Glenister saw that it was the Roanoke. As the hours passed and no boat put off, he tried to hire a crew, but the longshoremen spat wisely and shook their heads as they watched the surf.

"There's the devil of an undertow settin' along this beach," they told him, "and the water's too cold to drownd in comfortable." So he laid firm hands upon his impatience.

Every day meant many dollars to the watcher, and yet it seemed that nature was resolute in thwarting him, for that night the wind freshened and daylight saw the ship hugging the lee of Sledge Island, miles to the westward, while the surf, white as boiling milk, boomed and thundered against the shore.

Word had gone through the street that Bill Wheaton was aboard with a writ, or a subpoena, or an alibi, or whatever was necessary to put the "kibosh" on McNamara, so public excitement grew. McNamara hoarded his gold in the Alaska Bank, and it was taken for granted that there would lie the scene of the struggle. No one supposed for an instant that the usurper would part with the treasure peaceably.

On the third morning the ship lay abreast of the town again and a life-boat was seen to make off from her, whereupon the idle population streamed towards the beach.

"She'll make it to the surf all right, but then watch out."

"We'd better make ready to haul 'em out," said another. "It's mighty dangerous." And sure enough, as the skiff came rushing in through the breakers she was caught.

She had made it past the first line, soaring over the bar on a foamy roller-crest like a storm-driven gull winging in towards the land. The wiry figure of Bill Wheaton crouched in the stern while two sailors fought with their oars. As they gathered for their rush through the last zone of froth, a great comber rose out of the sea behind them, rearing high above their heads. The crowd at the surf's edge shouted. The boat wavered, sucked back into the ocean's angry maw, and with a crash the deluge engulfed them. There remained nothing but a swirling flood through which the life-boat emerged bottom up, amid a tangle of oars, gratings, and gear.

Men rushed into the water, and the next roller pounded them back upon the marble-hard sand. There came the sound of splitting wood, and then a group swarmed in waist-deep and bore out a dripping figure. It was a hempen-headed seaman, who shook the water from his mane and grinned when his breath had come.

A step farther down the beach the by-standers seized a limp form which the tide rolled to them. It was the second sailor, his scalp split from a blow of the gunwale. Nowhere was Wheaton.

Glenister had plunged to the rescue first, a heaving-line about his middle, and although buffeted about he had reached the wreck, only to miss sight of the lawyer utterly. He had time for but a glance when he was drawn outward by the undertow till the line at his waist grew taut, then the water surged over him and he was hurled high up on the beach again. He staggered dizzily back to the struggle, when suddenly a wave lifted the capsized cutter and righted it, and out from beneath shot the form of Wheaton, grimly clutching the life-ropes. They brought him in choking and breathless.

"I got it," he said, slapping his streaming breast. "It's all right, Glenister, I knew what delay meant so I took a long chance with the surf." The terrific ordeal he had undergone had blanched him to the lips, his legs wabbled uncertainly, and he would have fallen but for the young man, who thrust an arm about his waist and led him up into the town.

"I went before the Circuit Court of Appeals in 'Frisco," he explained later, "and they issued orders allowing an appeal from this court and gave me a writ of supersedeas directed against old Judge Stillman. That takes the litigation out of his hands altogether, and directs McNamara to turn over the Midas and all the gold he's got. What do you think of that? I did better than I expected."

Glenister wrung his hand silently while a great satisfaction came upon him. At last this waiting was over and his peaceful yielding to injustice had borne fruit; had proven the better course after all, as the girl had prophesied. He could go to her now with clean hands. The mine was his again. He would lay it at her feet, telling her once more of his love and the change it was working in him. He would make her see it, make her see that beneath the harshness his years in the wild had given him, his love for her was gentle and true and all absorbing. He would bid her be patient till she saw he had mastered himself, till he could come with his soul in harness.

"I am glad I didn't fight when they jumped us," he said. "Now we'll get our property back and all the money they took out—that is, if McNamara hasn't salted it."

"Yes; all that's necessary is to file the documents, then serve the Judge and McNamara. You'll be back on Anvil Creek to-morrow."

Having placed their documents on record at the court-house, the two men continued to McNamara's office. He met them with courtesy.

"I heard you had a narrow escape this morning, Mr. Wheaton. Too bad! What can I do for you?"

The lawyer rapidly outlined his position and stated in conclusion:

"I filed certified copies of these orders with the clerk of the court ten minutes ago, and now I make formal demand upon you to turn over the Midas to Messrs. Glenister and Dextry, and also to return all the gold-dust in your safe-deposit boxes in accordance with this writ." He handed his documents to McNamara, who tossed them on his desk without examination.

"Well," said the politician, quietly, "I won't do it."

Had he been slapped in the face the attorney would not have been more astonished.

"Why—you—"

"I won't do it, I said," McNamara repeated, sharply. "Don't think for a minute that I haven't gone into this fight armed for everything. Writs of supersedeas! Bah!" He snapped his fingers.

"We'll see whether you'll obey or not," said Wheaton and when he and Glenister were outside he continued:

"Let's get to the Judge quick."

As they neared the Golden Gate Hotel they spied McNamara entering. It was evident that he had slipped from the rear door of his office and beaten them to the judicial ear.

"I don't like that," said Glenister. "He's up to something."

So it appeared, for they were fifteen minutes in gaining access to the magistrate and then found McNamara with him. Both men were astounded at the change in Stillman's appearance. During the last month his weak face had shrunk and altered until vacillation was betrayed in every line, and he had acquired the habit of furtively watching McNamara's slightest movement. It seemed that the part he played sat heavily upon him.

The Judge examined the papers perfunctorily, and, although his air was deliberate, his fingers made clumsy work of it. At last he said:

"I regret that I am forced to doubt the authenticity of these documents."

"My Heavens, man!" Wheaton cried. "They're certified copies of orders from your superior court. They grant the appeal that you have denied us and take the case out of your hands altogether. Yes—and they order this man to surrender the mine and everything connected with it. Now, sir, we want you to enforce these orders."

Stillman glanced at the silent man in the window and replied:

"You will, of course, proceed regularly and make application in court in the proper way, but I tell you now that I won't do anything in the matter."

Wheaton stared at him fixedly until the old man snapped out:

"You say they are certified copies. How do I know they are? The signatures may all be false. Maybe you signed them yourself."

The lawyer grew very white at this and stammered until Glenister drew him out of the room.

"Come, come," he said, "we'll carry this thing through in open court. Maybe his nerve will go back on him then. McNamara has him hypnotized, but he won't dare refuse to obey the orders of the Circuit Court of Appeals."

"He won't, eh? Well, what do you think he's doing right now?" said Wheaton. "I must think. This is the boldest game I ever played in. They told me things while I was in 'Frisco which I couldn't believe, but I guess they're true. Judges don't disobey the orders of their courts of appeal unless there is power back of them."

They proceeded to the attorney's office, but had not been there long before Slapjack Simms burst in upon them.

"Hell to pay!" he panted. "McNamara's taking your dust out of the bank."

"What's that?" they cried.

"I goes into the bank just now for an assay on some quartz samples. The assayer is busy, and I walk back into his room, and while I'm there in trots McNamara in a hurry. He don't see me, as I'm inside the private office, and I overhear him tell them to get his dust out of the vault quick."

"We've got to stop that," said Glenister. "If he takes ours, he'll take the Swedes', too. Simms, you run up to the Pioneer Company and tell them about it. If he gets that gold out of there, nobody knows what'll become of it. Come on, Bill."

He snatched his hat and ran out of the room, followed by the others. That the loose-jointed Slapjack did his work with expedition was evidenced by the fact that the Swedes were close upon their heels as the two entered the bank. Others had followed, sensing something unusual, and the space within the doors filled rapidly. At the disturbance the clerks suspended their work, the barred doors of the safe-deposit vault clanged to, and the cashier laid hand upon the navy Colt's at his elbow. "What's the matter?" he cried.

"We want Alec McNamara," said Glenister.

The manager of the bank appeared, and Glenister spoke to him through the heavy wire netting.

"Is McNamara in there?"

No one had ever known Morehouse to lie. "Yes, sir." He spoke hesitatingly, in a voice full of the slow music of Virginia. "He is in here. What of it?"

"We hear he's trying to move that dust of ours and we won't stand for it. Tell him to come out and not hide in there like a dog."

At these words the politician appeared beside the Southerner, and the two conversed softly an instant, while the impatience of the crowd grew to anger. Some one cried:

"Let's go in and drag him out," and the rumble at this was not pleasant. Morehouse raised his hand.

"Gentlemen, Mr. McNamara says he doesn't intend to take any of the gold away."

"Then he's taken it already."

"No, he hasn't."

The receiver's course had been quickly chosen at the interruption. It was not wise to anger these men too much. Although he had planned to get the money into his own possession, he now thought it best to leave it here for the present. He could come back at any time when they were off guard and get it. Beyond the door against which he stood lay three hundred thousand dollars—weighed, sacked, sealed, and ready to move out of the custody of this Virginian whose confidence he had tried so fruitlessly to gain.

As McNamara looked into the angry eyes of the lean-faced men beyond the grating, he felt that the game was growing close, and his blood tingled at the thought. He had not planned on a resistance so strong and swift, but he would meet it. He knew that they hungered for his destruction and that Glenister was their leader. He saw further that the man's hatred now stared at him openly for the first time. He knew that back of it was something more than love for the dull metal over which they wrangled, and then a thought came to him.

"Some of your work, eh, Glenister?" he mocked. "Were you afraid to come alone, or did you wait till you saw me with a lady?"

At the same instant he opened a door behind him, revealing Helen Chester. "You'd better not walk out with me, Miss Chester. This man might—well, you're safer here, you know. You'll pardon me for leaving you." He hoped he could incite the young man to some rash act or word in the presence of the girl, and counted on the conspicuous heroism of his own position, facing the mob single-handed, one against fifty.

"Come out," said his enemy, hoarsely, upon whom the insult and the sight of the girl in the receiver's company had acted powerfully.

"Of course I'll come out, but I don't want this young lady to suffer any violence from your friends," said McNamara. "I am not armed, but

I have the right to leave here unmolested—the right of an American citizen." With that he raised his arms above his head. "Out of my way!" he cried. Morehouse opened the gate, and McNamara strode through the mob.

It is a peculiar thing that although under fury of passion a man may fire even upon the back of a defenceless foe, yet no one can offer violence to a man whose arms are raised on high and in whose glance is the level light of fearlessness. Moreover, it is safer to face a crowd thus than a single adversary.

McNamara had seen this psychological trick tried before and now took advantage of it to walk through the press slowly, eye to eye. He did it theatrically, for the benefit of the girl, and, as he foresaw, the men fell away before him—all but Glenister, who blocked him, gun in hand. It was plain that the persecuted miner was beside himself with passion. McNamara came within an arm's-length before pausing. Then he stopped and the two stared malignantly at each other, while the girl behind the railing heard her heart pounding in the stillness. Glenister raised his hand uncertainly, then let it fall. He shook his head, and stepped aside so that the other brushed past and out into the street.

Wheaton addressed the banker:

"Mr. Morehouse, we've got orders and writs of one kind or another from the Circuit Court of Appeals at 'Frisco directing that this money be turned over to us." He shoved the papers towards the other. "We're not in a mood to trifle. That gold belongs to us, and we want it."

Morehouse looked carefully at the papers.

"I can't help you," he said. "These documents are not directed to me. They're issued to Mr. McNamara and Judge Stillman. If the Circuit Court of Appeals commands me to deliver it to you I'll do it, but otherwise I'll have to keep this dust here till it's drawn out by order of the court that gave it to me. That's the way it was put in here, and that's the way it'll be taken out."

"We want it now."

"Well, I can't let my sympathies influence me"

"Then we'll take it out, anyway," cried Glenister. "We've had the worst of it everywhere else and we're sick of it. Come on, men."

"Stand back!—all of you!" cried Morehouse. "Don't lay a hand on that gate. Boys, pick your men."

He called this last to his clerks, at the same instant whipping from behind the counter a carbine, which he cocked. The assayer brought into view a shot-gun, while the cashier and clerks armed themselves. It was evident that the deposits of the Alaska Bank were abundantly safeguarded.

"I don't aim to have any trouble with you-all," continued the Southerner, "but that money stays here till it's drawn out right."

The crowd paused at this show of resistance, but Glenister railed at them:

"Come on—come on! What's the matter with you?" And from the light in his eye it was evident that he would not be balked.

Helen felt that a crisis was come, and braced herself. These men were in deadly earnest: the white-haired banker, his pale helpers, and those grim, quiet ones outside. There stood brawny, sun-browned men, with set jaws and frowning faces, and yellow-haired Scandinavians in whose blue eyes danced the flame of battle. These had been baffled at every turn, goaded by repeated failure, and now stood shoulder to shoulder in their resistance to a cruel law. Suddenly Helen heard a command from the street and the quick tramp of men, while over the heads before her she saw the glint of rifle barrels. A file of soldiers with fixed bayonets thrust themselves roughly through the crowd at the entrance.

"Clear the room!" commanded the officer.

"What does this mean?" shouted Wheaton.

"It means that Judge Stillman has called upon the military to guard this gold, that's all. Come, now, move quick." The men hesitated, then sullenly obeyed, for resistance to the blue of Uncle Sam comes only at the cost of much consideration.

"They're robbing us with our own soldiers," said Wheaton, when they were outside.

"Ay," said Glenister, darkly. "We've tried the law, but they're forcing us back to first principles. There's going to be murder here."

XII

Counterplots

Glenister had said that the Judge would not dare to disobey the mandates of the Circuit Court of Appeals, but he was wrong. Application was made for orders directing the enforcement of the writs—steps which would have restored possession of the Midas to its owners, as well as possession of the treasure in bank—but Stillman refused to grant them.

Wheaton called a meeting of the Swedes and their attorneys, advising a junction of forces. Dextry, who had returned from the mountains, was present. When they had finished their discussion, he said:

"It seems like I can always fight better when I know what the other feller's game is. I'm going to spy on that outfit."

"We've had detectives at work for weeks," said the lawyer for the Scandinavians; "but they can't find out anything we don't know already."

Dextry said no more, but that night found him busied in the building adjoining the one wherein McNamara had his office. He had rented a back room on the top floor, and with the help of his partner sawed through the ceiling into the loft and found his way thence to the roof through a hatchway. Fortunately, there was but little space between the two buildings, and, furthermore, each boasted the square fronts common in mining-camps, which projected high enough to prevent observation from across the way. Thus he was enabled, without discovery, to gain the roof adjoining and to cut through into the loft. He crept cautiously in through the opening, and out upon a floor of joists sealed on the lower side, then lit a candle, and, locating McNamara's office, cut a peep-hole so that by lying flat on the timbers he could command a considerable portion of the room beneath. Here, early the following morning, he camped with the patience of an Indian, emerging in the still of that night stiff, hungry, and atrociously cross. Meanwhile, there had been another meeting of the mine-owners, and it had been decided to send Wheaton, properly armed with affidavits and transcripts of certain court records, back to San Francisco on the return trip of the Santa Maria, which had arrived in port. He was to institute proceedings for contempt of court, and it was hoped that by extraordinary effort he could gain quick action.

At daybreak Dextry returned to his post, and it was midnight before he crawled from his hiding-place to see the lawyer and Glenister.

"They have had a spy on you all day, Wheaton," he began, "and they know you're going out to the States. You'll be arrested to-morrow morning before breakfast."

"Arrested! What for?"

"I don't just remember what the crime is—bigamy, or mayhem, or attainder of treason, or something—anyway, they'll get you in jail and that's all they want. They think you're the only lawyer that's wise enough to cause trouble and the only one they can't bribe."

"Lord! What'll I do? They'll watch every lighter that leaves the beach, and if they don't catch me that way, they'll search the ship."

"I've thought it all out," said the old man, to whom obstruction acted as a stimulant.

"Yes—but how?"

"Leave it to me. Get your things together and be ready to duck in two hours."

"I tell you they'll search the Santa Maria from stem to stern," protested the lawyer, but Dextry had gone.

"Better do as he says. His schemes are good ones," recommended Glenister, and accordingly the lawyer made preparation.

In the mean time the old prospector had begun at the end of Front Street to make a systematic search of the gambling-houses. Although it was very late they were running noisily, and at last he found the man he wanted playing "Black Jack," the smell of tar in his clothes, the lilt of the sea in his boisterous laughter. Dextry drew him aside.

"Mac, there's only two things about you that's any good—your silence and your seamanship. Otherwise, you're a disreppitable, drunken insect."

The sailor grinned.

"What is it you want now? If it's concerning money, or business, or the growed-up side of life, run along and don't disturb the carousals of a sailorman. If it's a fight, lemme get my hat."

"I want you to wake up your fireman and have steam on the tug in an hour, then wait for me below the bridge. You're chartered for twenty-four hours, and—remember, not a word."

"I'm on! Compared to me the Spinks of Egyp' is as talkative as a phonograph."

The old man next turned his steps to the Northern Theatre. The performance was still in progress, and he located the man he was hunting without difficulty.

Ascending the stairs, he knocked at the door of one of the boxes and called for Captain Stephens.

"I'm glad I found you, Cap," said he. "It saved me a trip out to your ship in the dark."

"What's the matter?"

Dextry drew him to an isolated corner. "Me an' my partner want to send a man to the States with you."

"All right."

"Well—er—here's the point," hesitated the miner, who rebelled at asking favors. "He's our law sharp, an' the McNamara outfit is tryin' to put the steel on him."

"I don't understand."

"Why, they've swore out a warrant an' aim to guard the shore to-morrow. We want you to—"

"Mr. Dextry, I'm not looking for trouble. I get enough in my own business."

"But, see here," argued the other, "we've GOT to send him out so he can make a pow-wow to the big legal smoke in 'Frisco. We've been cold-decked with a bum judge. They've got us into a corner an' over the ropes."

"I'm sorry I can't help you, Dextry, but I got mixed up in one of your scrapes and that's plenty."

"This ain't no stowaway. There's no danger to you," began Dextry, but the officer interrupted him:

"There's no need of arguing. I won't do it."

"Oh, you WON'T, eh?" said the old man, beginning to lose his temper. "Well, you listen to me for a minute. Everybody in camp knows that me an' the kid is on the square an' that we're gettin' the hunk passed to us. Now, this lawyer party must get away to-night or these grafters will hitch the horses to him on some phony charge so he can't get to the upper court. It'll be him to the bird-cage for ninety days. He's goin' to the States, though, an' he's goin'—in—your—wagon! I'm talkin' to you—man to man. If you don't take him, I'll go to the health inspector—he's a friend of mine—an' I'll put a crimp in you an' your steamboat, I don't want to do that—it ain't my reg'lar graft by no means—but this bet goes through as she lays. I never belched up a secret before. No, sir;

I am the human huntin'-case watch, an' I won't open my face unless you press me. But if I should, you'll see that it's time for you to hunt a new job. Now, here's my scheme." He outlined his directions to the sailor, who had fallen silent during the warning. When he had done, Stephens said:

"I never had a man talk to me like that before, sir—never. You've taken advantage of me, and under the circumstances I can't refuse. I'll do this thing—not because of your threat, but because I heard about your trouble over the Midas—and because I can't help admiring your blamed insolence." He went back into his stall.

Dextry returned to Wheaton's office. As he neared it, he passed a lounging figure in an adjacent doorway.

"The place is watched," he announced as he entered. "Have you got a back door? Good! Leave your light burning and we'll go out that way." They slipped quietly into an inky, tortuous passage which led back towards Second Street. Floundering through alleys and over garbage heaps, by circuitous routes, they reached the bridge, where, in the swift stream beneath, they saw the lights from Mac's tug.

Steam was up, and when the Captain had let them aboard Dextry gave him instructions, to which he nodded acquiescence. They bade the lawyer adieu, and the little craft slipped its moorings, danced down the current, across the bar, and was swallowed up in the darkness to seaward. "I'll put out Wheaton's light so they'll think he's gone to bed."

"Yes, and at daylight I'll take your place in McNamara's loft," said Glenister. "There will be doings to-morrow when they don't find him."

They returned by the way they had come to the lawyer's room, extinguished his light, went to their own cabin and to bed. At dawn Glenister arose and sought his place above McNamara's office.

To lie stretched at length on a single plank with eye glued to a crack is not a comfortable position, and the watcher thought the hours of the next day would never end. As they dragged wearily past, his bones began to ache beyond endurance, yet owing to the flimsy structure of the building he dared not move while the room below was tenanted. In fact, he would not have stirred had he dared, so intense was his interest in the scenes being enacted beneath him.

First had come the marshal, who imported his failure to find Wheaton.

"He left his room some time last night. My men followed him in and saw a light in his window until two o'clock this morning. At seven o'clock we broke in and he was gone."

"He must have got wind of our plan. Send deputies aboard the Santa Maria; search her from keel to topmast, and have them watch the beach close or he'll put off in a small boat. You look over the passengers that go aboard yourself. Don't trust any of your men for that, because he may try to slip through disguised. He's liable to make up like a woman. You understand—there's only one ship in port, and—he mustn't get away."

"He won't," said Voorhees, with conviction, and the listener overhead smiled grimly to himself, for at that moment, twenty miles offshore, lay Mac's little tug, hove to in the track of the outgoing steamship, and in her tiny cabin sat Bill Wheaton eating breakfast.

As the morning wore by with no news of the lawyer, McNamara's uneasiness grew. At noon the marshal returned with a report that the passengers were all aboard and the ship about to clear.

"By Heavens! He's slipped through you," stormed the politician.

"No, he hasn't. He may be hidden aboard somewhere among the coal-bunkers, but I think he's still ashore and aiming to make a quick run just before she sails. He hasn't left the beach since daylight, that's sure. I'm going out to the ship now with four men and search her again. If we don't bring him off you can bet he's lying out somewhere in town and we'll get him later. I've stationed men along the shore for two miles."

"I won't have him get away. If he should reach 'Frisco—Tell your men I'll give five hundred dollars to the one that finds him."

Three hours later Voorhees returned.

"She sailed without him."

The politician cursed. "I don't believe it. He tricked you. I know he did."

Glenister grinned into a half-eaten sandwich, then turned upon his back and lay thus on the plank, identifying the speakers below by their voices.

He kept his post all day. Later in the evening he heard Struve enter. The man had been drinking.

"So he got away, eh?" he began. "I was afraid he would. Smart fellow, that Wheaton."

"He didn't get away," said McNamara. "He's in town yet. Just let me land him in jail on some excuse! I'll hold him till snow flies." Struve sank into a chair and lit a cigarette with wavering hand.

"This's a hell of a game, ain't it, Mac? D'you s'pose we'll win?"

The man overhead pricked up his ears.

"Win? Aren't we winning? What do you call this? I only hope we can lay hands on Wheaton. He knows things. A little knowledge is a dangerous thing, but more is worse. Lord! If only I had a MAN for judge in place of Stillman! I don't know why I brought him."

"That's right. Too weak. He hasn't got the backbone of an angleworm. He ain't half the man that his niece is. THERE's a girl for you! Say! What'd we do without her, eh? She's a pippin!" Glenister felt a sudden tightening of every muscle. What right had that man's liquor-sodden lips to speak so of her?

"She's a brave little woman all right. Just look how she worked Glenister and his fool partner. It took nerve to bring in those instructions of yours alone; and if it hadn't been for her we'd never have won like this. It makes me laugh to think of those two men stowing her away in their state-room while they slept between decks with the sheep, and her with the papers in her bosom all the time. Then, when we got ready to do business, why, she up and talks them into giving us possession of their mine without a fight. That's what I call reciprocating a man's affection."

Glenister's nails cut into his flesh, while his face went livid at the words. He could not grasp it at once. It made him sick—physically sick—and for many moments he strove blindly to beat back the hideous suspicion, the horror that the lawyer had aroused. His was not a doubting disposition, and to him the girl had seemed as one pure, mysterious, apart, angelically incapable of deceit. He had loved her, feeling that some day she would return his affection without fail. In her great, unclouded eyes he had found no lurking-place for double-dealing. Now—God! It couldn't be that all the time she had KNOWN!

He had lost a part of the lawyer's speech, but peered through his observation-hole again.

McNamara was at the window gazing out into the dark street, his back towards the lawyer, who lolled in the chair, babbling garrulously of the girl. Glenister ground his teeth—a frenzy possessed him to loose his anger, to rip through the frail ceiling with naked hands and fall vindictively upon the two men.

"She looked good to me the first time I saw her," continued Struve. He paused, and when he spoke again a change had coarsened his features, "Say, I'm crazy about her, Mac. I tell you, I'm crazy—and she likes me—I know she does—or, anyway, she would—"

"Do you mean that you're in love with her?" asked the man at the window, without shifting his position. It seemed that utter indifference was in his question, although where the light shone on his hands, tight-clinched behind his back, they were bloodless.

"Love her? Well—that depends—ha! You know how it is—" he chuckled, coarsely. His face was gross and bestial. "I've got the Judge where I want him, and I'll have her—"

His miserable words died with a gurgle, for McNamara had silently leaped and throttled him where he sat, pinning him to the wall. Glenister saw the big politician shift his fingers slightly on Struve's throat and then drop his left hand to his side, holding his victim writhing and helpless with his right despite the man's frantic struggles. McNamara's head was thrust forward from his shoulders, peering into the lawyer's face. Strove tore ineffectually at the iron arm which was squeezing his life out, while for endless minutes the other leaned his weight against him, his idle hand behind his back, his legs braced like stone columns, as he watched his victim's struggles abate.

Struve fought and wrenched while his breath caught in his throat with horrid, sickening sounds, but gradually his eyes rolled farther and farther back till they stared out of his blackened visage, straight up towards the ceiling, towards the hole through which Glenister peered. His struggles lessened, his chin sagged, and his tongue protruded, then he sat loose and still. The politician flung him out into the room so that he fell limply upon his face, then stood watching him. Finally, McNamara passed out of the watcher's vision, returning with a water-bucket. With his foot he rolled the unconscious wretch upon his back, then drenched him. Replacing the pail, he seated himself, lit a cigar, and watched the return of life into his victim. He made no move, even to drag him from the pool in which he lay.

Struve groaned and shuddered, twisted to his side, and at last sat up weakly. In his eyes there was now a great terror, while in place of his drunkenness was only fear and faintness—abject fear of the great bulk that sat and smoked and stared at him so fishily. He felt uncertainly of his throat, and groaned again.

"Why did you do that?" he whispered; but the other made no sign. He tried to rise, but his knees relaxed; he staggered and fell. At last he gained his feet and made for the door; then, when his hand was on the knob, McNamara spoke through his teeth, without removing his cigar.

"Don't ever talk about her again. She is going to marry me."

When he was alone he looked curiously up at the ceiling over his head. "The rats are thick in this shack," he mused. "Seems to me I heard a whole swarm of them."

A few moments later a figure crept through the hole in the roof of the house next door and thence down into the street. A block ahead was the slow-moving form of Attorney Struve. Had a stranger met them both he would not have known which of the two had felt at his throat the clutch of a strangler, for each was drawn and haggard and swayed as he went.

Glenister unconsciously turned towards his cabin, but at leaving the lighted streets the thought of its darkness and silence made him shudder. Not now! He could not bear that stillness and the company of his thoughts. He dared not be alone. Dextry would be down-town, undoubtedly, and he, too, must get into the light and turmoil. He licked his lips and found that they were cracked and dry.

At rare intervals during the past years he had staggered in from a long march where, for hours, he had waged a bitter war with cold and hunger, his limbs clumsy with fatigue, his garments wet and stiff, his mind slack and sullen. At such extreme seasons he had felt a consuming thirst, a thirst which burned and scorched until his very bones cried out feverishly. Not a thirst for water, nor a thirst which eaten snow could quench, but a savage yearning of his whole exhausted system for some stimulant, for some coursing fiery fluid that would burn and strangle. A thirst for whiskey—for brandy! Remembering these occasional ferocious desires, he had become charitable to such unfortunates as were too weak to withstand similar temptations.

Now with a shock he caught himself in the grip of a thirst as insistent as though the cold bore down and the weariness of endless heavy miles wrapped him about. It was no foolish wish to drown his thoughts nor to banish the grief that preyed upon him, but only thirst! Thirst!—a crying, trembling, physical lust to quench the fires that burned inside. He remembered that it had been more than a year since he had tasted whiskey. Now the fever of the past few hours had parched his every tissue.

As he elbowed in through the crowd at the Northern, those next him made room at the bar for they recognized the hunger that peers thus from men's faces. Their manner recalled Glenister to his senses, and he wrenched himself away. This was not some solitary, snow-banked road-house. He would not stand and soak himself, shoulder to shoulder with stevedores and longshoremen. This was something to be done in secret. He had no pride in it. The man on his right raised a glass, and the young man strangled a madness to tear it from his hands. Instead, he hurried back to the theatre and up to a box, where he drew the curtains.

"Whiskey!" he said, thickly, to the waiter. "Bring it to me fast. Don't you hear? Whiskey!"

Across the theatre Cherry Malotte had seen him enter and jerk the curtains together. She arose and went to him, entering without ceremony.

"What's the matter, boy?" she questioned.

"Ah! I am glad you came. Talk to me."

"Thank you for your few well-chosen remarks," she laughed. "Why don't you ask me to spring some good, original jokes? You look like the finish to a six-day go-as-you please. What's up?"

She talked to him for a moment until the waiter entered, then, when she saw what he bore, she snatched the glass from the tray and poured the whiskey on the floor. Glenister was on his feet and had her by the wrist.

"What do you mean?" he said, roughly.

"It's whiskey, boy," she cried, "and you don't drink."

"Of course it's whiskey. Bring me another," he shouted at the attendant.

"What's the matter?" Cherry insisted. "I never saw you act so. You know you don't drink. I won't let you. It's booze—booze, I tell you, fit for fools and brawlers. Don't drink it, Roy. Are you in trouble?"

"I say I'm thirsty—and I will have it! How do you know what it is to smoulder inside, and feel your veins burn dry?"

"It's something about that girl," the woman said, with quiet conviction. "She's double-crossed you."

"Well, so she has—but what of it? I'm thirsty. She's going to marry McNamara. I've been a fool." He ground his teeth and reached for the drink with which the boy had returned.

"McNamara is a crook, but he's a man, and he never drank a drop in his life." The girl said it, casually, evenly, but the other stopped the glass half-way to his lips.

"Well, what of it? Goon. You're good at W. C. T. U. talk. Virtue becomes you."

She flushed, but continued, "It simply occurred to me that if you aren't strong enough to handle your own throat, you're not strong enough to beat a man who has mastered his."

Glenister looked at the whiskey a moment, then set it back on the tray.

"Bring two lemonades," he said, and with a laugh which was half a sob Cherry Malotte leaned forward and kissed him.

"You're too good a man to drink. Now, tell me all about it."

"Oh, it's too long! I've just learned that the girl is in, hand and glove, with the Judge and McNamara—that's all. She's an advance agent—their lookout. She brought in their instructions to Struve and persuaded Dex and me to let them jump our claim. She got us to trust in the law and in her uncle. Yes, she hypnotized my property out of me and gave it to her lover, this ward politician. Oh, she's smooth, with all her innocence! Why, when she smiles she makes you glad and good and warm, and her eyes are as honest and clear as a mountain pool, but she's wrong—she's wrong—and—great God! how I love her!" He dropped his face into his hands.

When she had pled with him for himself a moment before Cherry Malotte was genuine and girlish but now as he spoke thus of the other woman a change came over her which he was too disturbed to note. She took on the subtleness that masked her as a rule, and her eyes were not pleasant.

"I could have told you all that and more."

"More! What more?" he questioned.

"Do you remember when I warned you and Dextry that they were coming to search your cabin for the gold? Well, that girl put them on to you. I found it out afterwards. She keeps the keys to McNamara's safety vault where your dust lies, and she's the one who handles the Judge. It isn't McNamara at all." The woman lied easily, fluently, and the man believed her.

"Do you remember when they broke into your safe and took that money?"

"Yes."

"Well, what made them think you had ten thousand in there?"

"I don't know."

"I do. Dextry told her."

Glenister arose. "That's all I want to hear now. I'm going crazy. My mind aches, for I've never had a fight like this before and it hurts. You see, I've been an animal all these years. When I wanted to drink, I drank, and what I wanted, I got, because I've been strong enough to take it. This is new to me. I'm going down-stairs now and try to think of something else—then I'm going home."

When he had gone she pulled back the curtains, and, leaning her chin in her hands, with elbows on the ledge, gazed down upon the crowd. The show was over and the dance had begun, but she did not see it, for she was thinking rapidly with the eagerness of one who sees the end of a long and weary search. She did not notice the Bronco Kid beckoning to her nor the man with him, so the gambler brought his friend along and invaded her box. He introduced the man as Mr. Champian.

"Do you feel like dancing?" the new-comer inquired.

"No; I'd rather look on. I feel sociable. You're a society man, Mr. Champian. Don't you know anything of interest? Scandal or the like?"

"Can't say that I do. My wife attends to all that for the family. But I know there's lots of it. It's funny to me, the airs some of these people assume up here, just as though we weren't all equal, north of Fifty-three. I never heard the like."

"Anything new and exciting?" inquired Bronco, mildly interested.

"The last I heard was about the Judge's niece, Miss Chester."

Cherry Malotte turned abruptly, while the Kid slowly lowered the front legs of his chair to the floor.

"What was it?" she inquired.

"Why, it seems she compromised herself pretty badly with this fellow Glenister coming up on the steamer last spring. Mighty brazen, according to my wife. Mrs. Champian was on the same ship and says she was horribly shocked."

Ah! Glenister had told her only half the tale, thought the girl. The truth was baring itself. At that moment Champian thought she looked the typical creature of the dance-halls, the crafty, jealous, malevolent adventuress.

"And the hussy masquerades as a lady," she sneered.

"She Is a lady," said the Kid. He sat bolt upright and rigid, and the knuckles of his clinched hands were very white. In the shadow they did not note that his dark face was ghastly, nor did he say more except to bid Champian good-bye when he left, later on. After the door had closed, however, the Kid arose and stretched his muscles, not languidly, but as though to take out the cramp of long tension. He wet his lips, and his mouth was so dry that the sound caused the girl to look up.

"What are you grinning at?" Then, as the light struck his face, she started. "My! How you look! What ails you? Are you sick?" No one, from Dawson down, had seen the Bronco Kid as he looked to-night.

"No. I'm not sick," he answered, in a cracked voice.

Then the girl laughed harshly.

"Do You love that girl, too? Why, she's got every man in town crazy."

She wrung her hands, which is a bad sign in a capable person, and as Glenister crossed the floor below in her sight she said, "Ah-h—I could kill him for that!"

"So could I," said the Kid, and left her without adieu.

XIII

In Which a Man is Possessed of a Devil

For a long time Cherry Malotte sat quietly thinking, removed by her mental stress to such an infinite distance from the music and turmoil beneath that she was conscious of it only as a formless clamor. She had tipped a chair back against the door, wedging it beneath the knob so that she might be saved from interruption, then flung herself into another seat and stared unseeingly. As she sat thus, and thought, and schemed, harsh and hateful lines seemed to eat into her face. Now and then she moaned impatiently, as though fearing lest the strategy she was plotting might prove futile; then she would rise and pace her narrow quarters. She was unconscious of time, and had spent perhaps two hours thus, when amid the buzz of talk in the next compartment she heard a name which caused her to start, listen, then drop her preoccupation like a mantle. A man was speaking of Glenister. Excitement thrilled his voice.

"I never saw anything like it since McMaster's Night in Virginia City, thirteen years ago. He's Right."

"Well, perhaps so," the other replied, doubtfully, "but I don't care to back you. I never 'staked' a man in my life."

"Then Lend me the money. I'll pay it back in an hour, but for Heaven's sake be quick. I tell you he's as right as a golden guinea. It's the lucky night of his life. Why, he turned over the Black Jack game in four bets. In fifteen minutes more we can't get close enough to a table to send in our money with a messenger-boy—every sport in camp will be here."

"I'll stake you to fifty," the second man replied, in a tone that showed a trace of his companion's excitement.

So Glenister was gambling, the girl learned, and with such luck as to break the Black Jack game and excite the greed of every gambler in camp. News of his winnings had gone out into the street, and the sporting men were coming to share his fortune, to fatten like vultures on the adversity of their fellows. Those who had no money to stake were borrowing, like the man next door.

She left her retreat, and, descending the stairs, was greeted by a strange sight. The dance-hall was empty of all but the musicians, who blew and fiddled lustily in vain endeavor to draw from the rapidly swelling crowd that thronged the gambling-room and stretched to the door. The press was thickest about a table midway down the hall. Cherry could see nothing of what went on there, for men and women stood ten deep about it and others perched on chairs and tables along the walls. A roar arose suddenly, followed by utter silence; then came the clink and rattle of silver. A moment, and the crowd resumed its laughter and talk.

"All down, boys," sounded the level voice of the dealer. "The field or the favorite. He's made eighteen straight passes. Get your money on the line." There ensued another breathless instant wherein she heard the thud of dice, then followed the shout of triumph that told what the spots revealed. The dealer payed off. Glenister reared himself head and shoulders above the others and pushed out through the ring to the roulette-wheel. The rest followed. Behind the circular table they had quitted, the dealer was putting away his dice, and there was not a coin in his rack. Mexico Mullins approached Cherry, and she questioned him.

"He just broke the crap game," Mullins told her; "nineteen passes without losing the bones."

"How much did he win?"

"Oh, he didn't win much himself, but it's the people betting with him that does the damage! They're gamblers, most of them, and they play the limit. He took out the Black Jack bank-roll first, $4,000, then cleaned the 'Tub.' By that time the tin horns began to come in. It's the greatest run I ever see."

"Did you get in?"

"Now, don't you know that I never play anything but 'bank'? If he lasts long enough to reach the faro lay-out, I'll get mine."

The excitement of the crowd began to infect the girl, even though she looked on from the outside. The exultant voices, the sudden hush, the tensity of nerve it all betokened, set her a-thrill. A stranger left the throng and rushed to the spot where Cherry and Mexico stood talking. He was small and sandy, with shifting glance and chinless jaw. His eyes glittered, his teeth shone rat-like through his dry lips, and his voice was shrill. He darted towards them like some furtive, frightened little animal, unnaturally excited.

"I guess that isn't so bad for three bets!" He shook a sheaf of bank-notes at them.

"Why don't you stick?" inquired Mullins.

"I am too wise. Ha! I know when to quit. He can't win steady—he don't play any system."

"Then he has a good chance," said the girl.

"There he goes now," the little man cried as the uproar arose. "I told you he'd lose." At the voice of the multitude he wavered as though affected by some powerful magnet.

"But he won again," said Mexico.

"No! Did he? Lord! I quit too soon!"

He scampered back into the other room, only to return, hesitating, his money tightly clutched.

"Do you s'pose it's safe? I never saw a man bet so reckless. I guess I'd better quit, eh?" He noted the sneer on the woman's face, and without waiting a reply dashed off again. They saw him clamorously fight his way in towards a post at the roulette-table. "Let me through! I've got money and I want to play it!"

"Pah!" said Mullins, disgustedly. "He's one of them Vermont desperadoes that never laid a bet till he was thirty. If Glenister loses he'll hate him for life."

"There are plenty of his sort here," the girl remarked; "his soul would fit in a flea-track." She spied the Bronco Kid sauntering back towards her and joined him. He leaned against the wall, watching the gossamer thread of smoke twist upward from his cigarette, seemingly oblivious to the surroundings, and showing no hint of the emotion he had displayed two hours before.

"This is a big killing, isn't it?" said the girl. The gambler nodded, murmuring indifferently.

"Why aren't you dealing bank? Isn't this your shift?"

"I quit last night."

"Just in time to miss this affair. Lucky for you."

"Yes; I own the place now. Bought it yesterday."

"Good Heavens! Then it's YOUR money he's winning."

"Sure, at the rate of a thousand a minute."

She glanced at the long trail of devastated tables behind Glenister and his followers. At that instant the sound told that the miner had won again, and it dawned upon Cherry that the gambler beside her stood too quietly, that his hand and voice were too steady, his glance too cold to be natural. The next moment approved her instinct.

The musicians, grown tired of their endeavors to lure back the dancers, determined to join the excitement, and ceased playing. The leader laid down his violin, the pianist trailed up the key-board with a departing twitter and quit his stool. They all crossed the hall, headed for the crowd, some of them making ready to bet. As they approached the Bronco Kid, his lips thinned and slid apart slightly, while out of his heavy-lidded eyes there flared unreasoning rage. Stepping forward, he seized the foremost man and spun him about violently.

"Where are you going?"

"Why, nobody wants to dance, so we thought we'd go out front for a bit."

"Get back, damn you!" It was his first chance to vent the passion within him. A glance at his maddened features was sufficient for the musicians, and they did not delay. By the time they had resumed their duties, however, the curtains of composure had closed upon the Kid, masking his emotion again; but from her brief glimpse Cherry Malotte knew that this man was not of ice, as some supposed. He turned to her and said, "Do you mean what you said up-stairs?"

"I don't understand."

"You said you could kill Glenister."

"I could."

"Don't you love—"

"I Hate him," she interrupted, hoarsely. He gave her a mirthless smile, and spying the crap-dealer leaving his bankrupt table, called him over and said:

"Toby, I want you to 'drive the hearse' when Glenister begins to play faro. I'll deal. Understand?"

"Sure! Going to give him a little 'work,' eh?"

"I never dealt a crooked card in this camp," exclaimed the Kid, "but I'll 'lay' that man to-night or I'll kill him! I'll use a 'sand-tell,' see! And I want to explain my signals to you. If you miss the signs you'll queer us both and put the house on the blink."

He rapidly rehearsed his signals in a jargon which to a layman would have been unintelligible, illustrating them by certain almost imperceptible shiftings of the fingers or changes in the position of his hand, so slight as to thwart discovery. Through it all the girl stood by and followed his every word and motion with eager attention. She needed no explanation of the terms they used. She knew them all, knew that the "hearse-driver" was the man who kept the cases, knew all the code of the "inside life." To her it was all as an open page, and she memorized more quickly than did Toby the signs by which the Bronco

Kid proposed to signal what card he had smuggled from the box or held back.

In faro it is customary for the case-keeper to sit on the opposite side of the table from the dealer, with a device before him resembling an abacus, or Chinese adding-machine. When a card is removed from the faro-box by the dealer, the "hearse-driver" moves a button opposite a corresponding card on his little machine, in order that the players, at a glance, may tell what spots have been played or are still in the box. His duties, though simple, are important, for should he make an error, and should the position of his counters not tally with the cards in the box on the "last turn," all bets on the table are declared void. When honestly dealt, faro is the fairest of all gambling games, but it is intricate, and may hide much knavery. When the game is crooked, it is fatal, for out of the ingenuity of generations of card sharks there have been evolved a multitude of devices with which to fleece the unsuspecting. These are so carefully masked that none but the initiated may know them, while the freemasonry of the craft is strong and discovery unusual.

Instead of using a familiar arrangement like the "needle-tell," wherein an invisible needle pricks the dealer's thumb, thus signalling the presence of certain cards, the Bronco Kid had determined to use the "sand-tell." In other words, he would employ a "straight box," but a deck of cards, certain ones of which had been roughened or sand-papered slightly, so that, by pressing more heavily on the top or exposed card, the one beneath would stick to its neighbor above, and thus enable him to deal two with one motion if the occasion demanded. This roughness would likewise enable him to detect the hidden presence of a marked card by the faintest scratching sound when he dealt. In this manipulation it would be necessary, also, to shave the edges of some of the pasteboards a trifle, so that, when the deck was forced firmly against one side of the box, there would be exposed a fraction of the small figure in the left-hand corner of the concealed cards. Long practice in the art of jugglery lends such proficiency as to baffle discovery and rob the game of its uncertainty as surely as the player is robbed of his money. It is, of course, vital that the confederate case-keeper be able to interpret the dealer's signs perfectly in order to move the sliding ebony disks to correspond, else trouble will accrue at the completion of the hand when the cases come out wrong.

Having completed his instructions, the proprietor went forward, and Cherry wormed her way towards the roulette-wheel. She wished to watch Glenister, but could not get near him because of the crowd. The men would not make room for her. Every eye was glued upon the table as though salvation lurked in its rows of red and black. They were packed behind it until the croupier had barely room to spin the ball, and although he forced them back, they pressed forward again inch by inch, drawn by the song of the ivory, drunk with its worship, maddened by the breath of Chance.

Cherry gathered that Glenister was still winning, for a glimpse of the wheel-rack between the shoulders of those ahead showed that the checks were nearly out of it.

Plainly it was but a question of minutes, so she backed out and took her station beside the faro-table where the Bronco Kid was dealing. His face wore its colorless mask of indifference; his long white hands moved slowly with the certainty that betokened absolute mastery of his art. He was waiting. The ex-crap dealer was keeping cases.

The group left the roulette-table in a few moments and surrounded her, Glenister among the others. He was not the man she knew. In place of the dreary hopelessness with which he had left her, his face was flushed and reckless, his collar was open, showing the base of his great, corded neck, while the lust of the game had coarsened him till he was again the violent, untamed, primitive man of the frontier. His self-restraint and dignity were gone. He had tried the new ways, and they were not for him. He slipped back, and the past swallowed him.

After leaving Cherry he had sought some mental relief by idly risking the silver in his pocket. He had let the coins lie and double, then double again and again. He had been indifferent whether he won or lost, so assumed a reckless disregard for the laws of probability, thinking that he would shortly lose the money he had won and then go home. He did not want it. When his luck remained the same, he raised the stakes, but it did not change—he could not lose. Before he realized it, other men were betting with him, animated purely by greed and craze of the sport. First one, then another joined till game after game was closed, and each moment the crowd had grown in size and enthusiasm so that its fever crept into him, imperceptibly at first, but ever increasing, till the mania mastered him.

He paid no attention to Cherry as he took his seat. He had eyes for nothing but the "lay-out." She clenched her hands and prayed for his ruin.

"What's your limit, Kid?" he inquired.

"One hundred, and two," the Kid answered, which in the vernacular means that any sum up to $200 be laid on one card save only on the last turn, when the amount is lessened by half.

Without more ado they commenced. The Kid handled his cards smoothly, surely, paying and taking bets with machine-like calm. The on-lookers ceased talking and prepared to watch, for now came the crucial test of the evening. Faro is to other games as war is to jackstraws.

For a time Glenister won steadily till there came a moment when many stacks of chips lay on the deuce. Cherry saw the Kid "flash" to the case-keeper, and the next moment he had "pulled two." The deuce lost. It was his first substantial gain, and the players paid no attention. At the end of half an hour the winnings were slightly in favor of the "house." Then Glenister said, "This is too slow. I want action."

"All right," smiled the proprietor. "We'll double the limit."

Thus it became possible to wager $400 on a card, and the Kid began really to play. Glenister now lost steadily, not in large amounts, but with tantalizing regularity. Cherry had never seen cards played like this. The gambler was a revelation to her—his work was wonderful. Ill luck seemed to fan the crowd's eagerness, while, to add to its impatience, the cases came wrong twice in succession, so that those who would have bet heavily upon the last turn had their money given back. Cherry saw the confusion of the "hearse-driver" even quicker than did Bronco. Toby was growing rattled. The dealer's work was too fast for him, and yet he could offer no signal of distress for fear of annihilation at the hands of those crowded close to his shoulder. In the same way the owner of the game could make no objection to his helper's incompetence for fear that some by-stander would volunteer to fill the man's part—there were many present capable of the trick. He could only glare balefully across the table at his unfortunate confederate.

They had not gone far on the next game before Cherry's quick eye detected a sign which the man misinterpreted. She addressed him, quietly, "You'd better brush up your plumes."

In spite of his anger the Bronco Kid smiled. Humor in him was strangely withered and distorted, yet here was a thrust he would always remember and recount with glee in years to come. He feared there were other faro-dealers present who might understand the hint, but there was none save Mexico Mullins, whose face was a study—mirth seemed to be strangling him. A moment later the girl spoke to the case-keeper again.

"Let me take your place; your reins are unbuckled."

Toby glanced inquiringly at the Kid, who caught Cherry's reassuring look and nodded, so he arose and the girl slid into the vacant chair. This woman would make no errors—the dealer knew that; her keen wits were sharpened by hate—it showed in her face. If Glenister escaped destruction to-night it would be because human means could not accomplish his downfall.

In the mind of the new case-keeper there was but one thought—Roy must be broken. Humiliation, disgrace, ruin, ridicule were to be his. If he should be downed, discredited, and discouraged, then, perhaps, he would turn to her as he had in the by-gone days. He was slipping away from her—this was her last chance. She began her duties easily, and her alertness stimulated Bronco till his senses, too, grew sharper, his observation more acute and lightning-like. Glenister swore beneath his breath that the cards were bewitched. He was like a drunken man, now as truly intoxicated as though the fumes of wine had befogged his brain. He swayed in his seat, the veins of his neck thickened and throbbed, his features were congested. After a while he spoke.

"I want a bigger limit. Is this some boy's game? Throw her open."

The gambler shot a triumphant glance at the girl and acquiesced. "All right, the limit is the blue sky. Pile your checks to the roof-pole." He began to shuffle.

Within the crowded circle the air was hot and fetid with the breath of men. The sweat trickled down Glenister's brown skin, dripping from his jaw unnoticed. He arose and ripped off his coat, while those standing behind shifted and scuffed their feet impatiently. Besides Roy, there were but three men playing. They were the ones who had won heaviest at first. Now that luck was against them they were loath to quit.

Cherry was annoyed by stertorous breathing at her shoulder, and glanced back to find the little man who had been so excited earlier in the evening. His mouth was agape, his eyes wide, the muscles about his lips twitching. He had lost back, long since, the hundreds he had won and more besides. She searched the figures walling her about and saw no women. They had been crowded out long since. It seemed as though the table formed the bottom of a sloping pit of human faces—eager, tense, staring. It was well she was here, she thought, else this task might fail. She would help to blast Glenister, desolate him, humiliate him. Ah, but wouldn't she!

Roy bet $100 on the "popular" card. On the third turn he lost. He bet $200 next and lost. He set out a stack of $400 and lost for the third time. Fortune had turned her face. He ground his teeth and doubled until the stakes grew enormous, while the dealer dealt monotonously. The spots flashed and disappeared, taking with them wager after wager. Glenister became conscious of a raging, red fury which he had hard shift to master. It was not his money—what if he did lose? He would stay until he won. He would win. This luck would not, could not, last—and yet with diabolic persistence he continued to choose the losing cards. The other men fared better till be yielded to their judgment, when the dealer took their money also.

Strange to say, the fickle goddess had really shifted her banner at last, and the Bronco Kid was dealing straight faro now. He was too good a player to force a winning hand, and Glenister's ill-fortune became as phenomenal as his winning had been. The girl who figured in this drama was keyed to the highest tension, her eyes now on her counters, now searching the profile of her victim. Glenister continued to lose and lose and lose, while the girl gloated over his swift-coming ruin. When at long intervals he won a bet she shrank and shivered for fear he might escape. If only he would risk it all—everything he had. He would have to come to her then!

The end was closer than she realized. The throng hung breathless upon each move of the players, while there was no sound but the noise of shifting chips and the distant jangle of the orchestra. The lookout sat far forward upon his perch, his hands upon his knees, his eyes frozen to the board, a dead cigar clenched between his teeth. Crowded upon his platform were miners tense and motionless as statues. When a man spoke or coughed, a score of eyes stared at him accusingly, then dropped to the table again.

Glenister took from his clothes a bundle of bank-notes, so thick that it required his two hands to compass it. On-lookers saw that the bills were mainly yellow. No one spoke while he counted them rapidly, glanced at the dealer, who nodded, then slid them forward till they rested on the king. He placed a "copper" on the pile. A great sigh of indrawn breaths swept through the crowd. The North had never known a bet like this—it meant a fortune. Here was a tale for one's grandchildren—that a man should win opulence in an evening, then lose it in one deal. This final bet represented more than many of them had ever seen a one time before. Its fate lay on a single card.

Cherry Malotte's fingers were like ice and shook till the buttons of her case-keeper rattled, her heart raced till she could not breathe, while something rose up and choked her. If Glenister won this bet he would quit; she felt it. If he lost, ah! what could the Kid there feel, the man who was playing for a paltry vengeance, compared to her whose hope of happiness, of love, of life hinged on this wager?

Evidently the Bronco Kid knew what card lay next below, for he offered her no sign, and as Glenister leaned back he slowly and firmly pushed the top card out of the box. Although this was the biggest turn of his life, he betrayed no tremor. His gesture displayed the nine of diamonds, and the crowd breathed heavily. The king had not won. Would it lose? Every gaze was welded to the tiny nickelled box. If the face-card lay next beneath the nine-spot, the heaviest wager in Alaska would have been lost; if it still remained hidden on the next turn, the money would be safe for a moment.

Slowly the white hand of the dealer moved back; his middle finger touched the nine of diamonds; it slid smoothly out of the box, and there in its place frowned the king of clubs. At last the silence was broken.

Men spoke, some laughed, but in their laughter was no mirth. It was more like the sound of choking. They stamped their feet to relieve the grip of strained muscles. The dealer reached forth and slid the stack of bills into the drawer at his waist without counting. The case-keeper passed a shaking hand over her face, and when it came away she saw blood on her fingers where she had sunk her teeth into her lower lip. Glenister did not rise. He sat, heavy-browed and sullen, his jaw thrust forward, his hair low upon his forehead, his eyes bloodshot and dead.

"I'll sit the hand out if you'll let me bet the 'finger,'" said he.

"Certainly," replied the dealer.

When a man requests this privilege it means that he will call the amount of his wager without producing the visible stakes, and the dealer may accept or refuse according to his judgment of the bettor's responsibility. It is safe, for no man shirks a gambling debt in the North, and thousands may go with a nod of the head though never a cent be on the board.

There were still a few cards in the box, and the dealer turned them, paying the three men who played. Glenister took no part, but sat bulked over his end of the table glowering from beneath his shock of hair.

Cherry was deathly tired. The strain of the last hour had been so intense that she could barely sit in her seat, yet she was determined to finish the hand. As Bronco paused before the last turn, many of the by-standers made bets. They were the "case-players" who risked money only on the final pair, thus avoiding the chance of two cards of like denomination coming together, in which event ("splits" it is called) the dealer takes half the money. The stakes were laid at last and the deal about to start when Glenister spoke. "Wait! What's this place worth, Bronco?"

"What do you mean?"

"You own this outfit?" He waved his hand about the room. "Well, what does it stand you?"

The gambler hesitated an instant while the crowd pricked up its ears, and the girl turned wondering, troubled eyes upon the miner. What would he do now?

"Counting bank rolls, fixtures, and all, about a hundred and twenty thousand dollars. Why?"

"I'll pick the ace to lose, my one-half interest in the Midas against your whole damned lay-out!"

There was an absolute hush while the realization of this offer smote the on-lookers. It took time to realize it. This man was insane. There were three cards to choose from—one would win, one would lose, and one would have no action.

Of all those present only Cherry Malotte divined even vaguely the real reason which prompted the man to do this. It was not "gameness," nor altogether a brutish stubbornness which would not let him quit, It was something deeper. He was desolate and his heart was gone. Helen was lost to him—worse yet, was unworthy, and she was all he cared for. What did he want of the Midas with its lawsuits, its intrigues, and its trickery? He was sick of it all—of the whole game—and wanted to get away. If he won, very well. If he lost, the land of the Aurora would know him no more.

When he put his proposition, the Bronco Kid dropped his eyes as though debating. The girl saw that he studied the cards in his box intently and that his fingers caressed the top one ever so softly during the instant the eyes of the rest were on Glenister. The dealer looked up at last, and Cherry saw the gleam of triumph in his eye; he could not mask it from her, though his answering words were hesitating. She knew by the look that Glenister was a pauper.

"Come on," insisted Roy, hoarsely. "Turn the cards."

"You're on!"

The girl felt that she was fainting. She wanted to scream. The triumph of this moment stifled her—or was it triumph, after all? She heard the breath of the little man behind her rattle as though he were being throttled, and saw the lookout pass a shaking hand to his chin, then wet his parched lips. She saw the man she had helped to ruin bend forward, his lean face strained and hard, an odd look of pain and weariness in his eyes. She never forgot that look. The crowd was frozen in various attitudes of eagerness, although it had not yet recovered from the suspense of the last great wager. It knew the Midas and what it meant. Here lay half of it, hidden beneath a tawdry square of pasteboard. With maddening deliberation the Kid dealt the top card. Beneath it was the trey of spades. Glenister said no word nor made a move. Some one coughed, and it sounded like a gunshot. Slowly the dealer's fingers retraced their way. He hesitated purposely and leered at the girl, then the three-spot disappeared and beneath it lay the ace as the king had lain on that other wager. It spelled utter ruin to Glenister. He raised his eyes blindly, and then the deathlike silence of the room was shattered by a sudden crash. Cherry Malotte had closed her check-rack violently, at the same instant crying shrill and clear: "That bet is off! The cases are wrong!"

Glenister half rose, overturning his chair; the Kid lunged forward across the table, and his wonderful hands, tense and talon-like, thrust themselves forward as though reaching for the riches she had snatched away. They worked and writhed and trembled as though in dumb fury, the nails sinking into the oil-cloth table-cover. His face grew livid and cruel, while his eyes blazed at her till she shrank from him affrightedly, bracing herself away from the table with rigid arms.

Reason came slowly back to Glenister, and understanding with it. He seemed to awake from a nightmare. He could read all too plainly the gambler's look of baffled hate as the man sprawled on the table, his arms spread wide, his eyes glaring at the cowering woman, who shrank before him like a rabbit before a snake. She tried to speak, but choked. Then the dealer came to himself, and cried harshly through his teeth one word:

"Christ!"

He raised his fist and struck the table so violently that chips and coppers leaped and rolled, and Cherry closed her eyes to lose sight of his awful grimace. Glenister looked down on him and said:

"I think I understand; but the money was yours, anyhow, so I don't mind." His meaning was plain. The Kid suddenly jerked open the drawer before him, but Glenister clenched his right hand and leaned forward. The miner could have killed him with a blow, for the gambler was seated and at his mercy. The Kid checked himself, while his face began to twitch as though the nerves underlying it had broken bondage and were dancing in a wild, ungovernable orgy.

"You have taught me a lesson," was all that Glenister said, and with that he pushed through the crowd and out into the cool night air. Overhead the arctic stars winked at him, and the sea smells struck him, clean and fresh. As he went homeward he heard the distant, full-throated plaint of a wolf-dog. It held the mystery and sadness of the North. He paused, arid, baring his thick, matted head, stood for a long time gathering himself together. Standing so, he made certain covenants with himself, and vowed solemnly never to touch another card.

At the same moment Cherry Malotte came hurrying to her cottage door, fleeing as though from pursuit or from some hateful, haunted spot. She paused before entering and flung her arms outward into the dark in a wide gesture of despair.

"Why did I do it? Oh! WHY did I do it? I can't understand myself."

XIV

A Midnight Messenger

M y dear Helen, don't you realize that my official position carries with it a certain social obligation which it is our duty to discharge?"

"I suppose so, Uncle Arthur; but I would much rather stay at home."

"Tut, tut! Go and have a good time."

"Dancing doesn't appeal to me any more. I left that sort of thing back home. Now, if you would only come along—"

"No—I'm too busy. I must work to-night, and I'm not in a mood for such things, anyhow."

"You're not well," his niece said. "I have noticed it for weeks. Is it hard work or are you truly ill? You're nervous; you don't eat; you're growing positively gaunt. Why—you're getting wrinkles like an old man." She rose from her seat at the breakfast-table and went to him, smoothing his silvered head with affection.

He took her cool hand and pressed it to his cheek, while the worry that haunted him habitually of late gave way to a smile.

"It's work, little girl—hard and thankless work, that's all. This country is intended for young men, and I'm too far along." His eyes grew grave again, and he squeezed her fingers nervously as though at the thought. "It's a terrible country—this—I—I—wish we had never seen it."

"Don't say that," Helen cried, spiritedly. "Why, it's glorious. Think of the honor. You're a United States judge and the first one to come here. You're making history—you're building a State—people will read about you." She stooped and kissed him; but he seemed to flinch beneath her caress.

"Of course I'll go if you think I'd better," she said, "though I'm not fond of Alaskan society. Some of the women are nice, but the others—" She shrugged her dainty shoulders. "They talk scandal all the time. One would think that a great, clean, fresh, vigorous country like this would broaden the women as it broadens the men—but it doesn't."

"I'll tell McNamara to call for you at nine o'clock," said the Judge as he arose. So, later in the day she prepared her long unused finery to such good purpose that when her escort called for her that evening he believed her the loveliest of women.

Upon their arrival at the hotel he regarded her with a fresh access of pride, for the function proved to bear little resemblance to a mining-camp party. The women wore handsome gowns, and every man was in evening dress. The wide hall ran the length of the hotel and was flanked with boxes, while its floor was like polished glass and its walls effectively decorated.

"Oh, how lovely!" exclaimed Helen as she first caught sight of it. "It's just like home."

"I've seen quick-rising cities before," he said, "but nothing like this. Still, if these Northerners can build a railroad in a month and a city in a summer, why shouldn't they have symphony orchestras and Louis Quinze ballrooms?"

"I know you're a splendid dancer," she said.

"You shall be my judge and jury. I'll sign this card as often as I dare without the certainty of violence at the hands of these young men, and the rest of the time I'll smoke in the lobby. I don't care to dance with any one but you."

After the first waltz he left her surrounded by partners and made his way out of the ballroom. This was his first relaxation since landing in the North. It was well not to become a dull boy, he mused, and as he chewed his cigar he pictured with an odd thrill, quite unusual with him, that slender, gray-eyed girl, with her coiled mass of hair, her ivory shoulders, and merry smile. He saw her float past to the measure of a two-step, and caught himself resenting the thought of another man's enjoyment of the girl's charms even for an instant.

"Hold on, Alec," he muttered. "You're too old a bird to lose your head." However, he was waiting for her before the time for their next dance. She seemed to have lost a part of her gayety.

"What's the matter? Aren't you enjoying yourself?"

"Oh, yes!" she returned, brightly. "I'm having a delightful time."

When he came for his third dance, she was more distraite than ever. As he led her to a seat they passed a group of women, among whom were Mrs. Champian and others whom he knew to be wives of men prominent in the town. He had seen some of them at tea in Judge Stillman's house, and therefore was astonished when they returned his greeting but ignored Helen. She shrank slightly, and he realized that there was something wrong; he could not guess what. Affairs of men he could cope with, but the subtleties of women were out of his realm.

"What ails those people? Have they offended you?"

"I don't know what it is. I have spoken to them, but they cut me."

"Cut You?" he exclaimed.

"Yes." Her voice trembled, but she held her head high. "It seems as though all the women in Nome were here and in league to ignore me. It dazes me—I do not understand."

"Has anybody said anything to you?" he inquired, fiercely. "Any man, I mean?"

"No, no! The men are kind. It's the women."

"Come—we'll go home."

"Indeed, we will not," she said, proudly. "I shall stay and face it out. I have done nothing to run away from, and I intend to find out what is the matter."

When he had surrendered her, at the beginning of the next dance, McNamara sought for some acquaintance whom he might question. Most of the men in Nome either hated or feared him, but he espied one that he thought suited his purpose, and led him into a corner.

"I want you to answer a question. No beating about the bush. Understand? I'm blunt, and I want you to be."

"All right."

"Your wife has been entertained at Miss Chester's house. I've seen her there. To-night she refuses to speak to the girl. She cut her dead, and I want to know what it's about."

"How should I know?"

"If you don't know, I'll ask you to find out."

The other shook his head amusedly, at which McNamara flared up.

"I say you will, and you'll make your wife apologize before she leaves this hall, too, or you'll answer to me, man to man. I won't stand to have a girl like Miss Chester cold-decked by a bunch of mining-camp swells, and that goes as it lies." In his excitement, McNamara reverted to his Western idiom.

The other did not reply at once, for it is embarrassing to deal with a person who disregards the conventions utterly, and at the same time has the inclination and force to compel obedience. The boss's reputation had gone abroad.

"Well—er—I know about it in a general way, but of course I don't go much on such things. You'd better let it drop."

"Go on."

"There has been a lot of talk among the ladies about—well, er—the fact is, it's that young Glenister. Mrs. Champian had the next state-room to them—er—him—I should say—on the way up from the States, and she saw things. Now, as far as I'm concerned, a girl can do what she pleases, but Mrs. Champian has her own ideas of propriety. From what my wife could learn, there's some truth in the story, too, so you can't blame her."

With a word McNamara could have explained the gossip and made this man put his wife right, forcing through her an elucidation of the silly affair in such a way as to spare Helen's feelings and cover the busy-tongued magpies with confusion. Yet he hesitated. It is a wise skipper who trims his sails to every breeze. He thanked his informant and left him. Entering the lobby, he saw the girl hurrying towards him.

"Take me away, quick! I want to go home."

"You've changed your mind?'"

"Yes, let us go," she panted, and when they were outside she walked so rapidly that he had difficulty in keeping pace with her. She was silent, and he knew better than to question, but when they arrived at her house he entered, took off his overcoat, and turned up the light in the tiny parlor. She flung her wraps over a chair, storming back and forth like a little fury. Her eyes were starry with tears of anger, her face was flushed, her hands worked nervously. He leaned against the mantel, watching her through his cigar smoke.

"You needn't tell me," he said, at length. "I know all about it."

"I am glad you do. I never could repeat what they said. Oh, it was brutal!" Her voice caught and she bit her lip. "What made me ask them? Why didn't I keep still? After you left, I went to those women and faced them. Oh, but they were brutal? Yet, why should I care?" She stamped her slippered foot.

"I shall have to kill that man some day," he said, flecking his cigar ashes into the grate.

"What man?" She stood still and looked at him.

"Glenister, of course. If I had thought the story would ever reach you, I'd have shut him up long ago."

"It didn't come from him," she cried, hot with indignation. "He's a gentleman. It's that cat, Mrs. Champian."

He shrugged his shoulders the slightest bit, but it was eloquent, and she noted it. "Oh, I don't mean that he did it intentionally—he's too decent a chap for that—but anybody's tongue will wag to a beautiful girl! My lady Malotte is a jealous trick."

"Malotte! Who is she?" Helen questioned, curiously.

He seemed surprised. "I thought every one knew who she is. It's just as well that you don't."

"I am sure Mr. Glenister would not talk of me." There was a pause. "Who is Miss Malotte?"

He studied for a moment, while she watched him. What a splendid figure he made in his evening clothes! The cosey room with its shaded lights enhanced his size and strength and rugged outlines. In his eyes was that admiration which women live for. He lifted his bold, handsome face and met her gaze.

"I had rather leave that for you to find out, for I'm not much at scandal. I have something more important to tell you. It's the most important thing I have ever said to you, Helen." It was the first time he had used that name, and she began to tremble, while her eyes sought the door in a panic. She had expected this moment, and yet was not ready.

"Not to-night—don't say it now," she managed to articulate.

"Yes, this is a good time. If you can't answer, I'll come back to-morrow. I want you to be my wife. I want to give you everything the world offers, and I want to make you happy, girl. There'll be no gossip hereafter—I'll shield you from everything unpleasant, and if there is anything you want in life, I'll lay it at your feet. I can do it." He lifted his massive arms, and in the set of his strong, square face was the promise that she should have whatever she craved if mortal man could give it to her—love, protection, position, adoration.

She stammered uncertainly till the humiliation and chagrin she had suffered this night swept over her again. This town—this crude, half-born mining-camp—had turned against her, misjudged her cruelly. The women were envious, clacking scandal-mongers, all of them, who would ostracize her and make her life in the Northland a misery, make her an outcast with nothing to sustain her but her own solitary pride. She could picture her future clearly, pitilessly, and see herself standing alone, vilified, harassed in a thousand cutting ways, yet unable to run away, or to explain. She would have to stay and face it, for her life was bound up here during the next few years or so, or as long as her uncle remained a judge. This man would free her. He loved her; he offered her everything. He was bigger than all the rest combined. They were his playthings, and they knew it. She was not sure that she loved him, but his magnetism was overpowering, and her admiration intense. No other man she had ever known compared with him, except Glenister—Bah! The beast! He had insulted her at first; he wronged her now.

"Will you be my wife, Helen?" the man repeated, softly.

She dropped her head, and he strode forward to take her in his arms, then stopped, listening. Some one ran up on the porch and hammered loudly at the door. McNamara scowled, walked into the hall, and flung the portal open, disclosing Struve.

"Hello, McNamara! Been looking all over for you. There's the deuce to pay!" Helen sighed with relief and gathered up her cloak, while the hum of their voices reached her indistinctly. She was given plenty of time to regain her composure before they appeared. When they did, the politician spoke, sourly:

"I've been called to the mines, and I must go at once."

"You bet! It may be too late now. The news came an hour ago, but I couldn't find you," said Struve. "Your horse is saddled at the office. Better not wait to change your clothes."

"You say Voorhees has gone with twenty deputies, eh? That's good. You stay here and find out all you can."

"I telephoned out to the Creek for the boys to arm themselves and throw out pickets. If you hurry you can get there in time. It's only midnight now."

"What is the trouble?" Miss Chester inquired, anxiously.

"There's a plot on to attack the mines to-night," answered the lawyer. "The other side are trying to seize them, and there's apt to be a fight."

"You mustn't go out there," she cried, aghast. "There will be bloodshed."

"That's just why I MUST go," said McNamara. "I'll come back in the morning, though, and I'd like to see you alone. Good-night!" There was a strange, new light in his eyes as he left her. For one unversed in woman's ways he played the game surprisingly well, and as he hurried towards his office he smiled grimly into the darkness.

"She'll answer me to-morrow. Thank you, Mr. Glenister," he said to himself.

Helen questioned Struve at length, but gained nothing more than that secret-service men had been at work for weeks and had to-day unearthed the fact that Vigilantes had been formed. They had heard enough to make them think the mines would be jumped again to-night, and so had given the alarm.

"Have you hired spies?" she asked, incredulously.

"Sure. We had to. The other people shadowed us, and it's come to a point where it's life or death to one side or the other. I told McNamara we'd have bloodshed before we were through, when he first outlined the scheme—I mean when the trouble began."

She wrung her hands. "That's what uncle feared before we left Seattle. That's why I took the risks I did in bringing you those papers. I thought you got them in time to avoid all this."

Struve laughed a bit, eying her curiously.

"Does Uncle Arthur know about this?" she continued.

"No, we don't let him know anything more than necessary; he's not a strong man."

"Yes, yes. He's not well." Again the lawyer smiled. "Who is behind this Vigilante movement?"

"We think it is Glenister and his New Mexican bandit partner. At least they got the crowd together." She was silent for a time.

"I suppose they really think they own those mines."

"Undoubtedly."

"But they don't, do they?" Somehow this question had recurred to her insistently of late, for things were constantly happening which showed there was more back of this great, fierce struggle than she knew. It was impossible that injustice had been done the mine-owners, and yet scattered talk reached her which was puzzling. When she strove to follow it up, her acquaintances adroitly changed the subject. She was baffled on every side. The three local newspapers upheld the court. She read them carefully, and was more at sea than ever. There was a disturbing undercurrent of alarm and unrest that caused her to feel insecure, as though standing on hollow ground.

"Yes, this whole disturbance is caused by those two. Only for them we'd be all right."

"Who is Miss Malotte?"

He answered, promptly: "The handsomest woman in the North, and the most dangerous."

"In what way? Who is she?"

"It's hard to say who or what she is—she's different from other women. She came to Dawson in the early days—just came—we didn't know how, whence, or why, and we never found out. We woke up one morning and there she was. By night we were all jealous, and in a week we were most of us drivelling idiots. It might have been the mystery or, perhaps, the competition. That was the day when a dance-hall girl could make a homestake in a winter or marry a millionaire in a month, but she never bothered. She toiled not, neither did she spin on the waxed floors, yet Solomon in all his glory would have looked like a tramp beside her."

"You say she is dangerous?"

"Well, there was the young nobleman, in the winter of '98, Dane, I think—fine family and all that—big, yellow-haired boy. He wanted to marry her, but a faro-dealer shot him. Then there was Rock, of the mounted police, the finest officer in the service. He was cashiered. She knew he was going to pot for her, but she didn't seem to care—and there were others. Yet, with it all, she is the most generous person and the most tender-hearted. Why, she has fed every 'stew bum' on the Yukon, and there isn't a busted prospector in the country who wouldn't swear by her, for she has grubstaked dozens of them. I was horribly in love with her myself. Yes, she's dangerous, all right—to everybody but Glenister."

"What do you mean?"

"She had been across the Yukon to nurse a man with scurvy, and coming back she was caught in the spring break-up. I wasn't there, but it seems this Glenister got her ashore somehow when nobody else would tackle the job. They were carried five miles down-stream in the ice-pack before he succeeded."

"What happened then?"

"She fell in love with him, of course."

"And he worshipped her as madly as all the rest of you, I suppose," she said, scornfully.

"That's the peculiar part. She hypnotized him at first, but he ran away, and I didn't hear of him again till I came to Nome. She followed him, finally, and last week evened up her score. She paid him back for saving her."

"I haven't heard about it."

He detailed the story of the gambling episode at the Northern saloon, and concluded: "I'd like to have seen that 'turn,' for they say the excitement was terrific. She was keeping cases, and at the finish slammed her case-keeper shut and declared the bet off because she had made a mistake. Of course they couldn't dispute her, and she stuck to it. One of the by-standers told me she lied, though."

"So, in addition to his other vices, Mr. Glenister is a reckless gambler, is he?" said Helen, with heat. "I am proud to be indebted to such a character. Truly this country breeds wonderful species."

"There's where you're wrong," Struve chuckled. "He's never been known to bet before."

"Oh, I'm tired of these contradictions!" she cried, angrily. "Saloons, gambling-halls, scandals, adventuresses! Ugh! I hate it! I HATE it! Why did I ever come here?"

"Those things are a part of every new country. They were about all we had till this year. But it is women like you that we fellows need, Miss Helen. You can help us a lot." She did not like the way he was looking at her, and remembered that her uncle was up-stairs and asleep.

"I must ask you to excuse me now, for it's late and I am very tired."

The clock showed half-past twelve, so, after letting him out, she extinguished the light and dragged herself wearily up to her room. She removed her outer garments and threw over her bare shoulders a negligee of many flounces and bewildering, clinging looseness. As she took down her heavy braids, the story of Cherry Malotte returned to her tormentingly. So Glenister had saved HER life also at risk of his own. What a very gallant cavalier he was, to be sure! He should bear a coat of arms—a dragon, an armed knight, and a fainting maiden. "I succor ladies in distress—handsome ones," should be the motto on his shield. "The handsomest woman in the North," Struve had said. She raised her eyes to the glass and made a mouth at the petulant, tired reflection there. She pictured Glenister leaping from floe to floe with the hungry river surging and snapping at his feet, while the cheers of the crowd on shore gave heart to the girl crouching out there. She could see him snatch her up and fight his way back to safety over the plunging ice-cakes with death dragging at his heels. What a strong embrace he had! At this she blushed and realized with a shock that while she was mooning that very man might be fighting hand to hand in the darkness of a mountain-gorge with the man she was going to marry.

A moment later some one mounted the front steps below and knocked sharply. Truly this was a night of alarms. Would people never cease coming? She was worn out, but at the thought of the tragedy abroad and the sick old man sleeping near by, she lit a candle and slipped down-stairs to avoid disturbing him. Doubtless it was some message from McNamara, she thought, as she unchained the door.

As she opened it, she fell back amazed while it swung wide and the candle flame flickered and sputtered in the night air. Roy Glenister stood there, grim and determined, his soft, white Stetson pulled low, his trousers tucked into tan half-boots, in his hand a Winchester rifle. Beneath his corduroy coat she saw a loose cartridge-belt, yellow with shells, and the nickelled flash of a revolver. Without invitation he strode across the threshold, closing the door behind him.

"Miss Chester, you and the Judge must dress quickly and come with me."

"I don't understand."

"The Vigilantes are on their way here to hang him. Come with me to my house where I can protect you."

She laid a trembling hand on her bosom and the color died out of her face, then at a slight noise above they both looked up to see Judge Stillman leaning far over the banister. He had wrapped himself in a dressing-gown and now gripped the rail convulsively, while his features were blanched to the color of putty and his eyes were wide with terror, though puffed and swollen from sleep. His lips moved in a vain endeavor to speak.

XV

VIGILANTES

O n the morning after the episode in the Northern, Glenister awoke under a weight of discouragement and desolation. The past twenty-four hours with their manifold experiences seemed distant and unreal. At breakfast he was ashamed to tell Dextry of the gambling debauch, for he had dealt treacherously with the old man in risking half of the mine, even though they had agreed that either might do as he chose with his interest, regardless of the other. It all seemed like a nightmare, those tense moments when he lay above the receiver's office and felt his belief in the one woman slipping away, the frenzied thirst which Cherry Malotte had checked, the senseless, unreasoning lust for play that possessed him later. This lapse was the last stand of his old, untamed instincts. The embers of revolt in him were dead. He felt that he would never again lose mastery of himself, that his passions would never best him hereafter.

Dextry spoke. "We had a meeting of the 'Stranglers' last night." He always spoke of the Vigilantes in that way, because of his early Western training.

"What was done?"

"They decided to act quick and do any odd jobs of lynchin', claim-jumpin', or such as needs doin'. There's a lot of law sharps and storekeepers in the bunch who figure McNamara's gang will wipe them off the map next."

"It was bound to come to this."

"They talked of ejectin' the receiver's men and puttin' all us fellers back on our mines."

"Good. How many can we count on to help us?"

"About sixty. We've kept the number down, and only taken men with so much property that they'll have to keep their mouths shut."

"I wish we might engineer some kind of an encounter with the court crowd and create such an uproar that it would reach Washington. Everything else has failed, and our last chance seems to be for the government to step in; that is, unless Bill Wheaton can do something with the California courts."

"I don't count on him. McNamara don't care for California courts no more 'n he would for a boy with a pea-shooter—he's got too much pull at headquarters. If the 'Stranglers' don't do no good, we'd better go in an' clean out the bunch like we was killin' snakes. If that fails, I'm goin' out to the States an' be a doctor."

"A doctor? What for?"

"I read somewhere that in the United States every year there is forty million gallons of whiskey used for medical purposes."

Glenister laughed. "Speaking of whiskey, Dex—I notice that you've been drinking pretty hard of late—that is, hard for you."

The old man shook his head. "You're mistaken. It ain't hard for me."

"Well, hard or easy, you'd better cut it out."

It was some time later that one of the detectives employed by the Swedes met Glenister on Front Street, and by an almost imperceptible sign signified his desire to speak with him. When they were alone he said:

"You're being shadowed."

"I've known that for a long time."

"The district-attorney has put on some new men. I've fixed the woman who rooms next to him, and through her I've got a line on some of them, but I haven't spotted them all. They're bad ones—'up-river' men mostly—remnants of Soapy Smith's Skagway gang. They won't stop at anything."

"Thank you—I'll keep my eyes open."

A few nights after, Glenister had reason to recall the words of the sleuth and to realize that the game was growing close and desperate. To reach his cabin, which sat on the outskirts of the town, he ordinarily followed one of the plank walks which wound through the confusion of tents, warehouses, and cottages lying back of the two principal streets along the water front. This part of the city was not laid out in rectangular blocks, for in the early rush the first-comers had seized whatever pieces of ground they found vacant and erected thereon some kind of buildings to make good their titles. There resulted a formless jumble of huts, cabins, and sheds, penetrated by no cross streets and quite unlighted. At night, one leaving the illuminated portion of the town found this darkness intensified.

Glenister knew his course so well that he could have walked it blindfolded. Nearing a corner of the warehouse this evening he remembered that the planking at this point was torn up, so, to avoid the mud, he leaped lightly across. Simultaneously with his jump he detected a movement in the shadows that banked the wall at his elbow and saw the flaming spurt of a revolver-shot. The man had crouched behind the building and was so close that it seemed impossible to miss. Glenister fell heavily upon his side and the thought flashed over him, "McNamara's thugs have shot me."

His assailant leaped out from his hiding-place and ran down the walk, the sound of his quick, soft footfalls thudding faintly out into the silence. The young man felt no pain, however, so scrambled to his feet, felt himself over with care, and then swore roundly. He was untouched; the other had missed him cleanly. The report, coming while he was in the act of leaping, had startled him so that he had lost his balance, slipped upon the wet boards, and fallen. His assailant was lost in the darkness before he could rise. Pursuit was out of the question, so he continued homeward, considerably shaken, and related the incident to Dextry.

"You think it was some of McNamara's work, eh?" Dextry inquired when he had finished.

"Of course. Didn't the detective warn me to-day?"

Dextry shook his head. "It don't seem like the game is that far along yet. The time is coming when we'll go to the mat with them people, but they've got the aige on us now, so what could they gain by putting you away? I don't believe it's them, but whoever it is, you'd better be careful or you'll be got."

"Suppose we come home together after this," Roy suggested, and they arranged to do so, realizing that danger lurked in the dark corners and that it was in some such lonely spot that the deed would be tried again. They experienced no trouble for a time, though on nearing their cabin one night the younger man fancied that he saw a shadow glide away from its vicinity and out into the blackness of the tundra, as though some one had stood at his very door waiting for him, then became frightened at the two figures approaching. Dextry had not observed it, however, and Glenister was not positive himself, but it served to give him the uncanny feeling that some determined, unscrupulous force was bent on his destruction. He determined to go nowhere unarmed.

A few evenings later he went home early and was busied in writing when Dextry came in about ten o'clock. The old miner hung up his coat before speaking, lit a cigarette, inhaled deeply, then, amid mouthfuls of smoke, began:

"I had my own toes over the edge to-night. I was mistook for you, which compliment I don't aim to have repeated."

Glenister questioned him eagerly.

"We're about the same height an' these hats of ours are alike. Just as I come by that lumber-pile down yonder, a man hopped out an throwed a 'gat' under my nose. He was quicker than light, and near blowed my skelp into the next block before he saw who I was; then he dropped his weepon and said:

"'My mistake. Go on.' I accepted his apology."

"Could you see who he was?"

"Sure. Guess."

"I can't."

"It was the Bronco Kid."

"Lord!" exclaimed Glenister. "Do you think he's after me?"

"He ain't after nobody else, an', take my word for it, it's got nothin' to do with McNamara nor that gamblin' row. He's too game for that. There's some other reason."

This was the first mention Dextry had made of the night at the Northern.

"I don't know why he should have it in for me—I never did him any favors," Glenister remarked, cynically.

"Well, you watch out, anyhow. I'd sooner face McNamara an' all the crooks he can hire than that gambler."

During the next few days Roy undertook to meet the proprietor of the Northern face to face, but the Kid had vanished completely from his haunts. He was not in his gambling-hall at night nor on the street by day. The young man was still looking for him on the evening of the dance at the hotel, when he chanced to meet one of the Vigilantes, who inquired of him:

"Aren't you late for the meeting?"

"What meeting?"

After seeing that they were alone, the other stated:

"There's an assembly to-night at eleven o'clock. Something important, I think. I supposed, of course, you knew about it."

"It's strange I wasn't notified," said Roy. "It's probably an oversight. Ill go along with you."

Together they crossed the river to the less frequented part of town and knocked at the door of a large, unlighted warehouse, flanked by a high board fence. The building faced the street, but was enclosed on the other three sides by this ten-foot wall, inside of which were stored large quantities of coal and lumber. After some delay they were admitted, and, passing down through the dim-lit, high-banked lanes of merchandise, came to the rear room, where they were admitted again. This compartment had been fitted up for the warm storage of perishable goods during the cold weather, and, being without windows, made an ideal place for clandestine gatherings.

Glenister was astonished to find every man of the organization present, including Dextry, whom he supposed to have gone home an hour since. Evidently a discussion had been in progress, for a chairman was presiding, and the boxes, kegs, and bales of goods had been shoved back against the walls for seats. On these were ranged the threescore men of the "Stranglers," their serious faces lighted imperfectly by scattered lanterns. A certain constraint seized them upon Glenister's entrance; the chairman was embarrassed. It was but momentary, however. Glenister himself felt that tragedy was in the air, for it showed in the men's attitudes and spoke eloquently from their strained faces. He was about to question the man next to him when the presiding officer continued:

"We will assemble here quietly with our arms at one o'clock. And let me caution you again not to talk or do anything to scare the birds away."

Glenister arose. "I came late, Mr. Chairman, so I missed hearing your plan. I gather that you're out for business, however, and I want to be in it. May I ask what is on foot?"

"Certainly. Things have reached such a pass that moderate means are useless. We have decided to act, and act quickly. We have exhausted every legal resource and now we're going to stamp out this gang of robbers in our own way. We will get together in an hour, divide into three groups of twenty men, each with a leader, then go to the houses of McNamara, Stillman, and Voorhees, take them prisoners, and—" He waved his hand in a large gesture.

Glenister made no answer for a moment, while the crowd watched him intently.

"You have discussed this fully?" he asked.

"We have. It has been voted on, and we're unanimous."

"My friends, when I stepped into this room just now I felt that I wasn't wanted. Why, I don't know, because I have had more to do with organizing this movement than any of you, and because I have suffered just as much as the rest. I want to know if I was omitted from this meeting intentionally."

"This is an embarrassing position to put me in," said the chairman, gravely. "But I shall answer as spokesman for these men if they wish."

"Yes. Go ahead," said those around the room.

"We don't question your loyalty, Mr. Glenister, but we didn't ask you to this meeting because we know your attitude—perhaps I'd better say sentiment—regarding Judge Stillman's niece—er—family. It has come to us from various sources that you have been affected to the prejudice of your own and your partner's interest. Now, there isn't going to be any sentiment in the affairs of the Vigilantes. We are going to do justice, and we thought the simplest way was to ignore you in this matter and spare all discussion and hard feeling in every quarter."

"It's a lie!" shouted the young man, hoarsely. "A damned lie! You wouldn't let me in for fear I'd kick, eh? Well, you were right. I will kick. You've hinted about my feelings for Miss Chester. Let me tell you that she is engaged to marry McNamara, and that she's nothing to me. Now, then, let me tell you, further, that you won't break into her house and hang her uncle, even if he is a reprobate. No, sir! This isn't the time for violence of that sort—we'll win without it. If we can't, let's fight like men, and not hunt in a pack like wolves. If you want to do something, put us back on our mines and help us hold them, but, for God's sake, don't descend to assassination and the tactics of the Mafia!"

"We knew you would make that kind of a talk," said the speaker, while the rest murmured grudgingly. One of them spoke up.

"We've talked this over in cold blood, Glenister, and it's a question of their lives or our liberty. The law don't enter into it."

"That's right," echoed another at his elbow. "We can't seize the claims, because McNamara's got soldiers to back him up. They'd shoot us down. You ought to be the last one to object."

He saw that dispute was futile. Determination was stamped on their faces too plainly for mistake, and his argument had no more effect on them than had the pale rays of the lantern beside him, yet he continued:

"I don't deny that McNamara deserves lynching, but Stillman doesn't. He's a weak old man"—some one laughed derisively—"and there's a woman in the house. He's all she has in the world to depend upon, and you would have to kill her to get at him. If you Must follow this course, take the others, but leave him alone."

They only shook their heads, while several pushed by him even as he spoke. "We're going to distribute our favors equal," said a man as he left. They were actuated by what they called justice, and he could not sway them. The life and welfare of the North were in their hands, as they thought, and there was not one to hesitate. Glenister implored the chairman, but the man answered him:

"It's too late for further discussion, and let me remind you of your promise. You're bound by every obligation that exists for an honorable man—"

"Oh, don't think that I'll give the snap away!" said the other; "but I warn you again not to enter Stillman's house."

He followed out into the night to find that Dextry had disappeared, evidently wishing to avoid argument. Roy had seen signs of unrest beneath the prospector's restraint during the past few days, and indications of a fierce hunger to vent his spleen on the men who had robbed him of his most sacred rights. He was of an intolerant, vindictive nature that would go to any length for vengeance. Retribution was part of his creed.

On his way home, the young man looked at his watch, to find that he had but an hour to determine his course. Instinct prompted him to join his friends and to even the score with the men who had injured him so bitterly, for, measured by standards of the frontier, they were pirates with their lives forfeit. Yet, he could not countenance this step. If only the Vigilantes would be content with making an example—but he knew they would not. The blood hunger of a mob is easy to whet and hard to hold. McNamara would resist, as would Voorhees and the district-attorney, then there would be bloodshed, riot, chaos. The soldiers would be called out and martial law declared, the streets would become skirmish-grounds. The Vigilantes would rout them without question, for every citizen of the North would rally to their aid, and such men could not be stopped. The Judge would go down with the rest of the ring, and what would happen to—her?

He took down his Winchester, oiled and cleaned it, then buckled on a belt of cartridges. Still he wrestled with himself. He felt that he was being ground between his loyalty to the Vigilantes and his own conscience. The girl was one of the gang, he reasoned—she had schemed with them to betray him through his love, and she was pledged to the one man in the world whom he hated with fanatical fury. Why should he think of her in this hour? Six months back he would have looked with jealous eyes upon the right to lead the Vigilantes, but this change that had mastered him—what was it? Not cowardice, nor caution. No. Yet, being intangible, it was none the less marked, as his friends had shown him an hour since.

He slipped out into the night. The mob might do as it pleased elsewhere, but no man should enter her house. He found a light shining from her parlor window, and, noting the shade up a few inches, stole close. Peering through, he discovered Struve and Helen talking. He slunk back into the shadows and remained hidden for a considerable time after the lawyer left, for the dancers were returning from the hotel and passed close by. When the last group had chattered away down the street, he returned to the front of the house and, mounting the steps, knocked sharply. As Helen appeared at the door, he stepped inside and closed it after him.

The girl's hair lay upon her neck and shoulders in tumbled brown masses, while her breast heaved tumultuously at the sudden, grim sight of him. She stepped back against the wall, her wondrous, deep, gray eyes wide and troubled, the blush of modesty struggling with the pallor of dismay.

The picture pained him like a knife-thrust. This girl was for his bitterest enemy—no hope of her was for him. He forgot for a moment that she was false and plotting, then, recalling it, spoke as roughly as he might and stated his errand. Then the old man had appeared on the stairs above, speechless with fright at what he overheard. It was evident that his nerves, so sorely strained by the events of the past week, were now snapped utterly. A human soul naked and panic-stricken is no pleasant sight, so Glenister dropped his eyes and addressed the girl again:

"Don't take anything with you. Just dress and come with me."

The creature on the stairs above stammered and stuttered, inquiringly:

"What outrage is this, Mr. Glenister?"

"The people of Nome are up in arms, and I've come to save you. Don't stop to argue." He spoke impatiently.

"Is this some r-ruse to get me into your power?"

"Uncle Arthur!" exclaimed the girl, sharply. Her eyes met Glenister's and begged him to take no offence.

"I don't understand this atrocity. They must be mad!" wailed the Judge. "You run over to the jail, Mr. Glenister, and tell Voorhees to hurry guards here to protect me. Helen, 'phone to the military post and give the alarm. Tell them the soldiers must come at once."

"Hold on!" said Glenister. "There's no use of doing that—the wires are cut; and I won't notify Voorhees—he can take care of himself. I came to help you, and if you want to escape you'll stop talking and hurry up."

"I don't know what to do," said Stillman, torn by terror and indecision. "You wouldn't hurt an old man, would you? Wait! I'll be down in a minute."

He scrambled up the stairs, tripping on his robe, seemingly forgetting his niece till she called up to him, sharply:

"Stop, Uncle Arthur! You mustn't RUN AWAY." She stood erect and determined, "You wouldn't do THAT, would you? This is our house. You represent the law and the dignity of the government. You mustn't fear a mob of ruffians. We will stay here and meet them, of course."

"Good Lord!" said Glenister. "That's madness. These men aren't ruffians; they are the best citizens of Nome. You don't realize that this is Alaska and that they have sworn to wipe out McNamara's gang. Come along."

"Thank you for your good intentions," she said, "but we have done nothing to run away from. We will get ready to meet these cowards. You had better go or they will find you here."

She moved up the stairs, and, taking the Judge by the arm, led him with her. Of a sudden she had assumed control of the situation unfalteringly, and both men felt the impossibility of thwarting her. Pausing at the top, she turned and looked down.

"We are grateful for your efforts just the same. Good-night."

"Oh, I'm not going," said the young man. "If you stick I'll do the same." He made the rounds of the first-floor rooms, locking doors and windows. As a place of defence it was hopeless, and he saw that he would have to make his stand up-stairs. When sufficient time had elapsed he called up to Helen:

"May I come?"

"Yes," she replied. So he ascended, to find Stillman in the hall, half clothed and cowering, while by the light from the front chamber he saw her finishing her toilet.

"Won't you come with me—it's our last chance?" She only shook her head. "Well, then, put out the light. I'll stand at that front window, and when my eyes get used to the darkness I'll be able to see them before they reach the gate."

She did as directed, taking her place beside him at the opening, while the Judge crept in and sat upon the bed, his heavy breathing the only sound in the room. The two young people stood so close beside each other that the sweet scent of her person awoke in him an almost irresistible longing. He forgot her treachery again, forgot that she was another's, forgot all save that he loved her truly and purely, with a love which was like an agony to him. Her shoulder brushed his arm; he heard the soft rustling of her garment at her breast as she breathed. Some one passed in the street, and she laid a hand upon him fearfully. It was very cold, very tiny, and very soft, but he made no move to take it. The moments dragged along, still, tense, interminable. Occasionally she leaned towards him, and he stooped to catch her whispered words. At such times her breath beat warm against his cheek, and he closed his teeth stubbornly. Out in the night a wolfdog saddened the air, then came the sound of others wrangling and snarling in a near-by corral. This is a chickless land and no cock-crow breaks the midnight peace. The suspense enhanced the Judge's perturbation till his chattering teeth sounded like castanets. Now and then he groaned.

The watchers had lost track of time when their strained eyes detected dark blots materializing out of the shadows.

"There they come," whispered Glenister, forcing her back from the aperture; but she would not be denied, and returned to his side.

As the foremost figures reached the gate, Roy leaned forth and spoke, not loudly, but in tones that sliced through the silence, sharp, clean, and without warning.

"Halt! Don't come inside the fence." There was an instant's confusion; then, before the men beneath had time to answer or take action, he continued: "This is Roy Glenister talking. I told you not to molest these people and I warn you again. We're ready for you."

The leader spoke. "You're a traitor, Glenister."

He winced. "Perhaps I am. You betrayed me first, though; and, traitor or not, you can't come into this house."

There was a murmur at this, and some one said:

"Miss Chester is safe. All we want is the Judge. We won't hang him, not if he'll wear this suit we brought along. He needn't be afraid. Tar is good for the skin."

"Oh, my God!" groaned the limb of the law.

Suddenly a man came running down the planked pavement and into the group.

"McNamara's gone, and so's the marshal and the rest," he panted. There was a moment's silence, and then the leader growled to his men, "Scatter out and rush the house, boys." He raised his voice to the man in the window. "This is your work—you damned turncoat." His followers melted away to right and left, vaulted the fence, and dodged into the shelter of the walls. The click, click of Glenister's Winchester sounded through the room while the sweat stood out on him. He wondered if he could do this deed, if he could really fire on these people. He wondered if his muscles would not wither and paralyze before they obeyed his command.

Helen crowded past him and, leaning half out of the opening, called loudly, her voice ringing clear and true:

"Wait! Wait a moment. I have something to say. Mr. Glenister didn't warn them. They thought you were going to attack the mines and so they rode out there before midnight. I am telling you the truth, really. They left hours ago." It was the first sign she had made, and they recognized her to a man.

There were uncertain mutterings below till a new man raised his voice. Both Roy and Helen recognised Dextry.

"Boys, we've overplayed. We don't want THESE people—McNamara's our meat. Old bald-face up yonder has to do what he's told, and I'm ag'in' this twenty-to-one midnight work. I'm goin' home." There were some whisperings, then the original spokesman called for Judge Stillman. The old man tottered to the window, a palsied, terror-stricken object. The girl was glad he could not be seen from below.

"We won't hurt you this time, Judge, but you've gone far enough. We'll give you another chance, then, if you don't make good, we'll stretch you to a lamp-post. Take this as a warning."

"I—s-shall do my d-d-duty," said the Judge.

The men disappeared into the darkness, and when they had gone Glenister closed the window, pulled down the shades, and lighted a lamp. He knew by how narrow a margin a tragedy had been averted. If he had fired on these men his shot would have kindled a feud which would have consumed every vestige of the court crowd and himself among them. He would have fallen under a false banner, and his life would not have reached to the next sunset. Perhaps it was forfeit now— he could not tell. The Vigilantes would probably look upon his part as traitorous; and, at the very least, he had cut himself off from their support, the only support the Northland offered him. Henceforth he was a renegade, a pariah, hated alike by both factions. He purposely avoided sight of Stillman and turned his back when the Judge extended his hand with expressions of gratitude. His work was done and he wished to leave this house. Helen followed him down to the door and, as he opened it, laid her hand upon his sleeve.

"Words are feeble things, and I can never make amends for all you've done for us."

"For Us!" cried Roy, with a break in his voice. "Do you think I sacrificed my honor, betrayed my friends, killed my last hope, ostracized myself, for 'Us'? This is the last time I'll trouble you. Perhaps the last time I'll see you. No matter what else you've done, however, you've taught me a lesson, and I thank you for it. I have found myself at last. I'm not an Eskimo any longer—I'm a man!"

"You've always been that," she said. "I don't understand as much about this affair as I want to, and it seems to me that no one will explain it. I'm very stupid, I guess; but won't you come back to-morrow and tell it to me?"

"No," he said, roughly. "You're not of my people. McNamara and his are no friends of mine, and I'm no friend of theirs." He was half down the steps before she said, softly:

"Good-night, and God bless you—friend."

She returned to the Judge, who was in a pitiable state, and for a long time she labored to soothe him as though he were a child. She undertook to question him about the things which lay uppermost in her mind and which this night had half revealed, but he became fretful and irritated at the mention of mines and mining. She sat beside his bed till he dozed off, puzzling to discover what lay behind the hints she had heard, till her brain and body matched in absolute weariness. The reflex of the day's excitement sapped her strength till she could barely creep to her own couch, where she rolled and sighed—too tired to sleep at once. She awoke finally, with one last nervous flicker, before complete oblivion took her. A sentence was on her mind—it almost seemed as though she had spoken it aloud:

"The handsomest woman in the North. . . but Glenister ran away."

XVI

In Which the Truth Begins to Bare Itself

I t was nearly noon of the next day when Helen awoke to find that McNamara had ridden in from the Creek and stopped for breakfast with the Judge. He had asked for her, but on hearing the tale of the night's adventure would not allow her to be disturbed. Later, he and the Judge had gone away together.

Although her judgment approved the step she had contemplated the night before, still the girl now felt a strange reluctance to meet McNamara. It is true that she knew no ill of him, except that implied in the accusations of certain embittered men; and she was aware that every strong and aggressive character makes enemies in direct proportionate the qualities which lend him greatness. Nevertheless, she was aware of an inner conflict that she had not foreseen. This man who so confidently believed that she would marry him did not dominate her consciousness.

She had ridden much of late, taking long, solitary gallops beside the shimmering sea that she loved so well, or up the winding valleys into the foot-hills where echoed the roar of swift waters or glinted the flash of shovel blades. This morning her horse was lame, so she determined to walk. In her early rambles she had looked timidly askance at the rough men she met till she discovered their genuine respect and courtesy. The most unkempt among them were often college-bred, although, for that matter, the roughest of the miners showed abundant consideration for a woman. So she was glad to allow the men to talk to her with the fine freedom inspired by the new country and its wide spaces. The wilderness breeds a chivalry all its own.

Thus there seemed to be no danger abroad, though they had told the girl of mad dogs which roamed the city, explaining that the hot weather affects powerfully the thick-coated, shaggy "malamoots." This is the land of the dog, and whereas in winter his lot is to labor and shiver and starve, in summer he loafs, fights, grows fat, and runs mad with the heat.

Helen walked far and, returning, chose an unfamiliar course through the outskirts of the town to avoid meeting any of the women she knew, because of that vivid memory of the night before. As she walked swiftly along she thought that she heard faint cries far behind her. Looking up, she noted that it was a lonely, barren quarter and that the only figure in sight was a woman some distance away. A few paces farther on the shouts recurred—more plainly this time, and a gunshot sounded. Glancing back, she saw several men running, one bearing a smoking revolver, and heard, nearer still, the snarling hubbub of fighting dogs. In a flash the girl's curiosity became horror, for, as she watched, one of the dogs made a sudden dash through the now subdued group of animals and ran swiftly along the planking on which she stood. It was a handsome specimen of the Eskimo malamoot—tall, gray, and coated like a wolf, with the speed, strength, and cunning of its cousin. Its head hung low and swung from side to side as it trotted, the motion flecking foam and slaver. The creature had scattered the pack, and now, swift, menacing, relentless, was coming towards Helen. There was no shelter near, no fence, no house, save the distant one towards which the other woman was making her way. The men, too far away to protect her, shouted hoarse warnings.

Helen did not scream nor hesitate—she turned and ran, terror-stricken, towards the distant cottage. She was blind with fright and felt an utter certainty that the dog would attack her before she could reach safety. Yes—there was the quick patter of his pads close up behind her; her knees weakened; the sheltering door was yet some yards away. But a horse, tethered near the walk, reared and snorted as the flying pair drew near. The mad creature swerved, leaped at the horse's legs, and snapped in fury. Badly frightened at this attack, the horse lunged at his halter, broke it, and galloped away; but the delay had served for Helen, weak and faint, to reach the door. She wrenched at the knob. It was locked. As she turned hopelessly away, she saw that the other woman was directly behind her, and was, in her turn, awaiting the mad animal's onslaught, but calmly, a tiny revolver in her hand.

"Shoot!" screamed Helen. "Why don't you shoot?" The little gun spoke, and the dog spun around, snarling and yelping. The woman fired several times more before it lay still, and then remarked, calmly, as she "broke" the weapon and ejected the shells:

"The calibre is too small to be good for much."

Helen sank down upon the steps.

"How well you shoot!" she gasped. Her eyes were on the gray bundle whose death agonies had thrust it almost to her feet. The men had run up and were talking excitedly, but after a word with them the woman turned to Helen.

"You must come in for a moment and recover yourself," she said, and led her inside.

It was a cosey room in which the girl found herself—more than that—luxurious. There was a piano with scattered music, and many of the pretty, feminine things that Helen had not seen since leaving home. The hostess had stepped behind some curtains for an instant and was talking to her from the next room.

"That is the third mad dog I have seen this month. Hydrophobia is becoming a habit in this neighborhood." She returned, bearing a tiny silver tray with decanter and glasses.

"You're all unstrung, but this brandy will help you—if you don't object to a swallow of it. Then come right in here and lie down for a moment and you'll be all right." She spoke with such genuine kindness and sympathy that Helen flashed a grateful glance at her. She was tall, slender, and with a peculiar undulating suggestion in her movements, as though she had been bred to the clinging folds of silken garments. Helen watched the charm of her smile, the friendly solicitude of her expression, and felt her heart warm towards this one kind woman in Nome.

"You're very good," she answered; "but I'm all right now. I was badly frightened. It was wonderful, your saving me." She followed the other's graceful motion as she placed her burden on the table, and in doing so gazed squarely at a photograph of Roy Glenister.

"Oh—!" Helen exclaimed, then paused as it flashed over her who this girl was. She looked at her quickly. Yes, probably men would consider the woman beautiful, with that smile. The revelation came with a shock, and she arose, trying to mask her confusion.

"Thank you so much for your kindness. I'm quite myself now and I must go."

Her change of face could not escape the quick perceptions of one schooled by experience in the slights of her sex. Times without number Cherry Malotte had marked that subtle, scornful change in other women, and reviled herself for heeding it. But in some way this girl's manner hurt her worst of all. She betrayed no sign, however, save a widening of the eyes and a certain fixity of smile as she answered:

"I wish you would stay until you are rested, Miss—" She paused with out-stretched hand.

"Chester. My name is Helen Chester. I'm Judge Stillman's niece," hurried the other, in embarrassment.

Cherry Malotte withdrew her proffered hand and her face grew hard and hateful.

"Oh! So you are Miss Chester—and I—saved you!" She laughed harshly.

Helen strove for calmness. "I'm sorry you feel that way," she said, coolly. "I appreciate your service to me." She moved towards the door.

"Wait a moment. I want to talk to you." Then, as Helen paid no heed, the woman burst out, bitterly: "Oh, don't be afraid! I know you are committing an unpardonable sin by talking to me, but no one will see you, and in your code the crime lies in being discovered. Therefore, you're quite safe. That's what makes me an outcast—I was found out. I want you to know, however, that, bad as I am, I'm better than you, for I'm loyal to those that like me, and I don't betray my friends."

"I don't pretend to understand you," said Helen, coldly.

"Oh yes, you do! Don't assume such innocence. Of course it's your role, but you can't play it with me." She stepped in front of her visitor, placing her back against the door, while her face was bitter and mocking. "The little service I did you just now entitles me to a privilege, I suppose, and I'm going to take advantage of it to tell you how badly your mask fits. Dreadfully rude of me, isn't it? You're in with a fine lot of crooks, and I admire the way you've done your share of the dirty work, but when you assume these scandalized, supervirtuous airs it offends me."

"Let me out!"

"I've done bad things," Cherry continued, unheedingly, "but I was forced into them, usually, and I never, deliberately, tried to wreck a man's life just for his money."

"What do you mean by saying that I have betrayed my friends and wrecked anybody's life?" Helen demanded, hotly.

"Bah! I had you sized up at the start, but Roy couldn't see it. Then Struve told me what I hadn't guessed. A bottle of wine, a woman, and that fool will tell all he knows. It's a great game McNamara's playing and he did well to get you in on it, for you're clever, your nerve is good, and your make-up is great for the part. I ought to know, for I've turned a few tricks myself. You'll pardon this little burst of feeling—professional pique. I'm jealous of your ability, that's all. However, now that you realize we're in the same class, don't look down on me hereafter." She opened the door and bowed her guest out with elaborate mockery.

Helen was too bewildered and humiliated to make much out of this vicious and incoherent attack except the fact that Cherry Malotte accused her of a part in this conspiracy which every one seemed to believe existed. Here again was that hint of corruption which she encountered on all sides. This might be merely a woman's jealousy—and yet she said Struve had told her all about it—that a bottle of wine and a pretty face would make the lawyer disclose everything. She could believe it from what she knew and had heard of him. The feeling that she was groping in the dark, that she was wrapped in a mysterious woof of secrecy, came over her again as it had so often of late. If Struve talked to that other woman, why wouldn't he talk to her? She paused, changing her direction towards Front Street, revolving rapidly in her mind as she went her course of action. Cherry Malotte believed her to be an actress. Very well—she would prove her judgment right.

She found Struve busy in his private office, but he leaped to his feet on her entrance and came forward, offering her a chair.

"Good-morning, Miss Helen. You have a fine color, considering the night you passed. The Judge told me all about the affair; and let me state that you're the pluckiest girl I know."

She smiled grimly at the thought of what made her cheeks glow, and languidly loosened the buttons of her jacket.

"I suppose you're very busy, you lawyer man?" she inquired.

"Yes—but not too busy to attend to anything you want."

"Oh, I didn't come on business," she said, lightly. "I was out walking and merely sauntered in."

"Well, I appreciate that all the more," he said, in an altered tone, twisting his chair about. "I'm more than delighted." She judged she was getting on well from the way his professionalism had dropped off.

"Yes, I get tired of talking to uncle and Mr. McNamara. They treat me as though I were a little girl."

"When do you take the fatal step?"

"What step do you mean?"

"Your marriage. When does it occur? You needn't hesitate," he added. "McNamara told we about it a month ago."

He felt his throat gingerly at the thought, but his eyes brightened when she answered, lightly:

"I think you are mistaken. He must have been joking."

For some time she led him on adroitly, talking of many things, in a way to make him wonder at her new and flippant humor. He had never dreamed she could be like this, so tantalizingly close to familiarity, and yet so maddeningly aloof and distant. He grew bolder in his speech.

"How are things going with us?" she questioned, as his warmth grew pronounced. "Uncle won't talk and Mr. McNamara is as close-mouthed as can be, lately."

He looked at her quickly. "In what respect?"

She summoned up her courage and walked past the ragged edge of uncertainty.

"Now, don't you try to keep me in short dresses, too. It's getting wearisome. I've done my part and I want to know what the rest of you are doing." She was prepared for any answer.

"What do you want to know?" he asked, cautiously.

"Everything. Don't you think I can hear what people are saying?"

"Oh, that's it! Well, don't you pay any attention to what people say."

She recognized her mistake and continued, hurriedly:

"Why shouldn't I? Aren't we all in this together? I object to being used and then discarded. I think I'm entitled to know how the scheme is working. Don't you think I can keep my mouth shut?"

"Of course," he laughed, trying to change the subject of their talk; but she arose and leaned against the desk near him, vowing that she would not leave the office without piercing some part of this mystery. His manner strengthened her suspicion that there Was something behind it all. This dissipated, brilliant creature knew the situation thoroughly; and yet, though swayed by her efforts, he remained chained by caution. She leaned forward and smiled at him.

"You're just like the others, aren't you? You won't give me any satisfaction at all."

"Give, give, give," said Struve, cynically. "That's always the woman's cry. Give me this—give me that. Selfish sex! Why don't you offer something in return? Men are traders, women usurers. You are curious, hence miserable. I can help you, therefore I should, do it for a smile. You ask me to break my promises and risk my honor on your caprice. Well, that's woman-like, and I'll do it. I'll put myself in your power, but I won't do it gratis. No, we'll trade."

"It isn't curiosity," she denied, indignantly. "It is my due."

"No; you've heard the common talk and grown suspicious, that's all. You think I know something that will throw a new light or a new shadow on everything you have in the world, and you're worked up to such a condition that you can't take your own people's word; and, on the other hand, you can't go to strangers, so you come to me. Suppose I told you I had the papers you brought to me last spring in that safe and that they told the whole story—whether your uncle is unimpeachable or whether he deserved hanging by that mob. What would you do, eh? What would you give to see them? Well, they're there and ready to speak for themselves. If you're a woman you won't rest till you've seen them. Will you trade?"

"Yes, yes! Give them to me," she cried, eagerly, at which a wave of crimson rushed up to his eyes and he rose abruptly from his chair. He made towards her, but she retreated to the wall, pale and wide-eyed.

"Can't you see," she flung at him, "that I MUST know?"

He paused. "Of course I can, but I want a kiss to bind the bargain—to apply on account." He reached for her hand with his own hot one, but she pushed him away and slipped past him towards the door.

"Suit yourself," said he, "but if I'm not mistaken, you'll never rest till you've seen those papers. I've studied you, and I'll place a bet that you can't marry McNamara nor look your uncle in the eye till you know the truth. You might do either if you KNEW them to be crooks, but you couldn't if you only suspected it—that's the woman. When you get ready, come back; I'll show you proof, because I don't claim to be anything but what I am—Wilton Struve, bargainer of some mean ability. When they come to inscribe my headstone I hope they can carve thereon with truth, 'He got value received.'"

"You're a panther," she said, loathingly.

"Graceful and elegant brute, that," he laughed. "Affectionate and full of play, but with sharp teeth and sharper claws. To follow out the idea, which pleases me, I believe the creature owes no loyalty to its fellows and hunts alone. Now, when you've followed this conspiracy out and placed the blame where it belongs, won't you come and tell me about it? That door leads into an outer hall which opens into the street. No one will see you come or go."

As she hurried away she wondered dazedly why she had stayed to listen so long. What a monster he was! His meaning was plain, had always been so from the first day he laid eyes upon her, and he was utterly conscienceless. She had known all this; and yet, in her proud, youthful confidence, and in her need, every hour more desperate and urgent, to know the truth, she had dared risk herself with him. Withal, the man was shrewd and observant and had divined her mental condition with remarkable sagacity. She had failed with him; but the girl now knew that she could never rest till she found an answer to her questions. She MUST kill this suspicion that ate into her so. She thought tenderly of her uncle's goodness to her, clung with despairing faith to the last of her kin. The blood ties of the Chesters were close and she felt in dire need of that lost brother who was somewhere in this mysterious land—need of some one in whom ran the strain that bound her to the weak old man up yonder. There was McNamara; but how could he help her, how much did she know of him, this man who was now within the darkest shadow of her new suspicions?

Feeling almost intolerably friendless and alone, weakened both by her recent fright and by her encounter with Struve, Helen considered as calmly as her emotions would allow and decided that this was no day in which pride should figure. There were facts which it was imperative she should know, and immediately; therefore, a few minutes later, she knocked at the door of Cherry Malotte. When the girl appeared, Helen was astonished to see that she had been crying. Tears burn hottest and leave plainest trace in eyes where they come most seldom. The younger girl could not guess the tumult of emotion the other had undergone during her absence, the utter depths of self-abasement she had fathomed, for the sight of Helen and her fresh young beauty had roused in the adventuress a very tempest of bitterness and jealousy. Whether Helen Chester were guilty or innocent, how could Glenister hesitate between them? Cherry had asked herself. Now she stared at her visitor inhospitably and without sign.

"Will you let me come in?" Helen asked her. "I have something to say to you."

When they were inside, Cherry Malotte stood and gazed at her visitor with inscrutable eyes and stony face.

"It isn't easy for me to come back," Helen began, "but I felt that I had to. If you can help me, I hope you will. You said that you knew a great wrong was being done. I have suspected it, but I didn't know, and I've been afraid to doubt my own people. You said I had a part in it—that I'd betrayed my friends. Wait a moment," she hurried on, at the other's cynical smile. "Won't you tell me what you know and what you think my part has been? I've heard and seen things that make me think—oh, they make me afraid to think, and yet I can't find the Truth! You see, in a struggle like this, people will make all sorts of allegations, but do they Know, have they any proof, that my uncle has done wrong?"

"Is that all?"

"No. You said Struve told you the whole scheme. I went to him and tried to cajole the story out of him, but—" She shivered at the memory.

"What success did you have?" inquired the listener, oddly curious for all her cold dislike.

"Don't ask me. I hate to think of it."

Cherry laughed cruelly. "So, failing there, you came back to me, back for another favor from the waif. Well, Miss Helen Chester, I don't believe a word you've said and I'll tell you nothing. Go back to the uncle and the rawboned lover who sent you, and inform them that I'll speak when the time comes. They think I know too much, do they?—so they've sent you to spy? Well, I'll make a compact. You play your game and I'll play mine. Leave Glenister alone and I'll not tell on McNamara. Is it a bargain?"

"No, no, no! Can't you SEE? That's not it. All I want is the truth of this thing."

"Then go back to Struve and get it. He'll tell you; I won't. Drive your bargain with him—you're able. You've fooled better men—now, see what you can do with him."

Helen left, realizing the futility of further effort, though she felt that this woman did not really doubt her, but was scourged by jealousy till she deliberately chose this attitude.

Reaching her own house, she wrote two brief notes and called in her Jap boy from the kitchen.

"Fred, I want you to hunt up Mr. Glenister and give him this note. If you can't find him, then look for his partner and give the other to him." Fred vanished, to return in an hour with the letter for Dextry still in his hand.

"I don' catch dis feller," he explained. "Young mans say he gone, come back mebbe one, two, 'leven days."

"Did you deliver the one to Mr. Glenister?"

"Yes, ma'am."

"Was there an answer?"

"Yes, ma'am."

"Well, give it to me."

The note read:

DEAR MISS CHESTER,

A discussion of a matter so familiar to us both as the Anvil Creek controversy would be useless. If your inclination is due to the incidents of last night, pray don't trouble yourself. We don't want your pity. I am,

Your servant,
ROY GLENISTER

As she read the note, Judge Stillman entered, and it seemed to the girl that he had aged a year for every hour in the last twelve, or else the yellow afternoon light limned the sagging hollows and haggard lines of his face most pitilessly. He showed in voice and manner the nervous burden under which he labored.

"Alec has told me about your engagement, and it lifts a terrible load from me. I'm mighty glad you're going to marry him. He's a wonderful man, and he's the only one who can save us."

"What do you mean by that? What are we in danger of?" she inquired, avoiding discussion of McNamara's announcement.

"Why, that mob, of course. They'll come back. They said so. But Alec can handle the commanding officer at the post, and, thanks to him, we'll have soldiers guarding the house hereafter."

"Why—they won't hurt us—"

"Tut, tut! I know what I'm talking about. We're in worse danger now than ever, and if we don't break up those Vigilantes there'll be bloodshed—that's what. They're a menace, and they're trying to force me off the bench so they can take the law into their own hands again. That's what I want to see you about. They're planning to kill Alec and me—so he says—and we've got to act quick to prevent murder. Now, this young Glenister is one of them, and he knows who the rest are. Do you think you could get him to talk?"

"I don't think I quite understand you," said the girl, through whitening lips.

"Oh yes, you do. I want the names of the ring-leaders, so that I can jail them. You can worm it out of that fellow if you try."

Helen looked at the old man in a horror that at first was dumb. "You ask this of me?" she demanded, hoarsely, at last.

"Nonsense," he said, irritably. "This isn't any time for silly scruples. It's life or death for me, maybe, and for Alec, too." He said the last craftily, but she stormed at him:

"It's infamous! You're asking me to betray the very man who saved us not twelve hours ago. He risked his life for us."

"It isn't treachery at all, it's protection. If we don't get them, they'll get us. I wouldn't punish that young fellow, but I want the others. Come, now, you've got to do it."

But she said "No" firmly, and quietly went to her own room, where, behind the locked door, she sat for a long time staring with unseeing eyes, her hands tight clenched in her lap. At last she whispered:

"I'm afraid it's true. I'm afraid it's true."

She remained hidden during the dinner-hour, and pleaded a headache when McNamara called in the early evening. Although she had not seen him since he left her the night before, bearing her tacit promise to wed him, yet how could she meet him now with the conviction growing on her hourly that he was a master-rogue? She wrestled with the thought that he and her uncle, her own uncle who stood in the place of a father, were conspirators. And yet, at memory of the Judge's cold-blooded request that she should turn traitress, her whole being was revolted. If he could ask a thing like that, what other heartless, selfish act might he not be capable of? All the long, solitary evening she kept her room, but at last, feeling faint, slipped down-stairs in search of Fred, for she had eaten nothing since her late breakfast.

Voices reached her from the parlor, and as she came to the last step she froze there in an attitude of listening. The first sentence she heard through the close-drawn curtains banished all qualms at eavesdropping. She stood for many breathless minutes drinking in the plot that came to her plainly from within, then turned, gathered up her skirts, and tiptoed back to her room. Here she made haste madly, tearing off her house clothes and donning others.

She pressed her face to the window and noted that the night was like a close-hung velvet pall, without a star in sight. Nevertheless, she wound a heavy veil about her hat and face before she extinguished the light and stepped into the hall. Hearing McNamara's "Good-night" at the front-door, she retreated again while her uncle slowly mounted the stairs and paused before her chamber. He called her name softly, but when she did not answer continued on to his own room. When he was safely within she descended quietly, went out, and locked the front-door behind her, placing the key in her bosom. She hurried now, feeling her way through the thick gloom in a panic, while in her mind was but one frightened thought: "I'll be too late. I'll be too late."

XVII

The Drip of Water in the Dark

E ven after Helen had been out for some time she could barely see sufficiently to avoid collisions. The air, weighted by a low-hung roof of clouds, was surcharged with the electric suspense of an impending storm, and seemed to sigh and tremble at the hint of power in leash. It was that pause before the conflict wherein the night laid finger upon its lips.

As the girl neared Glenister's cabin she was disappointed at seeing no light there. She stumbled towards the door, only to utter a half-strangled cry as two men stepped out of the gloom and seized her roughly. Something cold and hard was thrust violently against her cheek, forcing her head back and bruising her. She struggled and cried out.

"Hold on—it's a woman!" exclaimed the man who had pinioned her arms, loosing his hold till only a hand remained on her shoulder. The other lowered the weapon he had jammed to her face and peered closely.

"Why, Miss Chester," he said. "What are you doing here? You came near getting hurt."

"I am bound for the Wilsons', but I must have lost my way in the darkness. I think you have cut my face." She controlled her fright firmly.

"That's too bad," one said. "We mistook you for—" And the other broke in, sharply, "You'd better run along. We're waiting for some one."

Helen hastened back by the route she had come, knowing that there was still time, and that as yet her uncle's emissaries had not laid hands upon Glenister. She had overheard the Judge and McNamara plotting to drag the town with a force of deputies, seizing not only her two friends, but every man suspected of being a Vigilante. The victims were to be jailed without bond, without reason, without justice, while the mechanism of the court was to be juggled in order to hold them until fall, if necessary. They had said that the officers were already busy, so haste was a crying thing. She sped down the dark streets towards the house of Cherry Malotte, but found no light nor answer to her knock. She was distracted now, and knew not where to seek next among the thousand spots which might hide the man she wanted. What chance had she against the posse sweeping the town from end to end? There was only one; he might be at the Northern Theatre. Even so, she could not reach him, for she dared not go there herself. She thought of Fred, her Jap boy, but there was no time. Wasted moments meant failure.

Roy had once told her that he never gave up what he undertook. Very well, she would show that even a girl may possess determination. This was no time for modesty or shrinking indecision, so she pulled the veil more closely about her face and took her good name into her hands. She made rapidly towards the lighted streets which cast a skyward glare, and from which, through the breathless calm, arose the sound of carousal. Swiftly she threaded the narrow alleys in search of the theatre's rear entrance, for she dared not approach from the front. In this way she came into a part of the camp which had lain hidden from her until now, and of the existence of which she had never dreamed.

The vices of a city, however horrible, are at least draped scantily by the mantle of convention, but in a great mining-camp they stand naked and without concealment. Here there were rows upon rows of crib-like houses clustered over tortuous, ill-lighted lanes, like blow-flies swarming to an unclean feast. From within came the noise of ribaldry and debauch. Shrill laughter mingled with coarse, maudlin songs, till the clinging night reeked with abominable revelry. The girl saw painted creatures of every nationality leaning from windows or beckoning from doorways, while drunken men collided with her, barred her course, challenged her, and again and again she was forced to slip from their embraces. At last the high bulk of the theatre building loomed a short distance ahead. Panting and frightened, she tried the door with weak hands, to find it locked. From behind it rose the blare of brass and the sound of singing. She accosted a man who approached her through the narrow alley, but he had cruised from the charted course in search of adventure and was not minded to go in quest of doormen; rather, he chose to sing a chantey, to the bibulous measures of which he invited her to dance with him, so she slipped away till he had teetered past. He was some longshoreman in that particular epoch of his inebriety where life had no burden save the dissipation of wages.

Returning, she pounded on the door, possessed of the sense that the man she sought was here, till at last it was flung open, framing the silhouette of a shirt-sleeved, thick-set youth, who shouted:

"What 'n 'ell do you want to butt in for while the show's on? Go round front." She caught a glimpse of disordered scenery, and before he could slam the door in her face thrust a silver dollar into his hand, at the same time wedging herself into the opening. He pocketed the coin and the door clicked to behind her.

"Well, speak up. The act's closin'." Evidently he was the directing genius of the performance, for at that moment the chorus broke into full cry, and he said, hurriedly:

"Wait a minute. There goes the finally," and dashed away to tend his drops and switches. When the curtain was down and the principals had sought their dressing-rooms he returned.

"Do you know Mr. Glenister?" she asked.

"Sure. I seen him to-night. Come here." He led her towards the footlights, and, pulling back the edge of the curtain, allowed her to peep past him out into the dance-hall. She had never pictured a place like this, and in spite of her agitation was astonished at its gaudy elegance. The gallery was formed of a continuous row of compartments with curtained fronts, in which men and women were talking, drinking, singing. The seats on the lower floor were disappearing, and the canvas cover was rolling back, showing the polished hardwood underneath, while out through the wide folding-doors that led to the main gambling-room she heard a brass-lunged man calling the commencement of the dance. Couples glided into motion while she watched.

"I don't see him," said her guide. "You better walk out front and help yourself." He indicated the stairs which led up to the galleried boxes and the steps leading down on to the main floor, but she handed him another coin, begging him to find Glenister and bring him to her. "Hurry; hurry!" she implored.

The stage-manager gazed at her curiously, remarking, "My! You spend your money like it had been left to you. You're a regular pie-check for me. Come around any time."

She withdrew to a dark corner and waited interminably till her messenger appeared at the head of the gallery stairs and beckoned to her. As she drew near he said, "I told him there was a thousand-dollar filly flaggin' him from the stage door, but he's got a grouch an' won't stir. He's in number seven." She hesitated, at which he said, "Go on—you're in right;" then continued, reassuringly: "Say, pal, if he's your white-haired lad, you needn't start no roughhouse, 'cause he don't flirt wit' these dames none whatever. Naw! Take it from me."

She entered the door her counsellor indicated to find Roy lounging back watching the dancers. He turned inquiringly—then, as she raised her veil, leaped to his feet and jerked the curtains to.

"Helen! What are you doing here?"

"You must go away quickly," she gasped. "They're trying to arrest you."

"They! Who? Arrest me for what?"

"Voorhees and his men—for riot, or something about last night."

"Nonsense," he said. "I had no part in it. You know that."

"Yes, yes—but you're a Vigilante, and they're after you and all your friends. Your house is guarded and the town is alive with deputies. They've planned to jail you on some pretext or other and hold you indefinitely. Please go before it's too late."

"How do you know this?" he asked, gravely.

"I overheard them plotting."

"Who?"

"Uncle Arthur and Mr. McNamara." She faced him squarely as she said it, and therefore saw the light flame up in his eyes as he cried:

"And you came here to save me—came HERE at the risk of your good name?"

"Of course. I would have done the same for Dextry." The gladness died away, leaving him listless.

"Well, let them come. I'm done, I guess. I heard from Wheaton to-night. He's down and out, too—some trouble with the 'Frisco courts about jurisdiction over these cases. I don't know that it's worth while to fight any longer."

"Listen," she said. "You must go. I am sure there is a terrible wrong being done, and you and I must stop it. I have seen the truth at last, and you're in the right. Please hide for a time at least."

"Very well. If you have taken sides with us there's some hope left. Thank you for the risk you ran in warning me."

She had moved to the front of the compartment and was peering forth between the draperies when she stifled a cry.

"Too late! Too late! There they are. Don't part the curtains. They'll see you."

Pushing through the gambling-hall were Voorhees and four others, seemingly in quest of some one.

"Run down the back stairs," she breathed, and pushed him through the door. He caught and held her hand with a last word of gratitude.

Then he was gone. She drew down her veil and was about to follow when the door opened and he reappeared.

"No use," he remarked, quietly. "There are three more waiting at the foot." He looked out to find that the officers had searched the crowd and were turning towards the front stairs, thus cutting off his retreat. There were but two ways down from the gallery and no outside windows from which to leap. As they had made no armed display, the presence of the officers had not interrupted the dance.

Glenister drew his revolver, while into his eyes came the dancing glitter that Helen had seen before, cold as the glint of winter sunlight.

"No, not that—for God's sake!" she shuddered, clasping his arm.

"I must for your sake, or they'll find you here, and that's worse than ruin. I'll fight it out in the corridors so that you can escape in the confusion. Wait till the firing stops and the crowd gathers." His hand was on the knob when she tore it loose, whispering hoarsely:

"They'll kill you. Wait! There's a better way. Jump." She dragged him to the front of the box and pulled aside the curtains. "It isn't high and they won't see you till it's too late. Then you can run through the crowd." He grasped her idea, and, slipping his weapon back into its holster, laid hold of the ledge before him and lowered himself down over the dancers. He swung out unhesitatingly, and almost before he had been observed had dropped into their midst. The gallery was but twice the height of a man's head from the floor, so he landed on his feet and had drawn his Colts even while the men at the stairs were shouting at him to halt.

At sight of the naked weapons there was confusion, wherein the commands of the deputies mingled with the shrieks of the women, the crash of overturned chairs, and the sound of tramping feet, as the crowd divided before Glenister and swept back against the wall in the same ominous way that a crowd in the street had once divided on the morning of Helen's arrival. The trombone player, who had sunk low in his chair with closed eyes, looked out suddenly at the disturbance, and his alarm was blown through the horn in a startled squawk. A large woman whimpered, "Don't shoot," and thrust her palms to her ears, closing her eyes tightly.

Glenister covered the deputies, from whose vicinity the by-standers surged as though from the presence of lepers.

"Hands up!" he cried, sharply, and they froze into motionless attitudes, one poised on the lowest step of the stairs, the other a pace forward. Voorhees appeared at the head of the flight and rushed down a few steps only to come abruptly into range and to assume a like rigidity, for the young man's aim shifted to him.

"I have a warrant for you," the officer cried, his voice loud in the hush.

"Keep it," said Glenister, showing his teeth in a smile in which there was no mirth. He backed diagonally across the hall, his boot-heels clicking in the silence, his eyes shifting rapidly up and down the stairs where the danger lay.

From her station Helen could see the whole tableau, all but the men on the stairs, where her vision was cut off. She saw the dance girls crouched behind their partners or leaning far out from the wall with parted lips, the men eager yet fearful, the bartender with a half-polished glass poised high. Then a quick movement across the hall suddenly diverted her absorbed attention. She saw a man rip aside the drapery of the box opposite and lean so far out that he seemed in peril of falling. He undertook to sight a weapon at Glenister, who was just passing from his view. At her first glance Helen gasped—her heart gave one fierce lunge, and she cried out.

The distance across the pit was so short that she saw his every line and lineament clearly; it was the brother she had sought these years and years. Before she knew or could check it the blood call leaped forth.

"Drury!" she cried, aloud, at which he whipped his head about, while amazement and some other emotion she could not gauge spread slowly over his features. For a long moment he stared at her without movement or sign while the drama beneath went on, then he drew back into his retreat with the dazed look of one doubting his senses, yet fearful of putting them to the test. For her part, she saw nothing except her brother vanishing slowly into the shadows as though stricken at her glance, the curtains closing before his livid face—and then pandemonium broke loose at her feet.

Glenister, holding his enemies at bay, had retreated to the double doors leading to the theatre. His coup had been executed so quickly and with such lack of turmoil that the throng outside knew nothing of it till they saw a man walk backward through the door. As he did so he reached forth and slammed the wide wings shut before his face, then turned and dashed into the press. Inside the dance-hall loud sounds arose as the officers clattered down the stairs and made after their quarry. They tore the barrier apart in time to see, far down the saloon, an eddying swirl as though some great fish were lashing through the lily-pads of a pond, and then the swinging doors closed behind Glenister.

Helen made her way from the theatre as she had come, unobserved and unobserving, but she walked in a dream. Emotions had chased each other too closely to-night to be distinguishable, so she went mechanically through the narrow alley to Front Street and thence to her home.

Glenister, meanwhile, had been swallowed up by the darkness, the night enfolding him without sign or trace. As he ran he considered what course to follow—whether to carry the call to his comrades in town or to make for the Creek and Dextry. The Vigilantes might still distrust him, and yet he owed them warning. McNamara's men were moving so swiftly that action must be speedy to forestall them. Another hour and the net would be closed, while it seemed that whichever course he chose they would snare one or the other—either the friends who remained in town, or Dex and Slapjack out in the hills. With daylight those two would return and walk unheeding into the trap, while if he bore the word to them first, then the Vigilantes would be jailed before dawn. As he drew near Cherry Malotte's house he saw a light through the drawn curtains. A heavy raindrop plashed upon his face, another followed, and then he heard the patter of falling water increasing swiftly. Before he could gain the door the storm had broken. It swept up the street with tropical violence, while a breath sighed out of the night, lifting the litter from underfoot and pelting him with flying particles. Over the roofs the wind rushed with the rising moan of a hurricane while the night grew suddenly noisy ahead of the tempest.

He entered the door without knocking, to find the girl removing her coat. Her face gladdened at sight of him, but he checked her with quick and cautious words, his speech almost drowned by the roar outside.

"Are you alone?" She nodded, and he slipped the bolt behind him, saying:

"The marshals are after me. We just had a 'run in' at the Northern, and I'm on the go. No—nothing serious yet, but they want the Vigilantes, and I must get them word. Will you help me?" He rapidly recounted the row of the last ten minutes while she nodded her quick understanding.

"You're safe here for a little while," she told him, "for the storm will check them. If they should come, there's a back door leading out from the kitchen and a side entrance yonder. In my room you'll find a French window. They can't corner you very well."

"Slapjack and Dex are out at the shaft house—you know—that quartz claim on the mountain above the Midas." He hesitated. "Will you lend me your saddle-horse? It's a black night and I may kill him."

"What about these men in town?"

"I'll warn them first, then hit for the hills."

She shook her head. "You can't do it. You can't get out there before daylight if you wait to rouse these people, and McNamara has probably telephoned the mines to send a party up to the quartz claim after Dex. He knows where the old man is as well as you do, and they'll raid him before dawn."

"I'm afraid so, but it's all I can offer. Will you give me the horse?"

"No! He's only a pony, and you'd founder him in the tundra. The mud is knee-deep. I'll go myself."

"Good Heavens, girl, in such a night! Why, it's worth your life! Listen to it! The creeks will be up and you'll have to swim. No, I can't let you."

"He's a good little horse, and he'll take me through." Then, coming close, she continued: "Oh, boy! Can't you see that I want to help? Can't you see that I—I'd DIE for you if it would do any good?" He gazed gravely into her wide blue eyes and said, awkwardly: "Yes, I know. I'm sorry things are—as they are—but you wouldn't have me lie to you, little woman?"

"No. You're the only true man I ever knew. I guess that's why I love you. And I do love you, oh, so much! I want to be good and worthy to love you, too."

She laid her face against his arm and caressed him with clinging tenderness, while the wind yelled loudly about the eaves and the windows drummed beneath the rain. His heavy brows knit themselves together as she whispered:

"I love you! I love you! I love you!" with such an agony of longing in her voice that her soft accents were sharply distinguishable above the turmoil. The growing wildness seemed a part of the woman's passion, which whipped and harried her like a willow in a blast.

"Things are fearfully jumbled," he said, finally. "And this is a bad time to talk about them. I wish they might be different. No other girl would do what you have offered to-night."

"Then why do you think of that woman?" she broke in, fiercely. "She's bad and false. She betrayed you once; she's in the play now; you've told me so yourself. Why don't you be a man and forget her?"

"I can't," he said, simply. "You're wrong, though, when you think she's bad. I found to-night that she's good and brave and honest. The part she played was played innocently, I'm sure of that, in spite of the fact that she'll marry McNamara. It was she who overheard them plotting and risked her reputation to warn me."

Cherry's face whitened, while the shadowy eagerness that had rested there died utterly. "She came into that dive alone? She did that?" He nodded, at which she stood thinking for some time, then continued: "You're honest with me, Roy, and I'll be the same with you. I'm tired of deceit, tired of everything. I tried to make you think she was bad, but in my own heart I knew differently all the time. She came here to-day and humbled herself to get the truth, humbled herself to me, and I sent her away. She suspected, but she didn't know, and when she asked for information I insulted her. That's the kind of a creature I am. I sent her back to Struve, who offered to tell her the whole story."

"What does that renegade want?"

"Can't you guess?"

"Why, I'd rather—" The young man ground his teeth, but Cherry hastened.

"You needn't worry; she won't see him again. She loathes the ground he walks on."

"And yet he's no worse than that other scoundrel. Come, girl, we have work to do; we must act, and act quickly." He gave her his message to Dextry, then she went to her room and slipped into a riding-habit. When she came out he asked: "Where is your raincoat? You'll be drenched in no time."

"I can't ride with it. I'll be thrown, anyway, and I don't want to be all bound up. Water won't hurt me."

She thrust her tiny revolver into her dress, but he took it and upon examination shook his head.

"If you need a gun you'll need a good one." He removed the belt from his own waist and buckled his Colts about her.

"But you!" she objected.

"I'll get another in ten minutes." Then, as they were leaving, he said: "One other request, Cherry. I'll be in hiding for a time, and I must get word to Miss Chester to keep watch of her uncle, for the big fight is on at last and the boys will hang him sure if they catch him. I owe her this last warning. Will you send it to her?"

"I'll do it for your sake, not for her—no, no; I don't mean that. I'll do the right thing all round. Leave it here and I'll see that she gets it to-morrow. And—Roy—be careful of yourself." Her eyes were starry and in their depths lurked neither selfishness nor jealousy now, only that mysterious glory of a woman who makes sacrifice.

Together they scurried back to the stable, and yet, in that short distance, she would have been swept from her feet had he not seized her. They blew in through the barn door, streaming and soaked by the blinding sheets that drove scythe-like ahead of the wind. He struck a light, and the pony whinnied at recognition of his mistress. She stroked the little fellow's muzzle while Glenister cinched on her saddle. Then, when she was at last mounted, she leaned forward:

"Will you kiss me once, Roy, for the last time?"

He took her rain-wet face between his hands and kissed her upon the lips as he would have saluted a little maid. As he did so, unseen by both of them, a face was pressed for an instant against the pane of glass in the stable wall.

"You're a brave girl and may God bless you," he said, extinguishing the light. He flung the door wide and she rode out into the storm. Locking the portal, he plunged back towards the house to write his hurried note, for there was much to do and scant time for its accomplishment, despite the helping hand of the hurricane. He heard the voice of Bering as it thundered on the Golden Sands, and knew that the first great storm of the fall had come. Henceforth he saw that the violence of men would rival the rising elements, for the deeds of this night would stir their passions as Æolus was rousing the hate of the sea.

He neglected to bolt the house door as he entered, but flung off his dripping coat and, seizing pad and pencil, scrawled his message. The wind screamed about the cabin, the lamp flared smokily, and Glenister felt a draught suck past him as though from an open door at his back as he wrote:

"I can't do anything more. The end has come and it has brought the hatred and bloodshed that I have been trying to prevent. I played the game according to your rules, but they forced me back to first principles in spite of myself, and now I don't know what the finish will be. To-morrow will tell. Take care of your uncle, and if you should wish to communicate with me, go to Cherry Malotte. She is a friend to both of us.

"Always your servant, ROY GLENISTER."

As he sealed this he paused, while he felt the hair on his neck rise and bristle and a chill race up his spine. His heart fluttered, then pounded onward till the blood thumped audibly at his ear-drums and he found himself swaying in rhythm to its beat. The muscles of his back cringed and rippled at the proximity of some hovering peril, and yet an irresistible feeling forbade him to turn. A sound came from close behind his chair—the drip, drip, drip of water. It was not from the eaves, nor yet from a faulty shingle. His back was to the kitchen door, through which he had come, and, although there were no mirrors before him, he felt a menacing presence as surely as though it had touched him. His ears were tuned to the finest pin-pricks of sound, so that he heard the faint, sighing "squish" of a sodden shoe upon which a weight had shifted. Still something chained him to his seat. It was as though his soul laid a restraining hand upon his body, waiting for the instant.

He let his hand seek his hip carelessly, but remembered where his gun was. Mechanically, he addressed the note in shaking characters, while behind him sounded the constant drip, drip, drip that he knew came from saturated garments. For a long moment he sat, till he heard the stealthy click of a gun-lock muffled by finger pressure. Then he set his face and slowly turned to find the Bronco Kid standing behind him as though risen from the sea, his light clothes wet and clinging, his feet centred in a spreading puddle. The dim light showed the convulsive fury of his features above the levelled weapon, whose hammer was curled back like the head of a striking adder, his eyes gleaming with frenzy. Glenister's mouth was powder dry, but his mind was leaping riotously like dust before a gale, for he divined himself to be in the deadliest peril of his life. When he spoke the calmness of his voice surprised himself.

"What's the matter, Bronco?" The Kid made no reply, and Roy repeated, "What do you want?"

"That's a hell of a question," the gambler said, hoarsely. "I want you, of course, and I've got you."

"Hold up! I am unarmed. This is your third try, and I want to know what's back of it."

"DAMN the talk!" cried the faro-dealer, moving closer till the light shone on his features, which commenced to twitch. He raised the revolver he had half lowered. "There's reason enough, and you know it."

Glenister looked him fairly between the eyes, gripping himself with firm hands to stop the tremor he felt in his bones. "You can't kill me," he said. "I am too good a man to murder. You might shoot a crook, but you can't kill a brave man when he's unarmed. You're no assassin." He remained rigid in his chair, however, moving nothing but his lips, meeting the other's look unflinchingly. The Kid hesitated an instant, while his eyes, which had been fixed with the glare of hatred, wavered a moment, betraying the faintest sign of indecision. Glenister cried out, exultantly:

"Ha! I knew it. Your neck cords quiver."

The gambler grimaced. "I can't do it. If I could, I'd have shot you before you turned. But you'll have to fight, you dog. Get up and draw."

Roy refused. "I gave Cherry my gun."

"Yes, and more too," the man gritted. "I saw it all."

Even yet Glenister had made no slightest move, realizing that a feather's weight might snap the gambler's nervous tension and bring the involuntary twitch that would put him out swifter than a whip is cracked.

"I have tried it before, but murder isn't my game." The Kid's eye caught the glint of Cherry's revolver where she had discarded it. "There's a gun—get it."

"It's no good. You'd carry the six bullets and never feel them. I don't know what this is all about, but I'll fight you whenever I'm heeled right."

"Oh, you black-hearted hound," snarled the Kid. "I want to shoot, but I'm afraid. I used to be a gentleman and I haven't lost it all, I guess. But I won't wait the next time. I'll down you on sight, so you'd better get ironed in a hurry." He backed out of the room into the semi-darkness of the kitchen, watching with lynx-like closeness the man who sat so quietly under the shaded light. He felt behind him for the outer door-knob and turned it to let in a white sheet of rain, then vanished like a storm wraith, leaving a parched-lipped man and a zigzag trail of water, which gleamed in the lamplight like a pool of blood.

XVIII

Wherein a Trap is Baited

Glenister did not wait long after his visitor's departure, but extinguished the light, locked the door, and began the further adventures of this night. The storm welcomed him with suffocating violence, sucking the very breath from his lips, while the rain beat through till his flesh was cold and aching. He thought with a pang of the girl facing this tempest, going out to meet the thousand perils of the night. And it remained for him to bear his part as she bore hers, smilingly.

The last hour had added another and mysterious danger to his full measure. Could the Kid be jealous of Cherry? Surely not. Then what else?

The tornado had driven his trailers to cover, evidently, for the streets were given over to its violence, and Roy encountered no hostile sign as he was buffeted from house to house. He adventured cautiously and yet with haste, finding certain homes where the marshals had been before him peopled now only by frightened wives and children. A scattered few of the Vigilantes had been taken thus, while the warring elements had prevented their families from spreading the alarm or venturing out for succor. Those whom he was able to warn dressed hurriedly, took their rifles, and went out into the drifting night, leaving empty cabins and weeping women. The great fight was on.

Towards daylight the remnants of the Vigilantes straggled into the big blank warehouse on the sand-spit, and there beneath the smoking glare of lanterns cursed the name of McNamara. As dawn grayed the ragged eastern sky-line, Dextry and Slapjack blew in through the spindrift, bringing word from Cherry and lifting a load from Glenister's mind.

"There's a game girl," said the old miner, as he wrung out his clothes. "She was half gone when she got to us, and now she's waiting for the storm to break so that she can come back."

"It's clearing up to the east," Slapjack chattered. "D'you know, I'm gettin' so rheumatic that ice-water don't feel comfortable to me no more."

"Uriatic acid in the blood," said Dextry. "What's our next move?" he asked of his partner. "When do we hang this politician? Seems like we've got enough able-bodied piano-movers here to tie a can onto the whole outfit, push the town site of Nome off the map, and start afresh."

"I think we had better lie low and watch developments," the other cautioned. "There's no telling what may turn up during the day."

"That's right. Stranglers is like spirits—they work best in the dark."

As the day grew, the storm died, leaving ramparts of clouds hanging sullenly above the ocean's rim, while those skilled in weather prophecy foretold the coming of the equinoctial. In McNamara's office there was great stir and the coming of many men. The boss sat in his chair smoking countless cigars, his big face set in grim lines, his hard eyes peering through the pall of blue at those he questioned. He worked the wires of his machine until his dolls doubled and danced and twisted at his touch. After a gusty interview he had dismissed Voorhees with a merciless tongue-lashing, raging bitterly at the man's failure.

"You're not fit to herd sheep. Thirty men out all night and what do you get? A dozen mullet-headed miners. You bag the mud-hens and the big game runs to cover. I wanted Glenister, but you let him slip through your fingers—now it's war. What a mess you've made! If I had even ONE helper with a brain the size of a flaxseed, this game would be a gift, but you've bungled every move from the start. Bah! Put a spy in the bull-pen with those prisoners and make them talk. Offer them anything for information. Now get out!"

He called for a certain deputy and questioned him regarding the night's quest, remarking, finally:

"There's treachery somewhere. Those men were warned."

"Nobody came near Glenister's house except Miss Chester," the man replied.

"What?"

"The Judge's niece. We caught her by mistake in the dark."

Later, one of the men who had been with Voorhees at the Northern asked to see the receiver and told him:

"The chief won't believe that I saw Miss Chester in the dance-hall last night, but she was there with Glenister. She must have put him wise to our game or he wouldn't have known we were after him."

His hearer made no comment, but, when alone, rose and paced the floor with heavy tread while his face grew savage and brutal.

"So that's the game, eh? It's man to man from now on. Very well, Glenister, I'll have your life for that, and then—you'll pay, Miss Helen." He considered carefully. A plot for a plot. If he could not swap intrigue with these miners and beat them badly, he deserved to lose. Now that the girl gave herself to their cause he would use her again and see how well she answered. Public opinion would not stand too great a strain, and, although he had acted within his rights last night, he dared not go much further. Diplomacy, therefore, must serve. He must force his enemies beyond the law and into his trap. She had passed the word once; she would do so again.

He hurried to Stillman's house and stormed into the presence of the Judge. He told the story so artfully that the Judge's astonished unbelief yielded to rage and cowardice, and he sent for his niece. She came down, white and silent, having heard the loud voices. The old man berated her with shrewish fury, while McNamara stood silent. The girl listened with entire self-control until her uncle made a reference to Glenister that she found intolerable.

"Hush! I will not listen!" she cried, passionately. "I warned him because you would have sacrificed him after he had saved our lives. That is all. He is an honest man, and I am grateful to him. That is the only foundation for your insult."

McNamara, with apparent candor, broke in:

"You thought you were doing right, of course, but your action will have terrible consequences. Now we'll have riot, bloodshed, and Heaven knows what. It was to save all this that I wanted to break up their organization. A week's imprisonment would have done it, but now they're armed and belligerent and we'll have a battle to-night."

"No, no!" she cried. "There mustn't be any violence."

"There is no use trying to check them. They are rushing to their own destruction. I have learned that they plan to attack the Midas to-night, and I'll have fifty soldiers waiting for them there. It is a shame, for they are decent fellows, blinded by ignorance and misled by that young miner. This will be the blackest night the North has ever seen."

With this McNamara left the house and went in search of Voorhees, remarking to himself: "Now, Miss Helen—send your warning—the sooner the better. If I know those Vigilantes, it will set them crazy, and yet not crazy enough to attack the Midas. They will strike for me, and when they hit my poor, unguarded office, they'll think hell has moved North."

"Mr. Marshal," said he to his tool, "I want you to gather forty men quietly and to arm them with Winchesters. They must be fellows who won't faint at blood—you know the kind. Assemble them at my office after dark, one at a time, by the back way. It must be done with absolute secrecy. Now, see if you can do this one thing and not get balled up. If you fail, I'll make you answer to me."

"Why don't you get the troops?" ventured Voorhees.

"If there's one thing I want to avoid, it's soldiers, either here or at the mines. When they step in, we step out, and I'm not ready for that just yet." The receiver smiled sinisterly.

Helen meanwhile had fled to her room, and there received Glenister's note through Cherry Malotte's messenger. It rekindled her worst fears and bore out McNamara's prophecy. The more she read of it the more certain she grew that the crisis was only a question of hours, and that with darkness, Tragedy would walk the streets of Nome. The thought of the wrong already done was lost in the lonely girl's terror of the crime about to happen, for it seemed to her she had been the instrument to set these forces in motion, that she had loosed this swift-speeding avalanche of greed, hatred, and brutality. And when the crash should come—the girl shuddered. It must not be. She would shriek a warning from the house-tops even at cost of her uncle, of McNamara, and of herself. And yet she had no proof that a crime existed. Although it all lay clear in her own mind, the certainty of it arose only from her intuition. If only she were able to take a hand—if only she were not a woman. Then Cherry Malotte's words anent Struve recurred to her, "A bottle of wine and a woman's face." They brought back the lawyer's assurance that those documents she had safeguarded all through the long spring-time journey really contained the proof. If they did, then they held the power to check this impending conflict. Her uncle and the boss would not dare continue if threatened with exposure and prosecution. The more she thought of it, the more urgent seemed the necessity to prevent the battle of to-night. There was a chance here, at least, and the only one.

Adding to her mental torment was the constant vision of that face in the curtains at the Northern. It was her brother, yet what mystery shrouded this affair, also? What kept him from her? What caused him to slink away like a thief discovered? She grew dizzy and hysterical.

Struve turned in his chair as the door to his private office opened, then leaped to his feet at sight of the gray-eyed girl standing there.

"I came for the papers," she said.

"I knew you would." The blood went out of his cheeks, then surged back up to his eyes. "It's a bargain, then?"

She nodded. "Give them to me first."

He laughed unpleasantly. "What do you take me for? I'll keep my part of the bargain if you'll keep yours. But this is no place, nor time. There's riot in the air, and I'm busy preparing for to-night. Come back to-morrow when it's all over."

But it was the terror of to-night's doings that led her into his power.

"I'll never come back," she said. "It is my whim to know to-day—yes, at once."

He meditated for a time. "Then to-day it shall be. I'll shirk the fight, I'll sacrifice what shreds of duty have clung to me, because the fever for you is in my bones, and it seems to me I'd do murder for it. That's the kind of a man I am, and I have no pride in myself because of it. But I've always been that way We'll ride to the Sign of the Sled. It's a romantic little road-house ten miles from here, perched high above the Snake River trail. We'll take dinner there together."

"But the papers?"

"I'll have them with me. We'll start in an hour."

"In an hour," she echoed, lifelessly, and left him.

He chuckled grimly and seized the telephone. "Central—call the Sled road-house—seven rings on the Snake River branch. Hello! That you, Shortz? This is Struve. Anybody at the house? Good. Turn them away if they come and say that you're closed. None of your business. I'll be out about dark, so have dinner for two. Spread yourself and keep the place clear. Good-bye."

Strengthened by Glenister's note, Helen went straight to the other woman and this time was not kept waiting nor greeted with sneers, but found Cherry cloaked in a shy dignity, which she clasped tightly about herself. Under her visitor's incoherence she lost her diffidence, however, and, when Helen had finished, remarked, with decision: "Don't go with him. He's a bad man."

"But I Must. The blood of those men will be on me if I don't stop this tragedy. If those papers tell the tale I think they do, I can call off my uncle and make McNamara give back the mines. You said Struve told you the whole scheme. Did you see the Proof?"

"No, I have only his word, but he spoke of those documents repeatedly, saying they contained his instructions to tie up the mines in order to give a foothold for the lawsuits. He bragged that the rest of the gang were in his power and that he could land them in the penitentiary for conspiracy. That's all."

"It's the only chance," said Helen. "They are sending soldiers to the Midas to lie in ambush, and you must warn the Vigilantes." Cherry paled at this and exclaimed:

"Good Lord! Roy said he'd lead an attack to-night." The two stared at each other.

"If I succeed with Struve I can stop it all—all of this injustice and crime—everything."

"Do you realize what you're risking?" Cherry demanded. "That man is an animal. You'll have to kill him to save yourself, and he'll never give up those proofs."

"Yes, he will," said Helen, fiercely, "and I defy him to harm me. The Sign of the Sled is a public roadhouse with a landlord, a telephone, and other guests. Will you warn Mr. Glenister about the troops?"

"I will, and bless you for a brave girl. Wait a moment." Cherry took from the dresser her tiny revolver. "Don't hesitate to use this. I want you to know also that I'm sorry for what I said yesterday."

As she hurried away, Helen realized with a shock the change that the past few months had wrought in her. In truth, it was as Glenister had said, his Northland worked strangely with its denizens. What of that shrinking girl who had stepped out of the sheltered life, strong only in her untried honesty, to become a hunted, harried thing, juggling with honor and reputation, in her heart a half-formed fear that she might kill a man this night to gain her end? The elements were moulding her with irresistible hands. Roy's contact with the primitive had not roughened him more quickly than had hers.

She met her appointment with Struve, and they rode away together, he talkative and elated, she silent and icy.

Late in the afternoon the cloud banks to the eastward assumed alarming proportions. They brought with them an early nightfall, and when they broke let forth a tempest which rivalled that of the previous night. During the first of it armed men came sifting into McNamara's office from the rear and were hidden throughout the building. Whenever he descried a peculiarly desperate ruffian the boss called him aside for private instruction and gave minute description of a wide-shouldered, erect, youth in white hat and half-boots. Gradually he set his trap with the men Voorhees had raked from the slums, and when it was done smiled to himself. As he thought it over he ceased to regret the miscarriage of last night's plan, for it had served to goad his enemies to the point he desired, to the point where they would rush to their own undoing. He thought with satisfaction of the role he would play in the United States press when the sensational news of this night's adventure came out. A court official who dared to do his duty despite a lawless mob. A receiver who turned a midnight attack into a rout and shambles. That is what they would say. What if he did exceed his authority thereafter? What if there were a scandal? Who would question? As to soldiers—no, decidedly no. He wished no help of soldiers at this time.

The sight of a ship in the offing towards dark caused him some uneasiness, for, notwithstanding the assurance that the course of justice in the San Francisco courts had been clogged, he knew Bill Wheaton to be a resourceful lawyer and a determined man. Therefore, it relieved him to note the rising gale, which precluded the possibility of interference from that source. Let them come to-morrow if they would. By that time some of the mines would be ownerless and his position strengthened a hundredfold.

He telephoned the mines to throw out guards, although he reasoned that none but madmen would think of striking there in the face of the warning which he knew must have been transmitted through Helen. Putting on his rain-coat he sought Stillman.

"Bring your niece over to my place to-night. There's trouble in the air and I'm prepared for it."

"She hasn't returned from her ride yet. I'm afraid she's caught in the storm." The Judge gazed anxiously into the darkness.

During all the long day the Vigilantes lay in hiding, impatient at their idleness and wondering at the lack of effort made towards their discovery, not dreaming that McNamara had more cleverly hidden plans behind. When Cherry's note of warning came they gathered in the back room and gave voice to their opinions.

"There's only one way to clear the atmosphere," said the chairman.

"You bet," chorussed the others. "They've garrisoned the mines, so let's go through the town and make a clean job of it. Let's hang the whole outfit to one post."

This met with general approval, Glenister alone demurring. Said he: "I have reasoned it out differently, and I want you to hear me through before deciding. Last night I got word from Wheaton that the California courts are against us. He attributes it to influence, but, whatever the reason, we are cut off from all legal help either in this court or on appeal. Now, suppose we lynch these officials to-night— what do we gain? Martial law in two hours, our mines tied up for another year, and who knows what else? Maybe a corrupter court next season. Suppose, on the other hand, we fail—and somehow I feel that we will, for that boss is no fool. What then? Those of us who don't find the morgue will end in jail. You say we can't meet the soldiers. I say we can and must. We must carry this row to them. We must jump it past the courts of Alaska, past the courts of California, and up to the White House, where there's one honest man, at least. We must do something to wake up the men in Washington. We must get out of politics, for McNamara can beat us there. Although he's a strong man he can't corrupt the President. We have one shot left, and it must reach the Potomac. When Uncle Sam takes a hand we'll get a square deal, so I say let us strike at the Midas to-night and take her if we can. Some of us will go down, but what of it?"

Following this harangue, he outlined a plan which in its unique daring took away their breaths, and as he filled in detail after detail they brightened with excitement and that love of the long chance which makes gamblers of those who thread the silent valleys or tread the edge of things. His boldness stirred them and enthusiasm did the rest.

"All I want for myself," he said, "is the chance to run the big risk. It's mine by right."

Dextry spoke, breathlessly, to Slapjack in the pause which ensued:

"Ain't he a heller?"

"We'll go you," the miners chimed to a man. And the chairman added: "Let's have Glenister lead this forlorn hope. I am willing to stand or fall on his judgment." They acquiesced without a dissenting voice and with the firm hands of a natural leader the young man took control.

"Let's hurry up," said one. "It's a long 'mush' and the mud is knee-deep."

"No walking for us," said Roy. "We'll go by train."

"By train? How can we get a train?"

"Steal it," he answered, at which Dextry grinned delightedly at his loose-jointed companion, and Slapjack showed his toothless gums in answer, saying:

"He sure is."

A few more words and Glenister, accompanied by these two, slipped out into the whirling storm, and a half-hour later the rest followed. One by one the Vigilantes left, the blackness blotting them up an arm's-length from the door, till at last the big, bleak warehouse echoed hollowly to the voice of the wind and water.

Over in the eastern end of town, behind dark windows upon which the sheeted rain beat furiously, other armed men lay patiently waiting—waiting some word from the bulky shadow which stood with folded arms close against a square of gray, while over their heads a wretched old man paced back and forth, wringing his hands, pausing at every turn to peer out into the night and to mumble the name of his sister's child.

XIX

DYNAMITE

Early in the evening Cherry Malotte opened her door to find the Bronco Kid on her step. He entered and threw off his rubber coat. Knowing him well, she waited for his disclosure of his errand. His sallow skin was without trace of color, his eyes were strangely tired, deep lines had gathered about his lips, while his hands kept up constant little nervous explorations as though for days and nights he had not slept and now hovered on the verge of some hysteria. He gave her the impression of a smouldering mine with the fire eating close up to the powder. She judged that his body had been racked by every passion till now it hung jaded and weary, yielding only to the spur of his restless, revengeful spirit.

After a few objectless remarks, he began, abruptly:

"Do you love Roy Glenister?" His voice, like his manner, was jealously eager, and he watched her carefully as she replied, without quibble or deceit:

"Yes, Kid; and I always shall. He is the only true man I have ever known, and I'm not ashamed of my feelings."

For a long time he studied her, and then broke into rapid speech, allowing her no time for interruption.

"I've held back and held back because I'm no talker. I can't be, in my business; but this is my last chance, and I want to put myself right with you. I've loved you ever since the Dawson days, not in the way you'd expect from a man of my sort, perhaps, but with the kind of love that a woman wants. I never showed my hand, for what was the use? That man outheld me. I'd have quit faro years back only I wouldn't leave this country as long as you were a part of it, and up here I'm only a gambler, fit for nothing else. I'd made up my mind to let you have him till something happened a couple of months ago, but now it can't go through. I'll have to down him. It isn't concerning you—I'm not a welcher. No, it's a thing I can't talk about, a thing that's made me into a wolf, made me skulk and walk the alleys like a dago. It's put murder into my heart. I've tried to assassinate him. I tried it here last night—but—I was a gentleman once—till the cards came. He knows the answer now, though, and he's ready for me—so one of us will go out like a candle when we meet. I felt that I had to tell you before I cut him down or before he got me."

"You're talking like a madman, Kid," she replied, "and you mustn't turn against him now. He has troubles enough. I never knew you cared for me. What a tangle it is, to be sure. You love me, I love him, he loves that girl, and she loves a crook. Isn't that tragedy enough without your adding to it? You come at a bad time, too, for I'm half insane. There's something dreadful in the air to-night—"

"I'll have to kill him," the man muttered, doggedly, and, plead or reason as she would, she could get nothing from him except those words, till at last she turned upon him fiercely.

"You say you love me. Very well—let's see if you do. I know the kind of a man you are and I know what this feud will mean to him, coming just at this time. Put it aside and I'll marry you."

The gambler rose slowly to his feet. "You do love him, don't you?" She bowed her face, and he winced, but continued: "I wouldn't make you my wife that way. I didn't mean it that way."

At this she laughed bitterly, "Oh, I see. Of course not. How foolish of me to expect it of a man like you. I understand what you mean now, and the bargain will stand just the same, if that is what you came for. I wanted to leave this life and be good, to go away and start over and play the game square, but I see it's no use. I'll pay. I know how relentless you are, and the price is low enough. You can have me—and that— marriage talk—I'll not speak of again. I'll stay what I am for his sake."

"Stop!" cried the Kid. "You're wrong. I'm not that kind of a sport." His voice broke suddenly, its vehemence shaking his slim body. "Oh, Cherry, I love you the way a man ought to love a woman. It's one of the two good things left in me, and I want to take you away from here where we can both hide from the past, where we can start new, as you say."

"You would marry me?" she asked.

"In an hour, and give my heart's blood for the privilege; but I can't stop this thing, not even if your own dear life hung upon it. I Must kill that man."

She approached him and laid her arms about his neck, every line of her body pleading, but he refused steadfastly, while the sweat stood out upon his brow.

She begged: "They're all against him, Kid. He's fighting a hopeless fight. He laid all he had at that girl's feet, and I'll do the same for you."

The man growled savagely. "He got his reward. He took all she had—"

"Don't be a fool. I guess I know. You're a faro-dealer, but you haven't any right to talk like that about a good woman, even to a bad one like me."

Into his dark eyes slowly crept a hungry look, and she felt him begin to tremble the least bit. He undertook to speak, paused, wet his lips, then carefully chose these words:

"Do you mean—that he did not—that she is—a good girl?"

"Absolutely."

He sat down weakly and passed a shaking hand over his face, which had begun to twitch and jerk again as it had on that night when his vengeance was thwarted.

"I may as well tell you that I know she's more than that. She's honest and high-principled. I don't know why I'm saying this, but it was on my mind and I was half distracted when you came. She's in danger to-night, though—at this minute. I don't dare to think of what may have happened, for she's risked everything to make reparation to Roy and his friends."

"What?"

"She's gone to the Sign of the Sled alone with Struve."

"Struve!" shouted the gambler, leaping to his feet. "Alone with Struve on a night like this?" He shook her fiercely, crying: "What for? Tell me quick!"

She recounted the reasons for Helen's adventure, while the man's face became terrible.

"Oh, Kid, I am to blame for letting her go. Why did I do it? I'm afraid—afraid."

"The Sign of the Sled belongs to Struve, and the fellow who runs it is a rogue." The Bronco looked at the clock, his eyes bloodshot and dull like those of a goaded, fly-maddened bull. "It's eight o'clock now—ten miles—two hours. Too late!"

"What ails you?" she questioned, baffled by his strange demeanor. "You called ME the one woman just now, and yet—"

He swung towards her heavily. "She's my sister."

"Your—sister? Oh, I—I'm glad. I'm glad—but don't stand there like a wooden man, for you've work to do. Wake up. Can't you hear? She's in peril!" Her words whipped him out of his stupor so that he drew himself somewhat under control. "Get into your coat. Hurry! Hurry!

My pony will take you there." She snatched his garment from the chair and held it for him while the life ran back into his veins. Together they dashed out into the storm as she and Roy had done, and as he flung the saddle on the buckskin, she said:

"I understand it all now. You heard the talk about her and Glenister; but it's wrong. I lied and schemed and intrigued against her, but it's over now. I guess there's a little streak of good in me somewhere, after all."

He spoke to her from the saddle. "It's more than a streak, Cherry, and you're my kind of people." She smiled wanly back at him under the lantern-light.

"That's left-handed, Kid. I don't want to be your kind. I want to be his kind—or your sister's kind."

Upon leaving the rendezvous, Glenister and his two friends slunk through the night, avoiding the life and lights of the town, while the wind surged out of the voids to seaward, driving its wet burden through their flapping slickers, pelting their faces as though enraged at its failure to wash away the purposes written there. Their course brought them to a cabin at the western outskirts of the city, where they paused long enough to adjust something beneath the brims of their hats.

Past them ran the iron rails of the narrow-gauged road which led out across the quaking tundra to the mountains and the mines. Upon this slender trail of steel there rolled one small, ungainly teapot of an engine which daily creaked and clanked back and forth at a snail's pace, screaming and wailing its complaint of the two high-loaded flat-cars behind. The ties beneath it were spiked to planks laid lengthwise over the semi-liquid road-bed, in places sagging beneath the surface till the humpbacked, short-waisted locomotive yawed and reeled and squealed like a drunken fish-wife. At night it panted wearily into the board station and there sighed and coughed and hissed away its fatigue as the coals died and the breath relaxed in its lungs.

Early to bed and early to rise was perforce the motto of its grimy crew, who lived near by. To-night they were just retiring when stayed by a summons at their door. The engineer opened it to admit what appeared to his astonished eyes to be a Krupp cannon propelled by a man in yellow-oiled clothes and white cotton mask. This weapon assumed the proportions of a great, one-eyed monster, which stared with baleful fixity at his vitals, giving him a cold and empty feeling. Away back beyond this Cyclops of the Sightless Orb were two other strangers likewise equipped.

The fireman arose from his chair, dropping an empty shoe with a thump, but, being of the West, without cavil or waste of wind, he stretched his hands above his head, balancing on one foot to keep his unshod member from the damp floor. He had unbuckled his belt, and now, loosened by the movement, his overalls seemed bent on sinking floorward in an ecstasy of abashment at the intrusion, whereupon with convulsive grip he hugged them to their duty, one hand and foot still elevated as though in the grand hailing-sign of some secret order. The other man was new to the ways of the North, so backed to the limit of his quarters, laid both hands protectingly upon his middle, and doubled up, remarking, fervidly:

"Don't point that damn thing at my stomach."

"Ha, ha!" laughed the fireman, with unnatural loudness. "Have your joke boys."

"This ain't no joke," said the foremost figure, its breath bellying out the mask at its mouth.

"Sure it is," insisted the shoeless one. "Must be—we ain't got anything worth stealing."

"Get into your clothes and come along. We won't hurt you." The two obeyed and were taken to the sleeping engine and there instructed to produce a full head of steam in thirty minutes or suffer a premature taking off and a prompt elision from the realms of applied mechanics. As stimulus to their efforts two of the men stood over them till the engine began to sob and sigh reluctantly. Through the gloom that curtained the cab they saw other dim forms materializing and climbing silently on to the cars behind; then, as the steam-gauge touched the mark, the word was given and the train rumbled out from its shelter, its shrill plaint at curb and crossing whipped away and drowned in the storm.

Slapjack remained in the cab, gun in lap, while Dextry climbed back to Glenister. He found the young man in good spirits, despite the discomfort of his exposed position, and striving to light his pipe behind the shelter of his coat.

"Is the dynamite aboard?" the old man questioned.

"Sure. Enough to ballast a battle-ship."

As the train crept out of the camp and across the river bridge, its only light or glimmer the sparks that were snatched and harried by the blast, the partners seated themselves on the powder cases and conversed guardedly, while about them sounded the low murmur of the men who risked their all upon this cry to duty, who staked their lives and futures upon this hazard of the hills, because they thought it right.

"We've made a good fight, whether we win or lose to-night," said Dextry.

Roy replied, "My fight is made and won."

"What does that mean?"

"My hardest battle had nothing to do with the Midas or the mines of Anvil. I fought and conquered myself."

"Awful wet night for philosophy," the first remarked. "It's apt to sour on you like milk in a thunder-storm. S'pose you put overalls an' gum boots on some of them Boston ideas an' lead 'em out where I can look 'em over an' find out what they're up to."

"I mean that I was a savage till I met Helen Chester and she made a man of me. It took sixty days, but I think she did a good job. I love the wild things just as much as ever, but I've learned that there are duties a fellow owes to himself, and to other people, if he'll only stop and think them out. I've found out, too, that the right thing is usually the hardest to do. Oh, I've improved a lot."

"Gee! but you're popular with yourself. I don't see as it helps your looks any. You're as homely as ever—an' what good does it do you after all? She'll marry that big guy."

"I know. That's what rankles, for he's no more worthy of her than I am. She'll do what's right, however, you may depend upon that, and perhaps she'll change him the way she did me. Why, she worked a miracle in my attitude towards life—my manner—"

"Oh, your manners are good enough as they lay," interrupted the other. "You never did eat with your knife."

"I don't believe in hara-kiri," Glenister laughed.

"No, when it comes to intimacies with decorum, you're right on the job along with any of them Easterners. I watched you close at them 'Frisco hotels last winter, and, say—you know as much as a horse. Why, you was wise to them tablewares and pickle-forks equal to a head-waiter, and it give me confidence just to be with you. I remember putting milk and sugar in my consomme the first time. It was pale and in a cup and looked like tea—but not you. No, sir! You savvied plenty and squeezed a lemon into yours—to clean your fingers, I reckon."

Roy slapped his partner's wet back, for he was buoyant and elated. The sense of nearing danger pulsed through him like wine. "That wasn't just what I meant, but it goes. Say, if we win back our mine, we'll hit for New York next—eh?"

"No, I don't aim to mingle with no higher civilization than I got in 'Frisco. I use that word 'higher' like it was applied to meat. Not that I wouldn't seem apropos, I'm stylish enough for Fifth Avenue or anywheres, but I like the West. Speakin' of modes an' styles, when I get all lit up in that gray woosted suit of mine, I guess I make the jaded sight-seers set up an' take notice—eh? Somethin' doin' every minute in the cranin' of necks—what? Nothin' gaudy, but the acme of neatness an' form, as the feller said who sold it to me."

Their common peril brought the friends together again, into that close bond which had been theirs without interruption until this recent change in the younger had led him to choose paths at variance with the old man's ideas; and now they spoke, heart to heart, in the half-serious, half-jesting ways of old, while beneath each whimsical irony was that mutual love and understanding which had consecrated their partnership.

Arriving at the end of the road, the Vigilantes debouched and went into the darkness of the canon behind their leader, to whom the trails were familiar. He bade them pause finally, and gave his last instructions.

"They are on the alert, so you want to be careful. Divide into two parties and close in from both sides, creeping as near to the pickets as possible without discovery. Remember to wait for the last blast. When it comes, cut loose and charge like Sioux. Don't shoot to kill at first, for they're only soldiers and under orders, but if they stand—well, every man must do his work."

Dextry appealed to the dim figures forming the circle.

"I leave it to you, gents, if it ain't better for me to go inside than for the boy. I've had more experience with giant powder, an' I'm so blamed used up an' near gone it wouldn't hurt if they did get me, while he's right in his prime—"

Glenister stopped him. "I won't yield the privilege. Come now—to your places, men."

They melted away to each side while the old prospector paused to wring his partner's hand.

"I'd ruther it was me, lad, but if they get you—God help 'em!" He stumbled after the departing shadows, leaving Roy alone. With his naked fingers, Glenister ripped open the powder cases and secreted the contents upon his person. Each cartridge held dynamite enough to devastate a village, and he loaded them inside his pockets, inside his shirt, and everywhere that he had room, till he was burdened and cased in an armor one-hundredth part of which could have blown him from the face of the earth so utterly as to leave no trace except, perhaps, a pit ripped out of the mountain-side. He looked to his fuses and saw that they were wrapped in oiled paper, then placed them in his hat. Having finished, he set out, walking with difficulty under the weight he carried.

That his choice of location had been well made was evidenced by the fact that the ground beneath his feet sloped away to a basin out of which bubbled a spring. It furnished the drinking supply of the Midas, and he knew every inch of the crevice it had worn down the mountain, so felt his way cautiously along. At the bottom of the hill where it ran out upon the level it had worn a considerable ditch through the soil, and into this he crawled on hands and knees. His bulging clothes handicapped him so that his gait was slow and awkward, while the rain had swelled the streamlet till it trickled over his calves and up to his wrists, chilling him so that his muscles cramped and his very bones cried out with it. The sharp schist cut into his palms till they were shredded and bleeding, while his knees found every jagged bit of bed-rock over which he dragged himself. He could not see an arm's-length ahead without rising, and, having removed his slicker for greater freedom of movement, the rain beat upon his back till he was soaked and sodden and felt streamlets cleaving downward between his ribs. Now and again he squatted upon his haunches, straining his eyes to either side. The banks were barely high enough to shield him. At last he came to a bridge of planks spanning the ditch and was about to rear himself for another look when he suddenly flattened into the stream bed, half damming the waters with his body. It was for this he had so carefully wrapped his fuses. A man passed over him so close above that he might have touched him. The sentry paused a few paces beyond and accosted another, then retraced his steps over the bridge. Evidently this was the picket-line, so Roy wormed his way forward till he saw the blacker blackness of the mine buildings, then drew himself dripping out from the bank. He had run the gauntlet safely.

Since evicting the owners, the receiver had erected substantial houses in place of the tents he had found on the mine. They were of frame and corrugated-iron, sheathed within and suited to withstand a moderate exposure. The partners had witnessed the operation from a distance, but knew nothing about the buildings from close examination.

A thrill of affection for this place wanned the young man. He loved this old mine. It had realized the dream of his boyhood, and had

REX BEACH

answered the hope he had clung to during his long fight against the Northland. It had come to him when he was disheartened, bringing cheer and happiness, and had yielded itself like a bride. Now it seemed a crime to ravage it.

He crept towards the nearest wall and listened. Within was the sound of voices, though the windows were dark, showing that the inhabitants were on the alert. Beneath the foundations he made mysterious preparations, then sought out the office building and cook-house, doing likewise. He found that back of the seeming repose of the Midas there was a strained expectancy.

Although suspense had lengthened the time out of all calculation, he judged he had been gone from his companions at least an hour and that they must be in place by now. If they were not—if anything failed at this eleventh hour—well, those were the fortunes of war. In every enterprise, however carefully planned, there comes a time when chance must take its turn.

He made his way inside the blacksmith-shop and fumbled for a match. Just as he was about to strike it he heard the swish of oiled clothes passing, and waited for some time. Then, igniting his punk and hiding it under his coat, he opened the door to listen. The wind had died down now and the rain sang musically upon the metal roofs.

He ran swiftly from house to house, and, when he had done, at the apices of the triangle he had traced three glowing coals were sputtering.

The final bolt was launched at last. He stepped down into the ditch and drew his .45, while to his tautened senses it seemed that the very hills leaned forth in breathless pause, that the rain had ceased, and the whole night hushed its thousand voices. He found his lower jaw set so stiffly that the muscles ached. Levelling his weapon at the eaves of the bunk-house, he pulled trigger rapidly—the bang, bang, bang, six times repeated, sounding dull and dead beneath the blanket of mist that overhung. A shout sounded behind him, and then the shriek of a Winchester ball close over his head. He turned in time to see another shot stream out of the darkness, where a sentry was firing at the flash of his gun, then bent himself double and plunged down the ditch.

With the first impact overhead the men poured forth from their quarters armed and bristling, to be greeted by a volley of gunshots, the thud of bullets, and the dwindling whine of spent lead. They leaped from shelter to find themselves girt with a fitful hoop of fire, for the

"Stranglers" had spread in the arc of a circle and now emptied their rifles towards the centre. The defenders, however, maintained surprising order considering the suddenness of their attack, and ran to join the sentries, whose positions could be determined by the nearer flashes. The voice of a man in authority shouted loud commands. No demonstration came from the outer voids, nothing but the wicked streaks that stabbed the darkness. Then suddenly, behind McNamara's men, the night glared luridly as though a great furnace-door had opened and then clanged shut, while with it came a hoarse thudding roar that silenced the rifle play. They saw the cook-house disrupt itself and disintegrate into a thousand flying timbers and twisted sheets of tin which soared upward and outward over their heads and into the night. As the rocking hills ceased echoing, the sound of the Vigilantes' rifles recurred like the cracking of dry sticks, then everywhere about the defenders the earth was lashed by falling debris while the iron roofs rang at the fusillade.

The blast had come at their very elbows, and they were too dazed and shaken by it to grasp its significance. Then, before they could realize what it boded, the depths lit up again till the raindrops were outlined distinct and glistening like a gossamer veil of silver, while the office building to their left was ripped and rended and the adjoining walls leaped out into sudden relief, their shattered windows looking like ghostly, sightless eyes. The curtain of darkness closed heavier than velvet, and the men cowered in their tracks, shielding themselves behind the nearest objects or behind one another's bodies, waiting for the sky to vomit over them its rain of missiles. Their backs were to the Vigilantes now, their faces to the centre. Many had dropped their rifles. The thunder of hoofs and the scream of terrified horses came from the stables. The cry of a maddened beast is weird and calculated to curdle the blood at best, but with it arose a human voice, shrieking from pain and fear of death. A wrenched and doubled mass of zinc had hurtled out of the heavens and struck some one down. The choking hoarseness of the man's appeal told the story, and those about him broke into flight to escape what might follow, to escape this danger they could not see but which swooped out of the blackness above and against which there was no defence. They fled only to witness another and greater light behind them by which they saw themselves running, falling, grovelling. This time they were hurled from their balance by a concussion which dwarfed the two preceding ones. Some few stood still, staring at the rolling smoke-bank as it was revealed by the explosion, their eyes gleaming white, while others buried their faces in their hollowed arms as if to shut out the hellish glare, or to shield themselves from a blow.

Out in the heart of the chaos rang a voice loud and clear:

"Beware the next blast!"

At the same instant the girdle of sharp-shooters rose up smiting the air with their cries and charged in like madmen through the rain of detritus. They fired as they came, but it was unnecessary, for there was no longer a fight. It was a rout. The defenders, feeling they had escaped destruction only by a happy chance in leaving the bunk-house the instant they did, were not minded to tarry here where the heavens fell upon their heads. To augment their consternation, the horses had broken from their stalls and were plunging through the confusion. Fear swept over the men—blind, unreasoning, contagious—and they rushed out into the night, colliding with their enemies, overrunning them in the panic to quit this spot. Some dashed off the bluff and fell among the pits and sluices. Others ran up the mountain-side, and cowered in the brush like quail.

As the "Stranglers" assembled their prisoners near the ruins, they heard wounded men moaning in the darkness, so lit torches and searched out the stricken ones. Glenister came running through the smoke pall, revolver in hand, crying: "Has any one seen McNamara?" No one had, and when they were later assembled to take stock of their injuries he was greeted by Dextry's gleeful announcement:

"That's the deuce of a fight. We 'ain't got so much as a cold sore among us."

"We have captured fourteen," another announced, "and there may be more out yonder in the brush."

Glenister noted with growing surprise that not one of the prisoners lined up beneath the glaring torches wore the army blue. They were miners all, or thugs and ruffians gathered from the camp. Where, he wondered, were the soldiers.

"Didn't you have troops from the barracks to help you?" he asked.

"Not a troop. We haven't seen a soldier since we went to work."

At this the young leader became alarmed. Had this whole attack miscarried? Had this been no clash with the United States forces, after all? If so, the news would never reach Washington, and instead of accomplishing his end, he and his friends had thrust themselves into the realms of outlawry, where the soldiers could be employed against them with impunity, where prices would rest upon their heads. Innocent blood had been shed, court property destroyed. McNamara had them where he wanted them at last. They were at bay.

The unwounded prisoners were taken to the boundaries of the Midas and released with such warnings as the imagination of Dextry could conjure up; then Glenister assembled his men, speaking to them plainly.

"Boys, this is no victory. In fact, we're worse off than we were before, and our biggest fight is coming. There's a chance to get away now before daylight and before we're recognized, but if we're seen here at sun-up we'll have to stay and fight. Soldiers will be sent against us, but if we hold out, and the struggle is fierce enough, it may reach to Washington. This will be a different kind of fighting now, though. It will be warfare pure and simple. How many of you will stick?"

"All of us," said they, in unison, and, accordingly, preparations for a siege were begun. Barricades were built, ruins removed, buildings transformed into blockhouses, and all through the turbulent night the tired men labored till ready to drop, led always by the young giant, who seemed without fatigue.

It was perhaps four hours after midnight when a man sought him out.

"Somebody's callin' you on the Assay Office telephone—says it's life or death."

Glenister hurried to the building, which had escaped the shock of the explosions, and, taking down the receiver, was answered by Cherry Malotte.

"Thank God, you're safe," she began. "The men have just come in and the whole town is awake over the riot. They say you've killed ten people in the fight—is it true?"

He explained to her briefly that all was well, but she broke in:

"Wait, wait! McNamara has called for troops and you'll all be shot. Oh, what a terrible night it has been! I haven't been to bed. I'm going mad. Now, listen, carefully—yesterday Helen went with Struve to the Sign of the Sled and she hasn't come back."

The man at the end of the wire cried out at this, then choked back his words to hear what followed. His free hand began making strange, futile motions as though he traced patterns in the air.

"I can't raise the road-house on the wire and—something dreadful has happened, I know."

"What made her go?" he shouted.

"To save you," came Cherry's faint reply. "If you love her, ride fast to the Sign of the Sled or you'll be too late. The Bronco Kid has gone there—"

At that name Roy crashed the instrument to its hook and burst out of the shanty, calling loudly to his men.

"What's up?"

"Where are you going?"

"To the Sign of the Sled," he panted.

"We've stood by you, Glenister, and you can't quit us like this," said one, angrily. "The trail to town is good, and we'll take it if you do." Roy saw they feared he was deserting, feared that he had heard some alarming rumor of which they did not know.

"We'll let the mine go, boys, for I can't ask you to do what I refuse to do myself, and yet it's not fear that's sending me. There's a woman in danger and I MUST go. She courted ruin to save us all, risked her honor to try and right a wrong—and—I'm afraid of what has happened while we were fighting here. I don't ask you to stay till I come back—it wouldn't be square, and you'd better go while you have a chance. As for me—I gave up the old claim once—I can do it again." He swung himself to the horse's back, settled into the saddle, and rode out through the lane of belted men.

XX

In Which Three Go to the Sign of the Sled and But Two Return

As Helen and her companion ascended the mountain, scarred and swept by the tempest of the previous night, they heard, far below, the swollen torrent brawling in its bowlder-ridden bed, while behind them the angry ocean spread southward to a blood-red horizon. Ahead, the bleak mountains brooded over forbidding valleys; to the west a suffused sun glared sullenly, painting the high-piled clouds with the gorgeous hues of a stormy sunset. To Helen the wild scene seemed dyed with the colors of flame and blood and steel.

"That rain raised the deuce with the trails," said Struve, as they picked their way past an unsightly "slip" whence a part of the overhanging mountain, loosened by the deluge, had slid into the gulch. "Another storm like that would wash out these roads completely."

Even in the daylight it was no easy task to avoid these danger spots, for the horses floundered on the muddy soil. Vaguely the girl wondered how she would find her way back in the darkness, as she had planned. She said little as they approached the road-house, for the thoughts within her brain had begun to clamor too wildly; but Struve, more arrogant than ever before, more terrifyingly sure of himself, was loudly garrulous. As they drew nearer and nearer, the dread that possessed the girl became of paralyzing intensity. If she should fail—but she vowed she would not, could not, fail.

They rounded a bend and saw the Sign of the Sled cradled below them where the trail dipped to a stream which tumbled from the comb above into the river twisting like a silver thread through the distant valley. A peeled flag-pole topped by a spruce bough stood in front of the tavern, while over the door hung a sled suspended from a beam. The house itself was a quaint structure, rambling and amorphous, from whose sod roof sprang blooming flowers, and whose high-banked walls were pierced here and there with sleepy windows. It had been built by a homesick foreigner of unknown nationality whom the army of "mushers" who paid for his clean and orderly hospitality had dubbed duly and as a matter of course a "Swede." When travel had changed to the river trail, leaving the house lonesome and high as though left by a receding wave, Struve had taken it over on a debt, and now ran it for the convenience of a slender traffic, mainly stampeders, who chose the higher route towards the interior. His hireling spent the idle hours in prospecting a hungry quartz lead and in doing assessment work on near-by claims.

Shortz took the horses and answered his employer's questions curtly, flashing a curious look at Helen. Under other conditions the girl would have been delighted with the place, for this was the quaintest spot she had found in the north country. The main room held bar and gold-scales, a rude table, and a huge iron heater, while its walls and ceiling were sheeted with white cloth so cunningly stitched and tacked that it seemed a cavern hollowed from chalk. It was filled with trophies of the hills, stuffed birds and animals, skins and antlers, from which depended, in careless confusion, dog harness, snow-shoes, guns, and articles of clothing. A door to the left led into the bunk-room where travellers had been wont to sleep in tiers three deep. To the rear was a kitchen and cache, to the right a compartment which Struve called the art gallery. Here, free reign had been allowed the original owner's artistic fancies, and he had covered the place with pictures clipped from gazettes of questionable repute till it was a bewildering arrangement of pink ladies in tights, pugilists in scanty trunks, prize bulldogs, and other less moral characters of the sporting world.

"This is probably the worst company you were ever in," Struve observed to Helen, with a forced attempt at lightness.

"Are there no guests here?" she asked him, her anxiety very near the surface.

"Travel is light at this time of the year. They'll come in later, perhaps."

A fire was burning in this pink room where the landlord had begun spreading the table for two, and its warmth was grateful to the girl. Her companion, thoroughly at his ease, stretched himself on a fur-covered couch and smoked.

"Let me see the papers, now, Mr. Struve," she began, but he put her off.

"No, not now. Business must wait on our dinner. Don't spoil our little party, for there's time enough and to spare."

She arose and went to the window, unable to sit still. Looking down the narrow gulch she saw that the mountains beyond were indistinct for it was growing dark rapidly. Dense clouds had rolled up from the east. A rain-drop struck the glass before her eyes, then another and another, and the hills grew misty behind the coming shower. A traveller with a pack on his back hurried around the corner of the building and past her to the door. At his knock, Struve, who had been watching Helen through half-shut eyes, arose and went into the other room.

"Thank Heaven, some one has come," she thought. The voices were deadened to a hum by the sod walls, till that of the stranger raised itself in such indignant protest that she distinguished his words.

"Oh, I've got money to pay my way. I'm no dead-head."

Shortz mumbled something back.

"I don't care if you are closed. I'm tired and there's a storm coming."

This time she heard the landlord's refusal and the miner's angry profanity. A moment later she saw the traveller plodding up the trail towards town.

"What does that mean?" she inquired, as the lawyer re-entered.

"Oh, that fellow is a tough, and Shortz wouldn't let him in. He's careful whom he entertains—there are so many bad men roaming the hills."

The German came in shortly to light the lamp, and, although she asked no further questions, Helen's uneasiness increased. She half listened to the stories with which Struve tried to entertain her and ate little of the excellent meal that was shortly served to them. Struve, meanwhile, ate and drank almost greedily, and the shadowy, sinister evening crept along. A strange cowardice had suddenly overtaken the girl; and if, at this late hour, she could have withdrawn, she would have done so gladly and gone forth to meet the violence of the tempest. But she had gone too far for retreat; and realizing that, for the present, apparent compliance was her wisest resource, she sat quiet, answering the man with cool words while his eyes grew brighter, his skin more flushed, his speech more rapid. He talked incessantly and with feverish gayety, smoking numberless cigarettes and apparently unconscious of the flight of time. At last he broke off suddenly and consulted his watch, while Helen remembered that she had not heard Shortz in the kitchen for a long time. Suddenly Struve smiled on her peculiarly, with confident cunning. As he leered at her over the disorder between them he took from his pocket a flat bundle which he tossed to her.

"Now for the bargain, eh?"

"Ask the man to remove these dishes," she said, as she undid the parcel with clumsy fingers.

"I sent him away two hours ago," said Struve, arising as if to come to her. She shrank back, but he only leaned across, gathered up the four corners of the tablecloth, and, twisting them together, carried the whole thing out, the dishes crashing and jangling as he threw his burden recklessly into the kitchen. Then he returned and stood with his back to the stove, staring at her while she perused the contents of the papers, which were more voluminous than she had supposed.

For a long time the girl pored over the documents. The purport of the papers was only too obvious; and, as she read, the proof of her uncle's guilt stood out clear and damning. There was no possibility of mistake; the whole wretched plot stood out plain, its darkest infamies revealed.

In spite of the cruelty of her disillusionment, Helen was nevertheless exalted with the fierce ecstasy of power, with the knowledge that justice would at last be rendered. It would be her triumph and her expiation that she, who had been the unwitting tool of this miserable clique, would be the one through whom restitution was made. She arose with her eyes gleaming and her lips set.

"It is here."

"Of course it is. Enough to convict us all. It means the penitentiary for your precious uncle and your lover." He stretched his chin upward at the mention as though to free his throat from an invisible clutch. "Yes, your lover particularly, for he's the real one. That's why I brought you here. He'll marry you, but I'll be the best man." The timbre of his voice was unpleasant.

"Come, let us go," she said.

"Go," he chuckled, mirthlessly. "That's a fine example of unconscious humor."

"What do you mean?"

"Well, first, no human being could find his way down to the coast in this tempest; second—but, by-the-way, let me explain something in those papers while I think of it." He spoke casually and stepped forward, reaching for the package, which she was about to give up, when something prompted her to snatch it behind her back; and it was well she did, for his hand was but a few inches away. He was no match for her quickness, however, and she glided around the table, thrusting the papers into the front of her dress. The sudden contact with Cherry's revolver gave her a certain comfort. She spoke now with determination.

"I intend to leave here at once. Will you bring my horse? Very well, I shall do it myself."

She turned, but his indolence vanished like a flash, and springing in front of the door he barred her way.

"Hold on, my lady. You ought to understand without my saying any more. Why did I bring you here? Why did I plan this little party? Why did I send that man away? Just to give you the proof of my complicity in a crime, I suppose. Well, hardly. You won't leave here to-night. And when you do, you won't carry those papers—my own safety depends on that and I am selfish, so don't get me started. Listen!" They caught the wail of the night crying as though hungry for sacrifice. "No, you'll stay here and—"

He broke off abruptly, for Helen had stepped to the telephone and taken down the receiver. He leaped, snatched it from her, and then, tearing the instrument loose from the wall, raised it above his head, dashed it upon the floor, and sprang towards her, but she wrenched herself free and fled across the room. The man's white hair was wildly tumbled, his face was purple, and his neck and throat showed swollen, throbbing veins. He stood still, however, and his lips cracked into his ever-present, cautious smile.

"Now, don't let's fight about this. It's no use, for I've played to win. You have your proof—now I'll have my price—or else I'll take it. Think over which it will be, while I lock up."

Far down the mountain-side a man was urging a broken pony recklessly along the trail. The beast was blown and spent, its knees weak and bending, yet the rider forced it as though behind him yelled a thousand devils, spurring headlong through gully and ford, up steep slopes and down invisible ravines. Sometimes the animal stumbled and fell with its master, sometimes they arose together, but the man was heedless of all except his haste, insensible to the rain which smote him blindingly, and to the wind which seized him savagely upon the ridges, or gasped at him in the gullies with exhausted malice. At last he gained the plateau and saw the road-house light beneath, so drove his heels into the flanks of the wind-broken creature, which lunged forward gamely. He felt the pony rear and drop away beneath him, pawing and scrambling, and instinctively kicked his feet free from the stirrups, striving to throw himself out of the saddle and clear of the thrashing hoofs. It seemed that he turned over in the air before something smote him and he lay still, his gaunt, dark face upturned to the rain, while about him the storm screamed exultantly.

The moment Struve disappeared into the outer room Helen darted to the window. It was merely a single sash, nailed fast and immovable, but seizing one of the little stools beside the stove she thrust it through the glass, letting in a smother of wind and water. Before she could escape, Struve bounded into the room, his face livid with anger, his voice hoarse and furious.

But as he began to denounce her he paused in amazement, for the girl had drawn Cherry's weapon and levelled it at him. She was very pale and her breast heaved as from a swift run, while her wondrous gray eyes were lit with a light no man had ever seen there before, glowing like two jewels whose hearts contained the pent-up passion of centuries. She had altered as though under the deft hand of a master-sculptor, her nostrils growing thin and arched, her lips tight pressed and pitiless, her head poised proudly. The rain drove in through the shattered window, over and past her, while the cheap red curtain lashed and whipped her as though in gleeful applause. Her bitter abhorrence of the man made her voice sound strangely unnatural as she commanded:

"Don't dare to stop me." She moved towards the door, motioning him to retreat before her, and he obeyed, recognizing the danger of her coolness. She did not note the calculating treachery of his glance, however, nor fathom the purposes he had in mind.

Out on the rain-swept mountain the prostrate rider had regained his senses and now was crawling painfully towards the road-house. Seen through the dark he would have resembled some misshapen, creeping monster, for he dragged himself, reptile-like, close to the ground. But as he came closer the man heard a cry which the wind seemed guarding from his ear, and, hearing it, he rose and rushed blindly forward, staggering like a wounded beast.

Helen watched her captive closely as he backed through the door before her, for she dared not lose sight of him until free. The middle room was lighted by a glass lamp on the bar and its rays showed that the front-door was secured by a large iron bolt. She thanked Heaven there was no lock and key.

Struve had retreated until his back was to the counter, offering no word, making no move, but the darting brightness of his eyes showed that he was alert and planning. But when the door behind Helen, urged by the wind through the broken casement, banged to, the man made his first lightning-like sign. He dashed the lamp to the floor, where it burst like an eggshell, and darkness leaped into the room as an animal pounces. Had she been calmer or had time for an instant's thought Helen would have hastened back to the light, but she was midway to her liberty and actuated by the sole desire to break out into the open air, so plunged forward. Without warning, she was hurled from her feet by a body which came out of the darkness upon her. She fired the little gun, but Struve's arms closed about her, the weapon was wrenched from her hand, and she found herself fighting against him, breast to breast, with the fury of desperation. His wine-burdened breath beat into her face and she felt herself bound to him as though by hoops, while the touch of his cheek against hers turned her into a terrified, insensate animal, which fought with every ounce of its strength and every nerve of its body. She screamed once, but it was not like the cry of a woman. Then the struggle went on in silence and utter blackness, Strove holding her like a gorilla till she grew faint and her head began to whirl, while darting lights drove past her eyes and there was the roar of a cataract in her ears. She was a strong girl, and her ripe young body, untried until this moment, answered in every fibre, so that she wrestled with almost a man's strength and he had hard shift to hold her. But so violent an encounter could not last. Helen felt herself drifting free from the earth and losing grip of all things tangible, when at last they tripped and fell against the inner door. This gave way, and at the same moment the man's strength departed as though it were a thing of darkness and dared not face the light that streamed over them. She tore herself from his clutch and staggered into the supper-room, her loosened hair falling in a gleaming torrent about her shoulders, while he arose from his knees and came towards her again, gasping:

"I'll show you who's master here—"

Then he ceased abruptly, cringingly, and threw up an arm before his face as if to ward off a blow. Framed in the window was the pallid visage of a man. The air rocked, the lamp flared, and Struve whirled completely around, falling back against the wall. His eyes filled with horror and shifted down where his hand had clutched at his breast, plucking at one spot as if tearing a barb from his bosom. He jerked his head towards the door at his elbow in quest of a retreat a shudder ran over him, his knees buckled and he plunged forward upon his face, his arm still doubled under him.

It had happened like a flash of light, and although Helen felt, rather than heard, the shot and saw her assailant fall, she did not realize the meaning of it till a drift of powder smoke assailed her nostrils. Even so, she experienced no shock nor horror of the sight. On the contrary, a savage joy at the spectacle seized her and she stood still, leaning slightly forward, staring at it almost gloatingly, stood so till she heard her name called, "Helen, little sister!" and, turning, saw her brother in the window.

That which he witnessed in her face he had seen before in the faces of men locked close with a hateful death and from whom all but the most elemental passions had departed—but he had never seen a woman bear the marks till now. No artifice nor falsity was there, nothing but the crudest, intensest feeling, which many people live and die without knowing. There are few who come to know the great primitive, passionate longings. But in this black night, fighting in defence of her most sacred self, this girl's nature had been stripped to its purely savage elements. As Glenister had predicted, Helen at last had felt and yielded to irresistibly powerful impulse.

Glancing backward at the creature sprawled by the door, Helen went to her brother, put her arms about his neck, and kissed him.

"He's dead?" the Kid asked her.

She nodded and tried to speak, but began to shiver and sob instead.

"Unlock the door," he begged her. "I'm hurt, and I must get in."

When the Kid had hobbled into the room, she pressed him to her and stroked his matted head, regardless of his muddy, soaking garments.

"I must look at him. He may not be badly hurt," said the Kid.

"Don't touch him!" She followed, nevertheless, and stood near by while her brother examined his victim. Struve was breathing, and, discovering this, the others lifted him with difficulty to the couch.

"Something cracked in here—ribs, I guess," the Kid remarked, gasping and feeling his own side. He was weak and pale, and the girl led him into the bunk-room, where he could lie down. Only his wonderful determination had sustained him thus far, and now the knowledge of his helplessness served to prevent Helen's collapse.

The Kid would not hear of her going for help till the storm abated or daylight came, insisting that the trails were too treacherous and that no time could be saved by doing so. Thus they waited for the dawn. At last they heard the wounded man faintly calling. He spoke to Helen hoarsely. There was no malice, only fear, in his tones:

"I said this was my madness—and I got what I deserved, but I'm going to die. O God—I'm going to die and I'm afraid." He moaned till the Bronco Kid hobbled in, glaring with unquenched hatred.

"Yes, you're going to die and I did it. Be game, can't you? I sha'n't let her go for help until daylight."

Helen forced her brother back to his couch, and returned to help the wounded man, who grew incoherent and began to babble.

A little later, when the Kid seemed stronger and his head clearer, Helen ventured to tell him of their uncle's villany and of the proof she held, with her hope of restoring justice. She told him of the attack planned that very night and of the danger which threatened the miners. He questioned her closely and, realizing the bearing of her story, crept to the door, casting the wind like a hound.

"We'll have to risk it," said he. "The wind is almost gone and it's not long till daylight."

She pleaded to go alone, but he was firm. "I'll never leave you again, and, moreover, I know the lower trail quite well. We'll go down the gulch to the valley and reach town that way. It's farther but it's not so dangerous."

"You can't ride," she insisted.

"I can if you'll tie me into the saddle. Come, get the horses."

It was still pitchy dark and the rain was pouring, but the wind only sighed weakly as though tired by its violence when she helped the Bronco into his saddle. The effort wrenched a groan from him, but he insisted upon her tying his feet beneath the horse's belly, saying that the trail was rough and he could take no chance of falling again; so, having performed the last services she might for Struve, she mounted her own animal and allowed it to pick its way down the steep descent behind her brother, who swayed and lurched drunkenly in his seat, gripping the horn before him with both hands.

They had been gone perhaps a half-hour when another horse plunged furiously out of the darkness and halted before the road-house door. Its rider, mud-stained and dishevelled, flung himself in mad haste to the ground and bolted in through the door. He saw the signs of confusion in the outer room, chairs upset and broken, the table wedged against the stove, and before the counter a shattered lamp in a pool of oil. He called loudly, but, receiving no answer, snatched a light which, he found burning and ran to the door at his left. Nothing greeted him but the empty tiers of bunks. Turning, he crossed to the other side and burst through. Another lamp was lighted beside the couch where Struve lay, breathing heavily, his lids half closed over his staring eyes. Roy noted the pool of blood at his feet and the broken window; then, setting down his lamp, he leaned over the man and spoke to him.

When he received no answer he spoke again loudly. Then, in a frenzy, Glenister shook the wounded man cruelly, so that he cried out in terror:

"I'm dying—oh, I'm dying." Roy raised the sick man up and thrust his own face before his eyes.

"This is Glenister. I've come for Helen—where is she?" A spark of recognition flickered into the dull stare.

"You're too late—I'm dying—and I'm afraid."

His questioner shook Struve again. "Where is she?" he repeated, time after time, till by very force of his own insistence he compelled realization in the sufferer.

"The Kid took her away. The Kid shot me," and then his voice rose till it flooded the room with terror. "The Kid shot me and I'm dying." He coughed blood to his lips, at which Roy laid him back and stood up. So there was no mistake, after all, and he had arrived too late. This was the Kid's revenge. This was how he struck. Lacking courage to face a man's level eyes, he possessed the foulness to prey upon a woman. Roy felt a weakening physical sickness sweep over him till his eye fell upon a sodden garment which Helen had removed from her brother's shoulders and replaced with a dry one. He snatched it from the floor and in a sudden fury felt it come apart in his hands like wet tissue-paper.

He found himself out in the rain, scanning the trampled soil by light of his lamp, and discerned tracks which the drizzle had not yet erased. He reasoned mechanically that the two riders could have no great start of him, so strode out beyond the house to see if they had gone farther into the hills. There were no tracks here, therefore they must have doubled back towards town. It did not occur to him that they might have left the beaten path and followed down the little creek to the river; but, replacing the light where he had found it, he remounted and lashed his horse into a stiff canter up towards the divide that lay between him and the city. The story was growing plainer to him, though as yet he could not piece it all together. Its possibilities stabbed him with such horror that he cried out aloud and beat his steed into faster time with both hands and feet. To think of those two ruffians fighting over this girl as though she were the spoils of pillage! He must overtake the Kid—he WOULD! The possibility that he might not threw him into such ungovernable mental chaos that he was forced to calm himself. Men went mad that way. He could not think of it. That gasping creature in the road-house spoke all too well of the Bronco's determination. And yet, who of those who had known the Kid in the past would dream that his vileness was so utter as this?

Away to the right, hidden among the shadowed hills, his friends rested themselves for the coming battle, waiting impatiently his return, and timing it to the rising sun. Down in the valley to his left were the two he followed, while he, obsessed and unreasoning, now cursing like a madman, now grim and silent, spurred southward towards town and into the ranks of his enemies.

XXI

THE HAMMER-LOCK

Day was breaking as Glenister came down the mountain. With the first light he halted to scan the trail, and having no means of knowing that the fresh tracks he found were not those of the two riders he followed, he urged his lathered horse ahead till he became suddenly conscious that he was very tired and had not slept for two days and nights. The recollection did not reassure the young man, for his body was a weapon which must not fail in the slightest measure now that there was work to do. Even the unwelcome speculation upon his physical handicap offered relief, however, from the agony which fed upon him whenever he thought of Helen in the gambler's hands. Meanwhile, the horse, groaning at his master's violence, plunged onward towards the roofs of Nome, now growing gray in the first dawn.

It seemed years since Roy had seen the sunlight, for this night, burdened with suspense, had been endlessly long. His body was faint beneath the strain, and yet he rode on and on, tired, dogged, stony, his eyes set towards the sea, his mind a storm of formless, whirling thoughts, beneath which was an undeviating, implacable determination.

He knew now that he had sacrificed all hope of the Midas, and likewise the hope of Helen was gone; in fact, he began to realize dimly that from the beginning he had never had the possibility of winning her, that she had never been destined for him, and that his love for her had been sent as a light by which he was to find himself. He had failed everywhere, he had become an outlaw, he had fought and gone down, certain only of his rectitude and the mastery of his unruly spirit. Now the hour had come when he would perform his last mission, deriving therefrom that satisfaction which the gods could not deny. He would have his vengeance.

The scheme took form without conscious effort on his part and embraced two things—the death of the gambler and a meeting with McNamara. Of the former, he had no more doubt than that the sun rising there would sink in the west. So well confirmed was this belief that the details did not engage his thought; but on the result of the other encounter he speculated with some interest. From the first McNamara had been a riddle to him, and mystery breeds curiosity. His blind, instinctive hatred of the man had assumed the proportions of a mania; but as to what the outcome would be when they met face to face, fate alone could tell. Anyway, McNamara should never have Helen—Roy believed his mission covered that point as well as her deliverance from the Bronco Kid. When he had finished—he would pay the price. If he had the luck to escape, he would go back to his hills and his solitude; if he did not, his future would be in the hands of his enemies.

He entered the silent streets unobserved, for the mists were heavy and low. Smoke columns arose vertically in the still air. The rain had ceased, having beaten down the waves which rumbled against the beach, filling the streets with their subdued thunder. A ship, anchored in the offing, had run in from the lee of Sledge Island with the first lull, while midway to the shore a tender was rising and falling, its oars flashing like the silvered feelers of a sea insect crawling upon the surface of the ocean.

He rode down Front Street heedless of danger, heedless of the comment his appearance might create, and, unseen, entered his enemy's stronghold. He passed a gambling-hall, through the windows of which came a sickly yellow gleam. A man came out unsteadily and stared at the horseman, then passed on.

Glenister's plan was to go straight to the Northern and from there to track down its owner relentlessly, but in order to reach the place his course led him past the office of Dunham & Struve. This brought back to his mind the man dying out there ten miles at his back. The scantiest humanity demanded that assistance be sent at once. Yet he dared not give word openly, thus betraying his presence, for it was necessary that he maintain his liberty during the next hour at all hazards. He suddenly thought of an expedient and reined in his horse, which stopped with wide-spread legs and dejected head while he dismounted and climbed the stairs to leave a note upon the door. Some one would see the message shortly and recognize its urgency.

In dressing for the battle at the Midas on the previous night he had replaced his leather boots with "mukluks," which are waterproof, light, and pliable footgear made from the skin of seal and walrus. He was thus able to move as noiselessly as though in moccasins. Finding neither pencil nor paper in his pocket, he tried the outer door of the office, to find it unlocked. He stepped inside and listened, then moved towards a table on which were writing materials, but in doing so heard a rustle in Struve's private office. Evidently his soft soles had not disturbed the man inside. Roy was about to tiptoe out as he had come when the hidden man cleared his throat. It is in these involuntary sounds that the voice retains its natural quality more distinctly even than in speaking, A strange eagerness grew in Glenister's face and he approached the partition stealthily. It was of wood and glass, the panes clouded and opaque to a height of some six feet; but stepping upon a chair he peered into the room beyond. A man knelt in a litter of papers before the open safe, its drawers and compartments removed and their contents scattered. The watcher lowered himself, drew his gun, and laid soft hand upon the door-knob, turning the latch with firm fingers. His vengeance had come to meet him.

After lying in wait during the long night, certain that the Vigilantes would spring his trap, McNamara was astounded at news of the battle at the Midas and of Glenister's success. He stormed and cursed his men as cowards. The Judge became greatly exercised over this new development, which, coupled with his night of long anxiety, reduced him to a pitiful hysteria.

"They'll blow us up next. Great Heavens! Dynamite! Oh, that is barbarous. For Heaven's sake, get the soldiers out, Alec."

"Ay, we can use them now." Thereupon McNamara roused the commanding officer at the post and requested him to accoutre a troop and have them ready to march at daylight, then bestirred the Judge to start the wheels of his court and invoke this military aid in regular fashion.

"Make it all a matter of record," he said. "We want to keep our skirts clear from now on."

"But the towns-people are against us," quavered Stillman. "They'll tear us to pieces."

"Let 'em try. Once I get my hand on the ringleader, the rest may riot and be damned."

Although he had made less display than had the Judge, the receiver was no less deeply worried about Helen, of whom no news came. His jealousy, fanned to red heat by the discovery of her earlier defection, was enhanced fourfold by the thought of this last adventure. Something told him there was treachery afoot, and when she did not return at dawn he began to fear that she had cast in her lot with the rioters. This aroused a perfect delirium of doubt and anger till he reasoned further that Struve, having gone with her, must also be a traitor. He recognized the menace in this fact, knowing the man's venality, so began to reckon carefully its significance. What could Struve do? What proof had he? McNamara started, and, seizing his hat, hurried straight to the lawyer's office and let himself in with the key he carried. It was light enough for him to decipher the characters on the safe lock as he turned the combination, so he set to work scanning the endless bundles within, hoping that after all the man had taken with him no incriminating evidence. Once the searcher paused at some fancied sound, but when nothing came of it drew his revolver and laid it before him just inside the safe door and close beneath his hand, continuing to run through the documents while his uneasiness increased. He had been engaged so for some time when he heard the faintest creak at his back, too slight to alarm and just sufficient to break his tension and cause him to jerk his head about. Framed in the open door stood Roy Glenister watching him.

McNamara's astonishment was so genuine that he leaped to his feet, faced about, and prompted by a secretive instinct swung to the safe door as though to guard its contents. He had acted upon the impulse before realizing that his weapon was inside and that now, although the door was not locked, it would require that one dangerous, yes, fatal, second to open it.

The two men stared at each other for a time, silent and malignant, their glances meeting like blades; in the older man's face a look of defiance, in the younger's a dogged and grim-purposed enmity. McNamara's first perturbation left him calm, alert, dangerous; whereas the continued contemplation of his enemy worked in Glenister to destroy his composure, and his purpose blazed forth unhidden.

He stood there unkempt and soiled, the clean sweep of jaw and throat overgrown with a three days' black stubble, his hair wet and matted, his whole left side foul with clay where he had fallen in the darkness. A muddy red streak spread downward from a cut above his temple, beneath his eyes were sagging folds, while the flicker at his mouth corners betrayed the high nervous pitch to which he was keyed.

"I have come for the last act, McNamara; now we'll have it out, man to man."

The politician shrugged his shoulders. "You have the drop on me. I am unarmed." At which the miner's face lighted fiercely and he chuckled.

"Ah, that's almost too good to be true. I have dreamed about such a thing and I have been hungry to feel your throat since the first time I saw you. It's grown on me till shooting wouldn't satisfy me. Ever had the feeling? Well, I'm going to choke the life out of you with my bare hands."

McNamara squared himself.

"I wouldn't advise you to try it. I have lived longer than you and I was never beaten, but I know the feeling you speak about. I have it now."

His eyes roved rapidly up and down the other's form, noting the lean thighs and close-drawn belt which lent the appearance of spareness, belied only by the neck and shoulders. He had beaten better men, and he reasoned that if it came to a physical test in these cramped quarters his own great weight would more than offset any superior agility the miner might possess. The longer he looked the more he yielded to his hatred of the man before him, and the more cruelly he longed to satisfy it.

"Take off your coat," said Glenister. "Now turn around. All right! I just wanted to see if you were lying about your gun."

"I'll kill you," cried McNamara.

Glenister laid his six-shooter upon the safe and slipped off his own wet garment. The difference was more marked now and the advantage more strongly with the receiver. Though they had avoided allusion to it, each knew that this fight had nothing to do with the Midas and each realized whence sprang their fierce enmity. And it was meet that they should come together thus. It had been the one certain and logical event which they had felt inevitably approaching from long back. And it was fitting, moreover, that they should fight alone and unwitnessed, armed only with the weapons of the wilderness, for they were both of the far, free lands, were both of the fighter's type, and had both warred for the first, great prize.

They met ferociously. McNamara aimed a fearful blow, but Glenister met him squarely, beating him off cleverly, stepping in and out, his arms swinging loosely from his shoulders like whalebone withes tipped with lead. He moved lightly, his footing made doubly secure by reason of his soft-soled mukluks. Recognizing his opponent's greater weight, he undertook merely to stop the headlong rushes and remain out of reach as long as possible. He struck the politician fairly in the mouth so that the man's head snapped back and his fists went wild, then, before the arms could grasp him, the miner had broken ground and whipped another blow across; but McNamara was a boxer himself, so covered and blocked it. The politician spat through his mashed lips and rushed again, sweeping his opponent from his feet. Again Glenister's fist shot forward like a lump of granite, but the other came on head down and the blow finished too high, landing on the big man's brow. A sudden darting agony paralyzed Roy's hand, and he realized that he had broken the metacarpal bones and that henceforth it would be useless. Before he could recover, McNamara had passed under his extended arm and seized him by the middle, then, thrusting his left leg back of Roy's, he whirled him from his balance, flinging him clear and with resistless force. It seemed that a fatal fall must follow, but the youth squirmed catlike in the air, landing with set muscles which rebounded like rubber. Even so, the receiver was upon him before he could rise, reaching for the young man's throat with his heavy hands. Roy recognized the fatal "strangle hold," and, seizing his enemy's wrists, endeavored to tear them apart, but his left hand was useless, so with a mighty wrench he freed himself, and, locked in each other's arms, the men strained and swayed about the office till their neck veins were bursting, their muscles paralyzed.

Men may fight duels calmly, may shoot or parry or thrust with cold deliberation; but when there comes the jar of body to body, the sweaty contact of skin to skin, the play of iron muscles, the painful gasp of exhaustion—then the mind goes skittering back into its dark recesses while every venomous passion leaps forth from its hiding-place and joins in the horrid war.

They tripped across the floor, crashing into the partition, which split, showering them with glass. They fell and rolled in it; then, by consent, wrenched themselves apart and rose, eye to eye, their jaws hanging, their lungs wheezing, their faces trickling blood and sweat. Roy's left hand pained him excruciatingly, while McNamara's macerated lips had turned outward in a hideous pout. They crouched so for an instant, cruel, bestial—then clinched again. The office-fittings were wrecked utterly and the room became a litter of ruins. The men's garments fell away till their breasts were bare and their arms swelled white and knotted through the rags. They knew no pain, their bodies were insensate mechanisms.

Gradually the older man's face was beaten into a shapeless mass by the other's cunning blows, while Glenister's every bone was wrenched and twisted under his enemy's terrible onslaughts. The miner's chief effort, it is true, was to keep his feet and to break the man's embraces. Never had he encountered one whom he could not beat by sheer strength till he met this great, snarling creature who worried him hither and yon as though he were a child. Time and again Roy beat upon the man's face with the blows of a sledge. No rules governed this solitary combat; the men were deaf to all but the roaring in their ears, blinded to all but hate, insensible to everything but the blood mania. Their trampling feet caused the building to rumble and shake as though some monster were running amuck.

Meanwhile a bareheaded man rushed out of the store beneath, bumping into a pedestrian who had paused on the sidewalk, and together they scurried up the stairs. The dory which Roy had seen at sea had shot the breakers, and now its three passengers were tracking through the wet sand towards Front Street, Bill Wheaton in the lead. He was followed by two rawboned men who travelled without baggage. The city was awakening with the sun which reared a copper rim out of the sea—Judge Stillman and Voorhees came down from the hotel and paused to gaze through the mists at a caravan of mule teams which trotted into the other end of the street with jingle and clank. The wagons were blue with soldiers, the early golden rays slanting from their Krags, and they were bound for the Midas.

Out of the fogs which clung so thickly to the tundra there came two other horses, distorted and unreal, on one a girl, on the other a figure of pain and tragedy, a grotesque creature that swayed stiffly to the motion of its steed, its face writhed into lines of suffering, its hands clutching cantle and horn.

It was as though Fate, with invisible touch, were setting her stage for the last act of this play, assembling the principals close to the Golden Sands where first they had made entrance.

The man and the girl came face to face with the Judge and marshal, who cried out upon seeing them, but as they reined in, out from the stairs beside them a man shot amid clatter and uproar.

"Give me a hand—quick!" he shouted to them.

"What's up?" inquired the marshal.

"It's murder! McNamara and Glenister!" He dashed back up the steps behind Voorhees, the Judge following, while muffled cries came from above.

The gambler turned towards the three men who were hurrying from the beach, and, recognizing Wheaton, called to him: "Untie my feet! Cut the ropes! Quick!"

"What's the trouble?" the lawyer asked, but on hearing Glenister's name bounded after the Judge, leaving one of his companions to free the rider. They could hear the fight now, and all crowded towards the door, Helen with her brother, in spite of his warning to stay behind.

She never remembered how she climbed those stairs, for she was borne along by that hypnotic power which drags one to behold a catastrophe in spite of his will. Reaching the room, she stood appalled; for the group she had joined watched two raging things that rushed at each other with inhuman cries, ragged, bleeding, fighting on a carpet of debris. Every loose and breakable thing had been ground to splinters as though by iron slugs in a whirling cylinder.

To this day, from Dawson to the Straits, from Unga to the Arctics, men tell of the combat wherever they foregather at flaring camp-fires or in dingy bunkhouses; and although some scout the tale, there are others who saw it and can swear to its truth. These say that the encounter was like the battle of bull moose in the rutting season, though more terrible, averring that two men like these had never been known in the land since the days of Vitus Bering and his crew; for their rancor had swollen till at feel of each other's flesh they ran mad and felt superhuman strength. It is true, at any rate, that neither was conscious of the filling room, nor the cries of the crowd, even when the marshal forced himself through the wedged door and fell upon the nearest, which was Glenister. He came at an instant when the two had paused at arm's-length, glaring with rage-drunken eyes, gasping the labored breath back into their lungs.

With a fling of his long arms the young man hurled the intruder aside so violently that his head struck the iron safe and he collapsed insensible. Then, without apparent notice of the interruption, the fight went on. It was seen during this respite that McNamara's mouth was running water as though he were deathly sick, while every retch brought forth a groan. Helen heard herself crying: "Stop them! Stop them!" But no one seemed capable of interference. She heard her brother muttering and his breath coming heavily like that of the fighters, his body swaying in time to theirs. The Judge was ashy, imbecile, helpless.

McNamara's distress was patent to his antagonist, who advanced upon him with the hunger of promised victory; but the young man's muscles obeyed his commands sluggishly, his ribs seemed broken, his back was weak, and on the inner side of his legs the flesh was quivering. As they came together the boss reached up his right hand and caught the miner by the face, burying thumb and fingers crab like into his cheeks, forcing his slack jaws apart, thrusting his head backward, while he centred every ounce of his strength in the effort to maim. Roy felt the flesh giving way and flung himself backward to break the hold, whereupon the other summoned his wasting energy and plunged towards the safe, where lay the revolver. Instinct warned Glenister of treachery, told him that the man had sought this last resource to save himself, and as he saw him turn his back and reach for the weapon, the youth leaped like a panther, seizing him about the waist, grasping McNamara's wrist with his right hand. For the first time during the combat they were not face to face, and on the instant Roy realized the advantage given him through the other's perfidy, realized the wrestler's hold that was his, and knew that the moment of victory was come.

The telling takes much time, but so quickly had these things happened that the footsteps of the soldiers had not yet reached the door when the men were locked beside the safe.

Of what happened next many garbled accounts have gone forth, for of all those present, none but the Bronco Kid knew its significance and ever recounted the truth concerning it. Some claim that the younger man was seized with a fear of death which multiplied his enormous strength, others that the power died in his adversary as reward for his treason; but it was not so.

No sooner had Roy encompassed McNamara's waist from the rear than he slid his damaged hand up past the other's chest and around the back of his neck, thus bringing his own left arm close under his enemy's left armpit, wedging the receiver's head forward, while with his other hand he grasped the politician's right wrist close to the revolver, thus holding him in a grasp which could not be broken. Now came the test. The two bodies set themselves rocklike and rigid. There was no lunging about. Calling up the final atom of his strength, Glenister bore backward with his right arm and it became a contest for the weapon which, clutched in the two hands, swayed back and forth or darted up and down, the fury of resistance causing it to trace formless patterns in the air with its muzzle. McNamara shook himself, but he was close against the safe and could not escape, his head bowed forward by the lock of the miner's left arm, and so he strained till the breath clogged in his throat. Despite the grievous toil his right hand moved back slightly. His feet shifted a bit, while the blood seemed bursting from his eyes, but he found that the long fingers encircling his wrist were like gyves weighted with the strength of the hills and the irresistible vigor of youth which knew no defeat. Slowly, inch by inch, the great man's arm was dragged back, down past his side, while the strangling labor of his breath showed at what awful cost. The muzzle of the gun described a semicircle and the knotted hands began to travel towards the left, more rapidly now, across his broad back. Still he struggled and wrenched, but uselessly. He strove to fire the weapon, but his fingers were woven about it so that the hammer would not work. Then the miner began forcing upward.

The white skin beneath the men's strips of clothing was stretched over great knots and ridges which sunk and swelled and quivered. Helen, watching in silent terror, felt her brother sinking his fingers into her shoulder and heard him panting, his face ablaze with excitement, while she became conscious that he had repeated time and again:

"It's the hammer-lock—the hammer-lock."

By now McNamara's arm was bent and cramped upon his back, and then they saw Glenister's shoulder dip, his elbow come closer to his side, and his body heave in one final terrific effort as though pushing a heavy weight. In the silence something snapped like a stick. There came a deafening report and the scream of a strong man overcome with agony. McNamara went to his knees and sagged forward on to his face as though every bone in his huge bulk had turned to water, while his master reeled back against the opposite wall, his heels dragging in the litter, bringing up with outflung arms as though fearful of falling, swaying, blind, exhausted, his face blackened by the explosion of the revolver, yet grim with the light of victory.

Judge Stillman shouted, hysterically:

"Arrest that man, quick! Don't let him go!"

It was the miner's first realization that others were there. Raising his head he stared at the faces close against the partition, then groaned the words:

"I beat the traitor and—and—I broke him with—my hands!"

XXII

The Promise of Dreams

Soldiers seized the young man, who made no offer at resistance, and the room became a noisy riot. Crowds surged up from below, clamoring, questioning, till some one at the head of the stairs shouted down:

"They've got Roy Glenister. He's killed McNamara," at which a murmur arose that threatened to become a cheer.

Then one of the receiver's faction called: "Let's hang him. He killed ten of our men last night." Helen winced, but Stillman, roused to a sort of malevolent courage, quieted the angry voices.

"Officer, hold these people back. I'll attend to this man. The law's in my hands and I'll make him answer."

McNamara reared himself groaning from the floor, his right arm swinging from the shoulder strangely loose and distorted, with palm twisted outward, while his battered face was hideous with pain and defeat. He growled broken maledictions at his enemy.

Roy, meanwhile, said nothing, for as the savage lust died in him he realized that the whirling faces before him were the faces of his enemies, that the Bronco Kid was still at large, and that his vengeance was but half completed. His knees were bending, his limbs were like leaden bars, his chest a furnace of coals. As he reeled down the lane of human forms, supported by his guards, he came abreast of the girl and her companion and paused, clearing his vision slowly.

"Ah, there you are!" he said, thickly, to the gambler, and began to wrestle with his captors, baring his teeth in a grimace of painful effort; but they held him as easily as though he were a child and drew him forward, his body sagging limply, his face turned back over his shoulder.

They had him near the door when Wheaton barred their way, crying: "Hold up a minute—it's all right, Roy—"

"Ay, Bill—it's all right. We did our—best, but we were done by a damned blackguard. Now he'll send me up—but I don't care. I broke him—with my naked hands. Didn't I, McNamara?" He mocked unsteadily at the boss, who cursed aloud in return, glowering like an evil mask, while Stillman ran up dishevelled and shrilly irascible.

"Take him away, I tell you! Take him to jail."

But Wheaton held his place while the room centred its eyes upon him, scenting some unexpected denouement. He saw it, and in concession to a natural vanity and dramatic instinct, he threw back his head and stuffed his hands into his coat-pockets while the crowd waited. He grinned insolently at the Judge and the receiver.

"This will be a day of defeats and disappointments to you, my friends. That boy won't go to jail because you will wear the shackles yourselves. Oh, you played a shrewd game, you two, with your senators, your politics, and your pulls; but it's our turn now, and we'll make you dance for the mines you gutted and the robberies you've done and the men you've ruined. Thank Heaven there's ONE honest court and I happened to find it." He turned to the strangers who had accompanied him from the ship, crying, "Serve those warrants," and they stepped forward.

The uproar of the past few minutes had brought men running from every direction till, finding no room on the stairs, they had massed in the street below while the word flew from lip to lip concerning this closing scene of their drama, the battle at the Midas, the great fight up-stairs, and the arrest by the 'Frisco deputies. Like Sindbad's genie, a wondrous tale took shape from the rumors. Men shouldered one another eagerly for a glimpse of the actors, and when the press streamed out, greeted it with volleys of questions. They saw the unconscious marshal borne forth, followed by the old Judge, now a palsied wretch, slinking beside his captor, a very shell of a man at whom they jeered. When McNamara lurched into view, an image of defeat and chagrin, their voices rose menacingly. The pack was turning and he knew it, but, though racked and crippled, he bent upon them a visage so full of defiance and contemptuous malignity that they hushed themselves, and their final picture of him was that of a big man downed, but unbeaten to the last. They began to cry for Glenister, so that when he loomed in the doorway, a ragged, heroic figure, his heavy shock low over his eyes, his unshaven face aggressive even in its weariness, his corded arms and chest bare beneath the fluttering streamers, the street broke into wild cheering. Here was a man of their own, a son of the Northland who labored and loved and fought in a way they understood, and he had come into his due.

But Roy, dumb and listless, staggered up the street, refusing the help of every man except Wheaton. He heard his companion talking, but grasped only that the attorney gloated and gloried.

"We have whipped them, boy. We have whipped them at their own game. Arrested in their very door-yards—cited for contempt of court—that's what they are. They disobeyed those other writs, and so I got them."

"I broke his arm," muttered the miner.

"Yes, I saw you do it! Ugh! it was an awful thing. I couldn't prove conspiracy, but they'll go to jail for a little while just the same, and we have broken the ring."

"It snapped at the shoulder," the other continued, dully, "just like a shovel handle. I felt it—but he tried to kill me and I had to do it."

The attorney took Roy to his cabin and dressed his wounds, talking incessantly the while, but the boy was like a sleep-walker, displaying no elation, no excitement, no joy of victory. At last Wheaton broke out:

"Cheer up! Why, man, you act like a loser. Don't you realize that we've won? Don't you understand that the Midas is yours? And the whole world with it?"

"Won?" echoed the miner. "What do you know about it, Bill? The Midas—the world—what good are they? You're wrong. I've lost—yes—I've lost everything she taught me, and by some damned trick of Fate she was there to see me do it. Now, go away; I want to sleep."

He sank upon the bed with its tangle of blankets and was unconscious before the lawyer had covered him over.

There he lay like a dead man till late in the afternoon, when Dextry and Slapjack came in from the hills, answering Wheaton's call, and fell upon him hungrily. They shook Roy into consciousness with joyous riot, pommelling him with affectionate roughness till he rose and joined with them stiffly. He bathed and rubbed the soreness from his muscles, emerging physically fit. They made him recount his adventures to the tiniest detail, following his description of the fight with absorbed interest till Dextry broke into mournful complaint:

"I'd have give my half of the Midas to see you bust him. Lord, I'd have screeched with soopreme delight at that."

"Why didn't you gouge his eyes out when you had him crippled?" questioned Slapjack, vindictively. "I'd 'a' done it."

Dextry continued: "They tell me that when he was arrested he swore in eighteen different languages, each one more refreshin'ly repulsive an' vig'rous than the precedin'. Oh, I have sure missed a-plenty to-day, partic'lar because my own diction is gettin' run down an' skim-milky of late, showin' sad lack of new ideas. Which I might have assim'lated somethin' robustly original an' expressive if I'd been here. No, sir; a nose-bag full of nuggets wouldn't have kept me away."

"How did it sound when she busted?" insisted the morbid Simms, but Glenister refused to discuss his combat.

"Come on, Slap," said the old prospector, "let's go down-town. I'm so het up I can't set still, an' besides, mebbe we can get the story the way it really happened, from somebody who ain't bound an' gagged an' chloroformed by such unbecomin' modesties. Roy, don't never go into vawdyville with them personal episodes, because they read about as thrillin' as a cook-book. Why, say, I've had the story of that fight from four different fellers already, none of which was within four blocks of the scrimmage, an' they're all diff'rent an' all better 'n your account."

Now that Glenister's mind had recovered some of its poise he realized what he had done.

"I was a beast, an animal," he groaned, "and that after all my striving. I wanted to leave that part behind, I wanted to be worthy of her love and trust even though I never won it, but at the first test I am found lacking. I have lost her confidence, yes—and what is worse, infinitely worse, I have lost my own. She's always seen me at my worst," he went on, "but I'm not that kind at bottom, not that kind. I want to do what's right, and if I have another chance I will, I know I will. I've been tried too hard, that's all."

Some one knocked, and he opened the door to admit the Bronco Kid and Helen.

"Wait a minute, old man," said the Kid. "I'm here as a friend." The gambler handled himself with difficulty, offering in explanation:

"I'm all sewed up in bandages of one kind or another."

"He ought to be in bed now, but he wouldn't let me come alone, and I could not wait," the girl supplemented, while her eyes avoided Glenister's in strange hesitation.

"He wouldn't let you. I don't understand."

"I'm her brother," announced the Bronco Kid. "I've known it for a long time, but I—I—well, you understand I couldn't let her know. All I can say is, I've gambled square till the night I played you, and I was as mad as a dervish then, blaming you for the talk I'd heard. Last night I learned by chance about Struve and Helen and got to the road-house in time to save her. I'm sorry I didn't kill him." His long white fingers writhed about the arm of his chair at the memory.

"Isn't he dead?" Glenister inquired.

"No. The doctors have brought him in and he'll get well. He's like half the men in Alaska—here because the sheriffs back home couldn't shoot straight. There's something else. I'm not a good talker, but give me time and I'll manage it so you'll understand. I tried to keep Helen from coming on this errand, but she said it was the square thing and she knows better than I. It's about those papers she brought in last spring. She was afraid you might consider her a party to the deal, but you don't, do you?" He glared belligerently, and Roy replied, with fervor:

"Certainly not. Go on."

"Well, she learned the other day that those documents told the whole story and contained enough proof to break up this conspiracy and convict the Judge and McNamara and all the rest, but Struve kept the bundle in his safe and wouldn't give it up without a price. That's why she went away with him—She thought it was right, and—that's all. But it seems Wheaton had succeeded in another way. Now, I'm coming to the point. The Judge and McNamara are arrested for contempt of court and they're as good as convicted; you have recovered your mine, and these men are disgraced. They will go to jail—"

"Yes, for six months, perhaps," broke in the other, hotly, "but what does that amount to? There never was a bolder crime consummated nor one more cruelly unjust. They robbed a realm and pillaged its people, they defiled a court and made Justice a wanton, they jailed good men and sent others to ruin; and for this they are to suffer—how? By a paltry fine or a short imprisonment, perhaps, by an ephemeral disgrace and the loss of their stolen goods. Contempt of court is the accusation, but you might as well convict a murderer for breach of the peace. We've thrown them off, it's true, and they won't trouble us again, but they'll never have to answer for their real infamy. That will go unpunished while their lawyers quibble over technicalities and rules of court. I guess it's true that there isn't any law of God or man north of Fifty-three; but if there is justice south of that mark, those people will answer for conspiracy and go to the penitentiary."

"You make it hard for me to say what I want to. I am almost sorry we came, for I am not cunning with words, and I don't know that you'll understand," said the Bronco Kid, gravely, "We looked at it this way: you have had your victory, you have beaten your enemies against odds, you have recovered your mine, and they are disgraced. To men like them that last will outlive and outweigh all the rest; but the Judge is our uncle and our blood runs in his veins. He took Helen when she was a baby and was a father to her in his selfish way, loving her as best he knew how. And she loves him."

"I don't quite understand you," said Roy.

And then Helen spoke for the first time eagerly, taking a packet from her bosom as she began:

"This will tell the whole wretched story, Mr. Glenister, and show the plot in all its vileness. It's hard for me to betray my uncle, but this proof is yours by right to use as you see fit, and I can't keep it."

"Do you mean that this evidence will show all that? And you're going to give it to me because you think it is your duty?"

"It belongs to you. I have no choice. But what I came for was to plead and to ask a little mercy for my uncle, who is an old, old man, and very weak. This will kill him."

He saw that her eyes were swimming while the little chin quivered ever so slightly and her pale cheeks were flushed. There rose in him the old wild desire to take her in his arms, a yearning to pillow her head on his shoulder and kiss away the tears, to smooth with tender caress the wavy hair, and bury his face deep in it till he grew drunk with the madness of her. But he knew at last for whom she really pleaded.

So he was to forswear this vengeance, which was no vengeance after all, but in verity a just punishment. They asked him—a man—a man's man—a Northman—to do this, and for what? For no reward, but on the contrary to insure himself lasting bitterness. He strove to look at the proposition calmly, clearly, but it was difficult. If only by freeing this other villain as well as her uncle he would do a good to her, then he would not hesitate. Love was not the only thing. He marvelled at his own attitude; this could not be his old self debating thus. He had asked for another chance to show that he was not the old Roy Glenister; well, it had come, and he was ready.

Roy dared not look at Helen any more, for this was the hardest moment he had ever lived.

"You ask this for your uncle, but what of—of the other fellow? You must know that if one goes free so will they both; they can't be separated."

"It's almost too much to ask," the Kid took up, uncertainly. "But don't you think the work is done? I can't help but admire McNamara, and neither can you—he's been too good an enemy to you for that—and—and—he loves Helen."

"I know—I know," said Glenister, hastily, at the same time stopping an unintelligible protest from the girl. "You've said enough." He straightened his slightly stooping shoulders and looked at the unopened package wearily, then slipped the rubber band from it, and, separating the contents, tore them up—one by one—tore them into fine bits without hurry or ostentation, and tossed the fragments away, while the woman began to sob softly, the sound of her relief alone disturbing the silence. And so he gave her his enemy, making his offer gamely, according to his code.

"You're right—the work is done. And now, I'm very tired."

They left him standing there, the glory of the dying day illumining his lean, brown features, the vision of a great loneliness in his weary eyes.

He did not rouse himself till the sky before him was only a curtain of steel, pencilled with streaks of soot that lay close down above the darker sea. Then he sighed and said, aloud:

"So this is the end, and I gave him to her with these hands"—he held them out before him curiously, becoming conscious for the first time that the left one was swollen and discolored and fearfully painful. He noted it with impersonal interest, realizing its need of medical attention—so left the cabin and walked down into the city. He encountered Dextry and Simms on the way, and they went with him, both flowing with the gossip of the camp.

"Lord, but you're the talk of the town," they began. "The curio hunters have commenced to pull Struve's office apart for souvenirs, and the Swedes want to run you for Congress as soon as ever we get admitted as a State. They say that at collar-an'-elbow holts you could lick any of them Eastern senators and thereby rastle out a lot of good legislation for us cripples up here."

"Speakin' of laws goes to show me that this here country is gettin' too blamed civilized for a white man," said Simms, pessimistically, "and now that this fight is ended up it don't look like there would be anything doin' fit to claim the interest of a growed-up person for a long while. I'm goin' west."

"West! Why, you can throw a stone into Bering Strait from here," said Roy, smiling.

"Oh, well, the world's round. There's a schooner outfittin' for Sibeery—two years' cruise. Me an' Dex is figgerin' on gettin' out towards the frontier fer a spell."

"Sure!" said Dextry. "I'm beginnin' to feel all cramped up hereabouts owin' to these fillymonarch orchestras an' French restarawnts and such discrepancies of scenery. They're puttin' a pavement on Front Street and there's a shoe-shinin' parlor opened up. Why, I'd like to get where I could stretch an' holler without disturbin' the pensiveness of some dude in a dress suit. Better come along, Roy; we can sell out the Midas."

"I'll think it over," said the young man.

The night was bright with a full moon when they left the doctor's office. Roy, in no mood for the exuberance of his companions, parted from them, but had not gone far before he met Cherry Malotte. His head was low and he did not see her till she spoke.

"Well, boy, so it's over at last!"

Her words chimed so perfectly with his thoughts that he replied: "Yes, it's all over, little girl."

"You don't need my congratulations—you know me too well for that. How does it feel to be a winner?"

"I don't know. I've lost."

"Lost what?"

"Everything—except the gold-mine."

"Everything except—I see. You mean that she—that you have asked her and she won't?" He never knew the cost at which she held her voice so steady.

"More than that. It's so new that it hurts yet, and it will continue to hurt for a long time, I suppose—but to-morrow I am going back to my hills and my valleys, back to the Midas and my work, and try to begin all over. For a time I've wandered in strange paths, seeking new gods, as it were, but the dazzle has died out of my eyes and I can see true again. She isn't for me, although I shall always love her. I'm sorry I can't forget easily, as some do. It's hard to look ahead and take an interest in things. But what about you? Where shall you go?"

"I don't know. It doesn't really matter—now." The dusk hid her white, set face and she spoke monotonously. "I am going to see the Bronco Kid. He sent for me. He's ill."

"He's not a bad sort," said Roy. "And I suppose he'll make a new start, too."

"Perhaps," said she, gazing far out over the gloomy ocean. "It all depends." After a moment, she added, "What a pity that we can't all sponge off the slate and begin afresh and—forget."

"It's part of the game," said he. "I don't know why it's so, but it is. I'll see you sometimes, won't I?"

"No, boy—I think not."

"I believe I understand," he murmured; "and perhaps it's better so." He took her two soft hands in his one good right and kissed them. "God bless you and keep you, dear, brave little Cherry."

She stood straight and still as he melted into the shadows, and only the moonlight heard her pitiful sob and her hopeless whisper:

"Good-bye, my boy, my boy."

He wandered down beside the sea, for his battle was not yet won, and until he was surer of himself he could not endure the ribaldry and rejoicing of his fellows. A welcome lay waiting for him in every public place, but no one there could know the mockery of it, no one could gauge the desolation that was his.

The sand, wet, packed, and hard as a pavement, gave no sound to his careless steps; and thus it was that he came silently upon the one woman as she stood beside the silver surf. Had he seen her first he would have slunk past in the landward shadows; but, recognizing his tall form, she called and he came, while it seemed that his lungs grew suddenly constricted, as though bound about with steel hoops. The very pleasure of her sight pained him. He advanced eagerly, and yet with hesitation, standing stiffly aloof while his heart fluttered and his tongue grew dumb. At last she saw his bandages and her manner changed abruptly. Coming closer she touched them with caressing fingers.

"It's nothing—nothing at all," he said, while his voice jumped out of all control. "When are you—going away?"

"I do not know—not for some time."

He had supposed she would go to-morrow with her uncle and—the other, to be with them through their travail.

With warm impetuosity she began: "It was a noble thing you did to-day. Oh, I am glad and proud."

"I prefer you to think of me in that way, rather than as the wild beast you saw this morning, for I was mad, perfectly mad with hatred and revenge, and every wild impulse that comes to a defeated man. You see, I had played and lost, played and lost, again and again, till there was nothing left. What mischance brought you there? It was a terribly brutal thing, but you can't understand."

"But I can understand. I do. I know all about it now. I know the wild rage of desperation; I know the exultation of victory; I know what hate and fear are now. You told me once that the wilderness had made you a savage, and I laughed at it just as I did when you said that my contact with big things would teach me the truth, that we're all alike, and that those motives are in us all. I see now that you were right and I was very simple. I learned a great deal last night."

"I have learned much also," said he. "I wish you might teach me more."

"I—I—don't think I could teach you any more," she hesitated.

He moved as though to speak, but held back and tore his eyes away from her.

"Well," she inquired, gazing at him covertly.

"Once, a long time ago, I read a Lover's Petition, and ever since knowing you I have made the constant prayer that I might be given the purity to be worthy the good in you, and that you might be granted the patience to reach the good in me—but it's no use. But at least I'm glad we have met on common ground, as it were, and that you understand, in a measure. The prayer could not be answered; but through it I have found myself and—I have known you. That last is worth more than a king's ransom to me. It is a holy thing which I shall reverence always, and when you go you will leave me lonely except for its remembrance."

"But I am not going," she said. "That is—unless—"

Something in her voice swept his gaze back from the shimmering causeway that rippled seaward to the rising moon. It brought the breath into his throat, and he shook as though seized by a great fear.

"Unless—what?"

"Unless you want me to."

"Oh, God! don't play with me!" He flung out his hand as though to stop her while his voice died out to a supplicating hoarseness. "I can't stand that."

"Don't you see? Won't you see?" she asked. "I was waiting here for the courage to go to you since you have made it so very hard for me—my pagan." With which she came close to him, looking upward into his face, smiling a little, shrinking a little, yielding yet withholding, while the moonlight made of her eyes two bottomless, boundless pools, dark with love, and brimming with the promise of his dreams.

The End

A Note About the Author

Rex Beach (1877–1949) was an American writer who was born in Michigan but raised in Florida. He attended multiple schools including Rollins College, Florida and the Chicago College of Law. He also spent five years in Alaska prospecting as part of the Klondike Goldrush. When he was unable to strike it rich, Beach turned to creative writing. In 1905, he published a collection of short stories called *Pardners*, followed by the novel *The Spoilers* (1906). Many of his titles have been adapted into feature films including *The Goose Woman* and *The Silver Horde*.

A Note from the Publisher

Spanning many genres, from non-fiction essays to literature classics to children's books and lyric poetry, Mint Edition books showcase the master works of our time in a modern new package. The text is freshly typeset, is clean and easy to read, and features a new note about the author in each volume. Many books also include exclusive new introductory material. Every book boasts a striking new cover, which makes it as appropriate for collecting as it is for gift giving. Mint Edition books are only printed when a reader orders them, so natural resources are not wasted. We're proud that our books are never manufactured in excess and exist only in the exact quantity they need to be read and enjoyed.

bookfinity™

Discover more of your favorite classics with Bookfinity™.

- Track your reading with custom book lists.
- Get great book recommendations for your personalized Reader Type.
- Add reviews for your favorite books.
- AND MUCH MORE!

Visit **bookfinity.com** and take the fun Reader Type quiz to get started.

Enjoy our classic and modern companion pairings!

Classic & Modern